PRISON PLAYPEN

M.C. SHAKIE

WAHIDA CLARK
PRESENTS
INNOVATIVE PUBLISHING

Wahida Clark Presents Publishing

P.O. BOX 383

Fairburn GA 30213

1(866) 910-6920

www.wclarkpublishing.com

Prison Playpen

Hardcover ISBN: 978-1-957954-11-0

Paperback ISBN: 978-1-957954-12-7

Ebook ISBN: 978-1-957954-13-4

1. LGBTQ 2. Prison 3. Relationship 4. Transgender 5. Abuse

Cover design and layout by:

Nuance Art & Tempertantrum Tina

Cover Model: Kway @blameitonkway

Editor: Chase Bolling, Alan Nixon

Printed in United States

M.C. SHAKIE
ACKNOWLEDGEMENTS

Thank you to my Creator for giving and saving my life.

This project was inspired by my own incarceration, where I as an effeminate gay man went through similar things that Summer did. But I recognize that a lot of people go through their own struggles while locked up in America's bullshit criminal justice system.

Thank **you** for taking this journey with me. So, first and foremost, I thank you, the reader, for making this project possible. It is your endless dedication that has made this book possible and gives me the inspiration to keep writing.

I would like to thank a host of family and friends that still tell me to write, write, write and kept pushing me to get this book out.

I must give a huge shout out to the Sippers of Sip Nation. I love you each, and you are who I do this for.

To Wahida Clark, you are amazing, Queen, and thank you for being my literary mother and giving me the opportunity. Thank you to Blame It Kway and his character, TiTi, who embodied my Summer on the stellar cover. To my Trap Queen, Candace Wilson, I love and thank you so much for everything.

To the team at Wahida Clark Presents … Lawd, what would I do without y'all? Thank you. Thank you. Thank you. This is just the beginning of our star-studded journey. I'm telling you. And that's tea!

To the love of my life, whenever they decide to come, know

I'm waiting on you, Bae, and I am writing this to let you know I love you and I am waiting for you.

To anyone one I failed to mention, know that I am thinking of you and love you.

Always,
    Rodney "M.C. Shakie" Roussell

PROLOGUE

"WHO'S COUNTERFEITING THESE CHECKS?" the burley, barrel-chested detective asked, placing his fisted Gorilla hands on the rickety silver table in front of Peyton.

He blew a flume of cigarette smoke right into Peyton's face. It was clear, he was going to be the bad cop in this meeting. Peyton lowered her head. She felt faint and the room spun a bit. She lifted her eyes and they locked with the menacing authority in front of her.

"I don't know. I'm telling you, I don't know." Peyton whimpered.

The detective let out a maniacal chortle and his nostrils flared as the last of his nasty cigarette smoke escaped them. He was tired of her.

"Listen, give me a break with the sad girl act. You're facing some serious charges," he pointed at her, the vein in his neck pulsing against his red neck.

The other detective stepped forward with a soothing smile. "Charges that we could drop if you give up your source," he said softly. He was the polar opposite of his partner. He was calm, slim, and kind of handsome.

He must be the good cop, Peyton thought to herself.

Peyton stopped sniffling and centered her attention on the nicer detective. "You can drop the charges?"

"Well...that..." the nice detective started, but his aggressive partner cut in. He just couldn't help himself. He had to be the asshole in the room. Peyton saw delight flicker over his expression.

"That depends on whether or not you give us your source. We want to know who's making these counterfeit checks," the mean detective said firmly.

Peyton squeezed her eyes shut for a second and swiped at her face with the back of her hand. Her legs swung under the table. Thoughts raced through her mind like the cars at the Indy 500. She had to make sure everything fell into place.

"Okay . . . Okay . . . I'll give you my source," she blurted, praying this worked.

"When?" the nice detective asked.

"Please, can you give me a couple of days?" Peyton pleaded.

The nice detective looked over at his partner, who had just lit up another Marlboro. His partner nodded. "All you got is a week. Not an hour, minute, or second more. You understand?"

Peyton's heart leaped in her chest. She had done it. A week, that's all she'd ever need.

Summer almost missed the call she was expecting from her best friend. But once she heard it ring, rushed to answer it. "Peyton? Girl, where are you? You should have been here."

"Hold your horses, bitch. I'm on my way," Summer said as she hung up and then washed her face. She listened to Cardi B on her iPhone, mouthing along to the song "Up". Summer threw on a red spencer dress and flip-flops. One look in the mirror was all she needed to kick-start her day.

She flashed her bright smile. She was convinced she favored her favorite artist Rihanna even more than usual. Her lips were glossed, which accentuated her cupid's bow. She tilted her chin up and pushed her shoulders back as she made kissy faces at herself in the mirror. Of course, it hadn't always been that way. In the back of her mind, she knew the mirror hadn't always been such a kind friend to her.

Summer hopped in her Range Rover and bee-lined it to Peyton's apartment across town.

Peyton came out on the first honk, wearing a monochrome lime green get-up. She carried a cream Aldo tote bag and her Candies' sunglasses hid her eyes.

Upon catching a view of Peyton, Summer had to admit to herself that her little white friend was fly. The graphic design Mill dress accentuated the soft touches of her curves.

"Come on, girl! We're running late," Peyton said.

"You need to hurry and get your car out of the shop," Summer replied.

Peyton rolled her eyes. Their friendship had seen better days. Summer had been through a tragic breakup with Peyton's cousin, Clayton, who'd beaten her nearly to death. Afterward, they didn't connect the same.

Summer had a photo shoot as she often did amateur modeling. Her exotic features and near-flawless foreign beauty afforded her the ability to accept gigs on the side. Summer's photo shoot was in Hyattsville, Maryland. It was a smaller modeling gig compared to some of her previous shoots, but she didn't like to pass up on any work in that field as it was her dream to break into it professionally. Summer hit the gas and sped off.

When they pulled up to the warehouse, a dark van swerved alongside Summer's truck as she parked, and three guys hopped out waving shotguns.

"Get out of the truck, bitch!" one of the masked gunmen said as he leveled the double-barrel shotgun to Summer's face. It took everything in Summer's power not to faint, and she immediately started sobbing. "I don't wanna die! Please don't kill me! I have some money in my purse!"

One of the masked gunmen was pulling Peyton around from the other side of the truck when he said, "Bitch, do you have eighty thousand dollars in your purse?"

Summer thought for literally one nanosecond to think of the answer. "I'm gonna die!" Summer cried, realizing she only had $80 in her purse.

"Shut the fuck up!" the masked gunman yelled.

It only took seconds before Summer heard Peyton being smacked to the ground. "Where's Ellis' money? You think you can play with somebody like Ellis? Bitch, you'll watch all your friends die first."

"I'm gonna get it," Peyton managed to say. Before she could finish explaining, one of the gunmen was already flinging stuff out of Summer's purse. That was until he found Summer's driver's license.

"By midnight, if you don't have that eighty grand, I'm going to kill your little girlfriend, and then tomorrow we'll find some-body else close to you to kill. Maybe your cousin, Clayton."

"No! Don't kill my friend."

"Well then, get that money, bitch!"

The masked man showed Summer her driver's license as if she didn't believe he had it. With one last shove to the ground, the three gunmen hopped in the van and skirted off.

"They gonna kill us!" Summer kept saying through sobs. There was no way in hell she could go through with her photo shoot. If those guys were telling the truth, they'd never have to worry about a photo shoot ever again.

It was too much for Summer. Peyton tried to hug her. She pushed her away, then tried to claw her eyes out. "They're gonna kill me because of you!"

Peyton was quicker than she looked. She jumped back and held her hands out in complete submission.

"Summer, wait! We can get the money. You know what we

gotta do. We can have it by tonight." Peyton kept a fair distance as Summer neared her.

"I can't ask my uncle. I told you about the situation between us."

"You know what I mean, Summer. We only have a little while left."

"You want me to cash some checks? Are you crazy!" Summer looked at Peyton in disbelief as if she had forgotten. "I nearly died the last time when I almost got caught."

"You're my only chance."

"It's your own fault! All you do is gamble. I can't believe you went to a loan shark like Ellis. He would rather clean his books with bullets than to be owed."

"Summer, please! I need your help." Peyton begged.

Summer went back to her Range Rover and sat down. She couldn't believe she was getting pulled into something she promised herself she'd never do again. She saw the tears sprouting from her friend's eyes with the promise of death lingering overhead and knew the decision was made for her.

"Get in the car."

Damn . . . Damn . . . Damn . . . Summer thought as she sped back to her apartment. She made one quick stop at Office Depot to get a pack of the specific set of checks she needed: blank payroll checks. She was a pro at this. She had been doing the scam for years until her tumultuous relationship with the love of her life, Clayton, had come to an end, and she moved back to town.

However, Summer didn't have any of her fraudware on hand, and she had to get everything together. She couldn't even look at Peyton when she got back in the truck after leaving Office Depot. The most she ever made cashing checks was eight to ten thousand in one day. Summer was afraid that it was impossible to pull off ten times that amount.

"I'm gonna drop you off at your apartment. Put on a nice, classy business suit and break out a briefcase. In about an hour, I'll come back and pick you up," Summer told Peyton. Neither girl met the other's gaze.

"Thank you," Peyton said softly as she smiled at her reflection in the rearview mirror.

Summer took a deep breath. She knew she couldn't be mad at her friend. "Don't worry. We'll have it by tonight."

After leaving Peyton's apartment, she kicked everything into gear. The first thing she had to do was get the account numbers from a guy she hadn't spoken to in over six months. Reluctantly, she made the connection and got several stolen business bank account numbers that she would then print on the blank checks.

To pull off the cashing of the checks, though, would take some convincing, so she quickly dressed in the sluttiest mini dress in her closet. She put on foundation, red lipstick, and slick black eyeliner. She pulled her hair into a neat ponytail and traded her flip-flops for a more seductive pair of Narciso Rodriguez wedges that stuck her pert ass up for display. After all that, she headed straight for the door.

She made it to Peyton's quickly, and Peyton was outside, awaiting Summer's arrival. Peyton looked the part well enough, but Summer still had her concerns. "We gotta cash these checks at their home branches. If they call on the check, leave immediately. We can go to the same banks and cash them together, but we must go in separately and do this while it's lunchtime," Summer explained.

Peyton rolled her eyes because she didn't need the pep talk for what she had in mind.

Bank of America on M Street was their first stop. Each check was made out for eight thousand, and if everything went according to Summer's plan, they'd be finished by the end of the lunch hour.

"You ready?" Summer asked.

"Yeah, I'm ready. I'm going to wait three minutes, and then I'll come in behind you."

"Okay. I'll see you after."

Summer went straight into the bank. Everything inside was quiet and orderly. The guard standing at the door smiled at her, and Summer nodded innocently in response.

As the line dwindled down to her, she noticed Peyton still hadn't come in yet. Summer pursed her lips as she approached the female bank teller. She should've let someone cut in front of her to ensure she had a male teller. It wouldn't be as easy to distract a woman.

Damn, shit isn't adding up, she thought to herself as she noticed that Peyton still had not walked in. Summer then remembered she had forgotten to put super glue on her fingertips to cover up her fingerprints. *Shit!* Everything in her mind told her to abandon this mission, but she couldn't just walk out with the threat of death hanging over her head. *Shit!* she said in her mind again when she realized that she didn't have her ID since the gunman took it.

"Can I help you?" the easy-going young bank teller asked.

Summer smiled kindly and naturally hid all the uneasiness building inside her.

"Yes. I'd like to cash this check."

"I'll just need a form of identification," replied the teller.

Of course, Summer thought. She fumbled through her purse, laying the check in front of the teller, hoping she could stall long enough while she thought of an excuse as to why she couldn't produce her license.

Peyton still wasn't anywhere in sight. What the fuck! Summer flashed a smile at the teller. "I must've left my ID in the car. Could you start the process while I run and grab it?"

The teller furrowed her brow as she held the check in her hands. "Certainly, but because of the amount, I will be having to call it in, so you have time," replied the teller.

Summer knew that if the bank teller called on the check, the owner of the account would certainly say that they never issued a check to Summer, and the next call the teller would make would be to the police.

Summer had to get control of this situation. "I'm really in a rush … my lunch break is almost up." Summer put on the best pleading eye face that she could.

The bank teller studied Summer for a second. "Oh alright, I won't need to call. How would you like your bills?"

"Large bills," Summer said. She could have kissed the lady as she cashed the check for eight thousand dollars. It brought back memories of days when she was on the top of her fraud game and finally made it out of the mud. "Thank you."

Summer nearly danced out of the bank's doors. She thought about the other four checks she had in her purse and was in the mood to quickly cash those as well. As she stepped into the warm afternoon sun, guns were drawn on her, and she was forcibly brought to the ground. It was unmistakable as a feeling that touched the pit of her soul swept over her and she blacked out after that moment.

———

"Bobby Moore, Bobby Moore, are you hearing me?" the detective asked.

Summer came to, her head pounding. The detective who had tackled her was standing over her now, a look of disgust on his face.

"Bobby Moore, we've got to talk," the detective got closer to Summer's face. She couldn't believe she was hearing someone say her dead name after all this time.

Bobby Moore had been gone a long time. She knew she was Summer from an early age. Once Summer realized why everything about being in her body had felt alien, she'd gone under the knife to add more bust to her bra size, then had her ribs removed to make her waist appear slenderer. By taking butt shots, she tailored her figure until she achieved her desired results. She went through evaluation after evaluation to get her hormone therapy started. The only thing left was to go all the way and have the sex change, which she put on hold after her break up with Clayton. Now she was sitting in an interrogation room, and a detective was asking for someone who had hardly ever existed.

The severity of the situation was becoming clearer. "Please, officer, you can't send me to prison. They'll kill me in there!" Summer couldn't contain herself as her worst fears came to life.

"Oh, please. You need to get ahold of yourself." The detective smelled like a deli, and he had mustard stains on his shirt and tie. He was a somewhat typical looking fat cop. The dark rings under his eyes didn't cover up the scattered moles, and his lips were too loose and gummy. Summer leaned back in the chair and tried to hold her breath. His badge said his name was Collins.

There was another officer in the room, sitting in the dim corner, and he was smirking in Summer's direction. He chuckled as she squirmed in her seat.

"The evidence is pretty damning, Mr. Moore. We don't think you're gonna get yourself out of this," he finally said.

"You don't understand! I'm not a man. I can't go to a men's prison. I won't survive!" Summer begged, placing her hands in front of her face, finally noticing the handcuffs on her wrists were already beginning to leave blisters. "Just take these off me! I promise I'll tell you everything."

The detectives smiled at one another.

"There isn't much you need to tell us we don't already know.

We have you on bank fraud, identity theft, forgery, counterfeiting, and manufacturing …"

"Uttering a forged instrument," the sitting detective, named Wallace, aided his partner's statement.

"You're going to get an enhanced sentence for sophisticated skills and a far lengthier sentence for the dollar amounts of the checks," Collins said, somehow still inching closer to Summer.

Summer heard nothing but her sobs. She couldn't believe that at this point in her life, things were still so difficult. She had always thought after she began her transition, things would be easier for her. Knowing she was a woman and living life as a woman was supposed to be the easy part. Now, this one mistake was going to cost her everything she had worked so hard for. She thought that there was no way she'd make it in prison. The near promise of being passed around like reefer in a group of Rastafarians made her throat dry and tight.

"Where did you get the account numbers from?" the detectives asked.

Before the words were off his lips, Summer said, "A dude named Glen! He gave them to me after I gave him some head and some butt!"

Despite Summer's distraught conditions, both detectives let out a laugh.

"It ain't funny!" Summer couldn't think of anything worse than being killed in prison by somebody who looked like Big Bubba on *Money Talks*. "I had stopped doing fraud, but my friend Peyton came to me because she owed Ellis, the loan shark, eighty grand, and I was only helping her out."

It all became clear to the detectives. They knew Ellis wouldn't loan money for gambling debts. From their investigation of him, he funded Black Market enterprises, not gambling debts. Peyton wasn't on the scene when Summer got caught at the bank. She was busy driving back to her place while on the phone with a 911 operator, placing an anonymous tip.

"Get him the fuck out of here," Wallace stood ignoring her transition, gesturing toward the door.

"I'm gonna kill myself," Summer said to the detectives.

"Tell it to the medic," said Collins.

"Get him some meds or tranquilize his ass," Wallace instructed Collins.

Collins escorted her to a holding cell in the Washington D.C. city jail, where she was instructed to change into a prison uniform. When she was done, she was led out into the hall again just as Peyton rounded the corner of the interrogation doorway.

Peyton stopped right in front of Summer and sweetly whispered her name. When Summer looked up, Peyton blinded her with a searing slap across her face. "Fuck you, you faggot bitch!"

Summer was held in the D.C. jail for the next six months, during which she was heavily sedated and dissociated. She could not remember the name of her assigned public defender, nor could she recall the look on the judge's face when he determined that the most appropriate sentence for her was an eighteen-month stint at a medium-security federal prison. Perhaps he felt bad for her, noticing the tremor in her plump lower lip as she sat shivering in the courtroom.

The judge might not have felt bad at all for the girl, since he did not see her as such. Either way, Summer was to leave the holding facility and go to a Federal Correctional Institute. The one they assigned her was in Schuylkill, Pennsylvania, an all-male facility.

No one, except Peyton, knew Summer was in jail those six months. She received one letter during her time there.

Summer, Bobby, or whatever you think you are, You should've seen this coming, messing with my cousin the way you did. Nobody but a twisted-freak faggot could fuck up my family the way you have. Now, you're exactly where you belong. Just know I would've done it even sooner if I had known the truth about what you are. I hope you rot in there. Whatever amount of time you got isn't long enough. Freaks like you will never deserve the light of day.

* Peyton

Summer tore the letter to pieces and flushed it down the toilet. She glanced blankly at the walls around her, all cinderblock and bare. They seemed to be extremely far away, and she was engulfed in an exceedingly empty space. Her mind was playing a vicious game of sanity and insanity with her, and she was losing.

One day when the guards passed out razors for the inmates to shave, she elected not to shave but she took out the blade by popping the razor head on the cinder blocks and deeply sliced both her wrists. *It just would be better this way,* she thought, than to die at some unknown time later down the road at Schuylkill. She climbed under her bunk before she fainted.

An officer making rounds to pick up the razors found her just a few minutes later, blood slowly seeping from her arms like water passing through wool. She was placed on suicide watch until she made a full recovery and then sent immediately to FCI Schuylkill.

CHAPTER 1
HOW WOULD SHE SURVIVE?

THE UNITED STATES MARSHALS SERVICE did all the transporting for the Federal Bureau of Prisons. On this day, after fifty or more inmates were cuffed and shackled, they were loaded onto the bus for transportation. The bus was old and rickety, like a standard school bus but painted a dull grey and everybody called it The Grey Goose. Summer joined other inmates climbing onto the bus, high-yellow from not seeing the son after months of administrative segregation from her failed suicide attempt and ten pounds lighter than she was the day she got arrested because she just could not vibe with the whole jail food thing.

"What you in for?" a Mexican man who was shackled next to her asked Summer as he took the seat next to her. He wore dark glasses that had to be corrective wear, or the D.C. jail wouldn't have let him wear them. His mustache was perfectly trimmed, and his hair was slicked back.

Summer studied him for a few seconds, and she decided after months alone with her thoughts she wanted to talk. "Bank fraud."

"What are you? Dominican?" he asked, his accent was heavy

but understandable. It made Summer want to continue speaking with him.

"No, I'm Black," Summer said.

He nodded in response. "Everybody calls me Sosa."

"I'm Summer." A hint of a smile spread across her face.

"Damn, I wish you Mexicana."

"What for?"

"To have you for my cellmate. I come from Schuylkill a year back. I went back to Mexico, and the Feds come get me. Now they give me thirty years."

They were silent. Summer didn't know it, but he was the underboss of a notorious drug lord in Mexico. She also didn't know how to respond to someone who was sentenced to thirty years, and she only had 18 months. She immediately thought about how on earth she would start doing a thirty-year sentence.

"But I own that pinche yarda. When I get back to Schuylkill, they gonna make me shot caller. Since I been locked down, I always called shots for my people. They got funny names for shot-callers. They call us reps or representatives. Like we in the congress."

They laughed.

"But I spend lots of money every month."

If Summer didn't know any better, she would have thought he was over-exaggerating by the animated and excited way he spoke.

"Every month," he continued, "I send five hundred dollars on ten different commissary accounts. I spend the shit like it's water."

Summer looked around to see if anybody was watching or looking. It was still dark outside, being that it couldn't be any later than 5:45 a.m. Everybody on the bus was either asleep or in their own little world.

"You must be rich," Summer said.

"Listen to me." Sosa's accent was heavy and forceful. "I'm

from Sinaloa. I know a lot of mero-mero. I think you call them bosses. But listen, I want you to give me your name and register number."

"Register number?" Summer asked, interrupting him.

"Yeah, it's the number everybody has in the federal prison system. I think I'm saying it right." He organized the sequence of words in his head. "Yes, Federal prison system." He was pleased with himself, almost forgetting his train of thought. "Yes, I want your information."

"For what?" Summer was somewhat defensive, but couldn't help being intrigued.

"So, I can send you some money, mami!"

Summer looked away when he said that. Prison could be filled with dangerous people; although Sosa seemed to have character and integrity, she thought it better to keep her guard up.

"Why haven't you said anything? Did I offend you?" Sosa brought Summer out of her musing. He smiled at her.

"No, I'm not offended," she said innocently.

"Then I send you money. I worried, with you being morena."

"Morena?" Summer asked quizzically.

"Yeah," he laughed, amused by his own forward behavior. He wanted to fuck Summer so much it hurt. He knew it would be several years before he could touch a woman again and, in his mind, she was very close to one. "Morena means Black in Spanish. We also say Negra or Negro, but we no say it 'cause we think it offend you."

"I'm not offended."

"I know, 'cause I not call you Negra. I say Morena. Morena deliciosa", he said with a seductive smile.

They laughed.

"See, I know you gonna cause mucho problema," Sosa said with charming eyes.

"Why do you say that?"

"You're gonna see, morena deliciosa. When those guys get

one look at you, they're gonna get so hungry, they'll do anything to get some of you. I be able to smell you from the other side of la yarda. You smell so sweet. I wanna fuck you right here."

They laughed again. Sosa couldn't be older than forty-five years old, but he still had a lot of youth.

"You're playing." She was hoping that was not the case because she was non-confrontational. She knew she wouldn't stand a chance if otherwise.

"I no lie. I tell you this; those morenos from D.C. marry each other."

"Marry?"

He excitedly shook his head. "When you get married, you married wherever you go."

Married! Good grief! Summer thought. She didn't know it was a binding non-legal process equivalent to slaves hopping the broom. Though, it did let other inmates know whose ass was claimed and by who.

"I can protect you, morena deliciosa." Sosa's face became stern then. There was only one thing Summer heard.

"I'ma need protection?" Summer asked, the sun finally peaking from the horizon outside of the bus.

Sosa sat up straight and looked ahead of him, taking notice of the other inmates glancing in Summer's direction. He nodded in response to Summer's question.

CHAPTER 2
THE ARRIVAL

A GUARD STOOD in a watchtower and watched the bus pull into the long driveway leading up to the prison's gate. When they arrived at the entrance, a thorough search ensued. Correctional Officers inspected the inside and underside of the bus in search of any contraband the new bloods might be trying to smuggle in. Summer was still sitting beside Sosa, though they hadn't spoken much since they departed from D.C.

As the bus was being inspected, Summer looked over at Sosa, who looked as if he was preparing himself for whatever awaited his arrival. As Summer observed the other passengers on the bus, everybody's expression was the same. As the COs passed her, she received multiple second glances and smirks.

She very clearly stood out from the rest of the inmates around her, with her soft features and awkward shuffling. Of course, they knew what she was, so they attempted to disregard her outward appearance and handle her presence as they would with any other new arrival. Roughly, and without concern for their fears or general well-being.

Once outside the bus, a team of COs removed the handcuffs, belly chains, and ankle braces as the inmates disembarked the bus. They were marched inside Receiving and Discharge, and they sat for what seemed like endless hours waiting to be processed inside the system.

Summer was appalled by the intake and screening process necessary to enter the institution. It was a tedious task of being strip-searched and dressed within unwashed, smelly garbs that made her gag. She held the disgusting underwear away from her body, with shit stains still present, stark against the white of the garment. She opted to wear the jailhouse khaki pants without the underwear.

She was shoved in front of a camera and her mug shot was taken. She briefly saw the image appear on a screen and, noticing how unrecognizable she'd become, gently touched her hair with trembling hands. Her perm was completely worn out, replaced by the kinkiness of her natural hair. She'd been having her hair styled for years, never allowing it to be seen natural. Now, she had no choice in the matter.

Summer went to the health department, where she was asked personal questions by a tall, white male nurse who had a shit-eating grin on his face the whole time she was interviewed.

"When was the last time you had sex?" the nurse asked with a hinting smile.

"None of your fucking business," Summer answered.

The nurse, whose badge read, CNA Eddings, acted as if he enjoyed the exchange. "When was the last time you had an HIV test?"

"D.C. jail, when I almost bled to death."

"Let me look . . . Oh good, you're negative. Let's hope it stays that way. Last thing we need is an outbreak in here." Nurse Eddings held the paper in his hand out to Summer. The paper was authorization that she had been medically cleared to go to the compound.

Summer was ushered into what the door read was a Case Manager's office. She soon found it was Case Manager Attenberger's office. He would assign her to a unit, and he had the final say so if she would go to the compound or not.

"Are you going to be a problem?" Attenberger asked.

"Excuse me?" Summer responded. She was tired, she was hungry, and the attitude in her voice and hands on her hips displayed it.

"You heard me. Are you going to be a problem?" Attenberger repeated.

"Why would I be a problem?"

Attenberger smirked. "Let's just say you're obviously gay, and you don't look like a man at all. I'm impressed myself. But do you know what's out there?"

"I'm not gay. I am a transwoman, first of all," corrected Summer, "and I'm pretty sure there are men out there," Summer smiled wanly.

"You know what," rhetorically asked Attenberger, "you're going to the SHU till the Captain signs off on you."

"The SHU? What's that?" Summer said as if the fear in her voice could keep her from going.

"Oh, you *are* all woman," Attenberger added, referring to what was written in her pre-sentence investigation report, which was prepared by the probation officer. The report was an intrusive history file about Summer's life, and all Summer could remember from the interview was how violating it was.

Attenberger continued, "SHU is an acronym that stands for Special Housing Unit, or administrative confinement of sorts. Some of the guys around here call it the hole."

"But I didn't do nothing."

"You can't go to the compound anyways, not today. There are no available cells. But in case you do go, if you're so much as found kissing or obscenely touching anybody, I promise you we'll ship you to that underground joint in Colorado. Have you heard of ADX?"

"No."

"I didn't think so. That's where we send our incorrigible inmates. Let's just say you wouldn't last five minutes."

There was no doubt in Summer's mind she couldn't last two minutes, let alone five. "I'm not going to do nothing."

"You'd better not. Now get out of my office," Attenberger said. Before she left, he almost forgot to ask some key questions. "One last thing, do you have any separatees at this joint?"

Summer didn't know what he was talking about. "Any what?"

"Boy, you are green. This must be your first time in jail. What are you in for?" Attenberger asked. He didn't want to waste time fingering through her file in his hands.

"Bank fraud and identity theft," Summer answered sheepishly.

"Did you testify against anybody? Or did anybody testify against you?"

"No," Summer lied. She technically didn't testify, but she did cooperate.

"Are you in a gang?"

"No," Summer snickered.

"I had to ask. This all determines if you'll go to the compound or not. You can leave now."

As Summer walked through the door to leave, Attenberger yelled for the next inmate to enter. Summer went to a holding tank that was crammed to the max, and everybody made way for her, keeping their distance. Many didn't want to be seen with a homosexual, gay, fag, gump, or sissy. It could make them far more vulnerable than they already were.

At least that's what Summer thought. Remembering her awful experience at the D.C. jail, she knew homophobia was something all gay men had to face while in prison. From Summer's point of view, it usually left them to deal with loneliness and isolation. She knew if one wasn't strong, they would lose the sense of balance. Summer read in an article, that nine out of every ten gay men in prison took psych meds to help them cope with the loneliness and open hostility coming from inmates and correctional officers.

The officers put lunch bags through the trap in the door of the holding tank. It was a wet bag of low-quality lunch meat, a rotten apple, molded bread, and milk so spoiled it had lumps in it.

Summer held the lunch bag away from her body to offer it to anybody because she couldn't stomach, let alone bear, the foul-smelling meat. Nobody approached her offering. Moments later, a big, dark-skinned guy arrived; he was the biggest, by far, in the holding tank. Once he saw Summer, he headed straight for her. His voice was aggressive by nature.

"You're not going to eat that?" he asked her.

"No, you can have it," Summer said, as she scooted over so he wouldn't sit on her.

"Where you from?"

"D.C.," Summer answered, thinking where Sosa's presence was warm and welcoming, this guy was coarse and unsettling.

"I'm from Northeast, and when I seen you, shorty, I kind of figured you were from D.C.," he said. He'd seen other girls like Summer from the area. "What part you from?" he asked.

"Southeast," Summer answered, still unsure of who the guy was, or what he really wanted. He seemed as if he had an ulterior motive.

"My name is Black, and I've already been to this joint for three years. I had to go back to court on a state case. "Now, it's a rack of homies here, so you ain't gonna have no problems. But if you do, come and holler at me." His eyes glimmered until their conversation was cut short when the officers opened the door and yelled out the inmates' names.

Once the inmates exited the door, they were given bedrolls, which consisted of a comb, toothbrush, toothpaste, shampoo, and soap that were stuffed inside a plastic cup. All the contents were wrapped inside two bed sheets and a cover. Some were off to the compound, while others were off to SHU. They moved like cattle through the halls of the facility, each with their own feelings about where they were headed and what got them there.

Summer was ushered to her cell in handcuffs, with two officers on either side of her. They took her through the small maze of halls to a cell, which, from the rectangular window in the door, looked dirty, cold, and empty.

They closed the door behind Summer and took her handcuffs off through the trap in the door. She looked around at the cell and there was a toilet off to the side with an attached sink, table, shower, and a bunk bed.

Summer was so exhausted from the four-hour bus ride, she collapsed on the bed without making it up. She wrapped herself in the covers, discarding the toiletries inside the bedroll.

She had fallen asleep for what seemed like two minutes when the officers opened the trap to the door and told her to cuff up. When Summer went to the door, she heard the most obnoxious voice.

"And you bet tuh not put me in the cell with just anybody! I don't play dat shit, and I ain't scared of you crackas," said a man, with clearly effeminate inflection. He didn't have any feminine features like Summer, but he was a ball of fire, sassy and pretentious as any diva would be.

"Adams, shut the hell up. It's one of your kind in there. You should be happy," one of the white COs said, not giving a fuck about being politically correct.

"What do you mean one of my kind? You bet not be talking about because I'm black?"

"Not 'cause you're black, it's because you're gay," the same CO added as the other CO handcuffed Summer through the trap.

"Hmmm, a sus, I guess I'm all right with that," he smacked his lips as he looked at Summer through the window. "By the way, you're kind of cute, Mr. Officer."

"Not a chance in a lifetime, Adams," the CO responded, realizing the inmate was speaking to him.

The COs waited impatiently for the control center, which was a command center that opened the automatic cell doors. They controlled the SHU through the surveillance cameras, and when the COs in front of Summer's cell waved at the camera, they opened the door. And to the CO's statement, the inmate said, "I don't blame you 'cause if you saw how big momma was packing, you'd probably doubt your sexuality."

"Get your ass in there!" the CO said brusquely. "Shut cell number 118," he said into his walkie-talkie.

The COs took the handcuffs off Summer and the other inmate then left. Once they were gone, the new inmate didn't introduce himself.

"Gurl, how can you lay down on that nasty bed without cleaning it first?"

"Clean it for what?" Summer asked and then sat back down on the bed.

"So, you won't get staph infection, scabies, crabs. Honey, you can take your pick," the inmate retorted.

"I don't care," replied Summer blankly.

Summer's new cellmate looked at her with understanding eyes. "What is it? Heartbroken? The judge gave you too much time, or your first time being locked up?"

"All the above."

"How much time did they give you?"

"Eighteen months," Summer replied.

Summer's cellmate laughed in her face. "Are you crazy? That's nothing! I know it may seem like the end of the world, but it's nothing. You probably did twelve months at D.C. jail and should already be ready to go home. Gurl, you can't be no older than nineteen."

"I'm twenty."

"Did you cooperate?" The new cellie, short for cellmate, knew the question had to be asked.

"What do you mean?"

"Duh! Did you snitch on anybody ... hello?"

Summer's eyes became as big as an owl's eye. She knew how other inmates would treat her if they knew she snitched and she didn't want to answer the question.

"Bitch, don't get all weird on me all of a sudden because the fool that didn't tell wish he had, let me tell you. But make sure you keep whatever you did on the down-low because they'd love to fuck you around with that."

"Is it dangerous?" asked Summer sheepishly.

"You don't have nothing at all to worry about. There's a lot of guys perpetrating like they ain't going, but when they with you by themselves, it's completely different . . . trust. My name is Buffy Da Body, and if you ain't already got a nickname, they'll give you one."

"My name's Summer. But maybe the guys around here will call me Morena," Summer said, thinking about Sosa.

"Uh, I don't know 'bout that, gurl. You don't want nobody thinking you Spanish, or that you're fuckin' with the Mexicans in here. That'd be bad news."

Damn, Summer thought. *How am I ever going to make it out of here?* She was confused as to why Sosa would come on to her if there was any sort of racial tension building within the facility's walls.

"But Sosa said he'd protect me," Summer whispered to herself.

"Sosa?" Buffy asked. It jolted Summer out of her inner cognition.

"Sosa, he said he used to be here and was a shot-caller."

"Sosa! Gurl, he came back?" Buffy asked with added amazement. "My God, they're gonna tear the compound up because of you, let me tell you."

CHAPTER 3
HE HAD TO CONQUER THE WORLD

ATWATER LOVED to feel the steel in his hands. He loved the thought that his body produced enough power to lift 405 pounds. He unracked the weight and took it slowly down on his chest. The weight felt good, and he was getting his mind and body right because he was preparing to go home.

He pushed the steel, and the 405 pounds came up with ease. He was going to make sure he was strong enough to handle what was waiting for him once he was back on the streets.

He was so focused that he could not hear the loud banter around him by the other guys lifting weights. He knew his future was again on the chopping block. This was a chance he wouldn't get again. *Shit*, he thought to himself, somebody had to pay for robbing him of 18 years.

He racked the weights and hopped up and then curled 135 pounds on his arms until he felt them swell. He then threw them down and could see somewhat of a visible future where the stakes were high, and he'd have his foot on the fuckers' necks who buried him alive for 18 summers.

His mind was intent on delivering that justice. Atwater felt like there was an integral part missing from his plan. His mind searched for what it was when his concentration was interrupted.

"Atwater, come here," Old School said. Old School was a well-respected old-timer from Chicago. He was serving a life sentence. No matter the life sentence, or the time he had already served, he looked considerably good for his age.

Atwater went over to him, and they shook hands and embraced, as only true gangsters do.

"Islam Moor," Old School paid Atwater the greetings of the Moorish Americans, a religious group who were similar in dedication to the Nation of Islam but followed the teachings of Noble Drew Ali. Atwater was not only a member; he held rank as the Assistant Grand Sheik in their group.

"That's my Atwater," Old School said proudly. "How's your wife, Shonda?"

"She's doing well. She's been riding out with a brother for these eighteen years, which seem like eighteen different lifetimes."

"It hasn't been wasted, young blood. You understand that it's direction that gives vision, and mismanagement that leads to collision."

Atwater looked at Old School admiringly. "You still speak in riddles, old man."

"It's not the riddle that's spoken, but the decipherment once it's broken. I can place wisdom like a dessert before your face, but what you choose is according to your taste." Old School continued, "I've helped you elevate your game. Your wife is now an accountant at a reputable accounting firm. And she has you to thank for that."

"Islam, and I have you to thank."

It was music to Old School's ears. For one to be grateful and appreciative when somebody taught him something said a lot about his character.

"Game is to be sold, not told," Old School said. "I'll life out in here. I just want you to pass the game on to those who are receptive, selective, and a little deceptive. What I teach you ten years back about your right to choose who you walk with, be it friend or foe?"

"To always exercise that right and to keep from allowing no-gooders to get under me," Atwater answered by rote.

"Right, because lames are always looking for some protection. That's what they make gangs, organizations, and armies for. It's a sort of protection program because real men stand on their own two feet. Others use the gangs, organizations, and armies to make themselves feel like real men because they can't think outside of the box. When a gang begins to exceed its usefulness, then cut it loose."

Atwater could never fully digest that teaching. "I feel you, Old School, but what about loyalty?"

"You are loyal, loyal to yaself, your ambition, and your success. Those fools are on autopilot to crash. You'd get run over trying to stop them. The only loyalty they understand is a face you put on to deal with them. You're in a whole other class. And what I teach you about classism?"

"The haves and the have-nots."

Old School had to smile at his pupil; he had learned his lessons well. And without showing his true satisfaction, Old School asked, "And at what time do you tie your fate with the have-nots?"

"At no time. Pimping ain't tender dick and kind-heartedness. The mack has to accumulate funds at the expense of a woman's virtue. But along with her virtue goes his own sense of humanity."

"Don't tell me you still pray?" Old School tested Atwater more.

"Never that, Old School. I don't pray, I prey."

"Calculation, misinformation, and mass manipulation are what rules the nation. You can never pluck a flower till after you've given her a mental orgasm. What you wear, drive, and speak does all of that."

One of Atwater's friends, who was working out, interrupted Old School. "Atwater, come on, man. You still gonna do squats?"

Old School and Atwater ignored him as Old School said, "You see how a have-not thinks? He thinks everything is brute force and physical strength. All these fools out here lifting crude instruments when the master chess players have aircraft carriers posted in front of their new victim's shores. New countries with new slaves to play to the master's tunes. But game is to be sold, not told. I told you, Atwater, to elevate your pimping, and I'm quite impressed at what you've accomplished. But I want you to take it one step further. Remember that a tender dick ain't got the applesauce to pimp."

Atwater laughed from the trance Old School had him in, the trance he was already in when he was plotting his future.

"All right, Old Man. Much love and I'm gonna take this pimping to a whole other level; that's my word."

"Your access has been granted."

CHAPTER 4
THE SHU HAD ITS WAY OF OFFERING SOLACE

SUMMER HAD NEVER BEEN inside a cage like she was at that time. As she looked around the cell, she felt she was going to be a victim of a degenerative disease or worse. Her skin crawled now that she was up and realized this prison wasn't a nightmare, but a living hell.

The cell itself was suffocating, with minor accommodations of a metal shower, a washbowl, and a toilet that was some sort of hybrid stuck together. The two-bed bunk was as comfortable as sleeping on a concrete slab.

Summer had spent one day in the SHU with Buffy, and after they did their best to clean everything, the cell was only slightly less nasty.

Buffy made the time go by a little easier with his light-hearted quips and buck-toothed smile. Summer had taken an instant liking to him, and Buffy spent the majority of the time telling Summer what to expect once she was released to the compound in his overly pretentious and feminine manner.

"Let me tell you," Buffy said as he smacked his lips and spoke with a pronounced and unnecessary lisp that made him sound as if he was sucking on a lollipop, "I don't care what anybody tells you about Schuylkill. It's the bomb out there. It's a rack of fine ass niggas who are most definitely going. I had to come here to take a break."

"You never told me why you're back here," Summer asked, excited from the stories Buffy told.

"Gurl," Buffy said, "it would be easier to say why I ain't back here. Let's just say I got caught in a compromising position. I was hunched over getting stuffed like a bell pepper with a yard of dick in the recreation bathroom."

They laughed.

"You got caught?"

"Yeah, and that ain't it. Lieutenant Muncy, who usually never gives a fuck, got all saintly, and he got the nerve to call me a black faggot, so I smacked that asshole in the face. They about snatched a bitch out of her panties and dragged me here."

"You're crazy!" Summer laughed.

"These scrapes on my legs look like rug burns as if I slept with King Mandingo himself."

Summer had to hold her stomach because she was laughing so hard.

"Gurl," Buffy smacked. "Let me tell you. From the other jails I've been to, this place is okay. T Roy, Banks, Eddie, Milk, Atwater, and Lazy Eyes... they all fine as fuck. That's just to name a few, but don't sleep with nobody that's been with Britney Spears 'cause *that* bitch got the bug."

"The what?"

She smacked her lips. "The big bug, bitch, Miss HIV. Hello!"

"Oh my God!" Summer said. She'd never met anyone her age with HIV. A lot had changed since the eighties.

"Don't sound so shocked, bitch. You better be extra careful, or you'll get more than a sore ass."

"Is there protection around here?" Summer asked.

Buffy looked as if he'd been asked the dumbest question in the universe. "Go to the chapel, make a wooden cross, and get a spray bottle full of Holy Water, let me tell you, 'cause ain't nothing on God's green earth gonna keep a bitch from getting some dick."

"You've completely lost your mind!" Summer said, still giggling.

"Other than that, you can try and use latex gloves, or a lot of prayer. Because most of the time ya ain't gonna wanna mess with a wee-wee that can fit in a finger of a glove, let me tell ya. Sometimes I like it when I can't sit down for a couple of days."

"I know what you mean . . . something that lingers!" Summer agreed as they slapped hands in full accord. She reminisced about how well-endowed Clayton had been.

"Listen to me, lil sister," Buffy said on a serious note, "be careful out there. Not only with your health, but with your heart, let me tell you. Don't get ya head involved 'cause some guys are too pussy to be seen with you in public. They won't even acknowledge you. But it's the life we have in here and in the free world, let me tell you. Don't even mess with nobody if you can't control your emotions because it will get you messed up. Plus, that's how a lot of people be getting stabbed. And you already lookin' psycho-ish."

Summer laughed. "What! No, I don't!"

"Please. What kind of medicine they have you on?" Summer didn't answer.

Buff grabbed her hands and looked at her wrists. "That's what I thought. How many times have you tried to kill yaself?" Buffy asked, seeing scars on Summer's wrist.

"Too many to count," Summer answered.

"Gurl, what is it? You hate the isolation, the ridicule, or the fact that you're always a secret in your lover's life? I know what's up. But ya's a crazy bitch for trynna to kill yaself. I ain't never went that far. I love dick too much, let me tell you."

They both laughed, feeling more comfortable around each other as they spoke. They were interrupted when they heard the

COs bringing somebody down the hall, their keys jangling against their uniformed legs.

Buffy ran to the door to see if he could peep down the hall through the crack in the door, but he could barely make out the image of Fats, who was coming down the hall.

"Stephens, make sure my cellie packs me out. I don't know if I'm going back to the compound," Fats said to the guard who brought him to the back, hoping his cellmate would send all his property to him in the SHU.

Somebody in another cell screamed. "Ya bet not go to the pound again, ya hot bitch!"

Fats ignored the guy screaming and said to the CO,

"Yo, CO, you see what I mean? I need all my property."

"Fats, is that you?" Buffy screamed because he loved him some Fats. Not only was Fats funny and a good time, but Fats also smuggled drugs into the prison.

"Hey, Buffy," Fats said warmly, "What the hell you doing back here? Don't answer that. I already know."

"Did you see Bad Breath Britney out there?" Buffy asked.

"Hold up. Let me get in my cell first."

The COs put Fats into an empty cell as they kicked his bedroll in, closed the door, and uncuffed him through the trap. He waited till the COs left before he resumed his conversation with Buffy. It required talking over other inmates' conversations, who screamed from cell to cell as they trafficked property underneath the doors by using strings torn from bedsheets and toothpaste tubes to launch the line.

The entire time the COs were putting Fats in his cell, Buffy was telling Summer who he was.

"Gurl, we done came up! Fats is my baby. He be having wine, cigarettes, cocaine, heroin, and whatever else you like."

"Damn! That's exactly what I need right now, something to calm my nerves."

"Oh, I hope he brought something back with him. Anything."

"How would he bring anything back here? They strip-searched me," Summer asked.

Buffy looked at Summer, coming to understand how green she really was. "You don't know who Keester is?"

Summer scrunched up her face. "No, who's he?"

Buffy shook his head. "It's when you hide something in ya ass."

"My God!" Summer said as Buffy laughed.

"Buffy!" Fats called.

Buffy ran back to the door.

"Fats?" Buffy called him for the fifth time, and he was getting agitated with Fats ignoring him.

"Buffy, I got something for you. You have a car?"

"Of course, I do," Buffy said, running over to his bed and ripping his bedsheet. He tied a small toothpaste tube to one end of the string.

"Baby, I told you we're going to Venus tonight," he said to Summer and danced with glee.

"What he got?" Summer asked.

"Bitch, how the hell do I know?" Buffy laughed. "Fats, I'm sending the car down."

Fats went to the door to steer the line in. Buffy had to keep trying to get the toothpaste to land in front of his cell door, but the shit seemed nearly impossible.

"Right there! It's in front of my cell. Hold up!"

Buffy looked over at Summer because they were about to get higher than kites.

"Pull the line!" Fats hollered back.

Buffy pulled the line in until the small package of goodies arrived.

Summer ran to the door to see what it was. It was two pin-sized cigarettes with a striking match.

"What is that?" Summer asked.

"Let me see," Buffy said as he unraveled it to find a mixture of marijuana, heroin, or crack.

"We know there's weed in there. But we'll figure out the rest once we're high," he laughed.

"Damn, bitch, you didn't even thank me!" Fats yelled.

With much affection, Buffy yelled, "Thanks, Fats!" He then turned his attention back to the items in his hand. He turned the shower on and put a towel under the door to trap the smell from going outside the room. And when they blazed, it became a puff-puff-pass rhythm between the two of them until their faces and heads felt heady, numb, and good!

They both wanted to get fucked, but they both knew that it wouldn't work out like that. So, they crawled into Summer's bed and held each other, wishing the other was someone else.

Summer's dreams took her deeper into a trance.

Her mind was drugged, and her vision was watery. Behind her eyelids, a vision from her childhood played out, as if she was right back there in the schoolyard.

"You're a sissy! You're a faggot, and you act like a girlllllllllllllllll," a group of kids teased. It was the rhythm of a song, and Summer was backed against a wall, totally trapped.

"I'm not, I'm not. Stop it!"

But they wouldn't, no matter how much she screamed. She didn't know if she was fighting to free herself from the corner that the kids had backed her into, or if she was struggling to be freed from the nightmare she had collapsed into. Once she realized she couldn't escape from the corner, she covered her ears. She looked down and saw a body she'd not been acquainted with for some time. Her small, rug-burned legs covered in pants, and she was wearing tennis shoes and a t-shirt. She hated the feeling of being in that body! It was nauseating, as she fought against the teasing, the kids, and the dream itself.

In the watery vision, Summer sensed Buffy walking around the cell, and she heard Fats call out to Buffy.

But Summer was still stuck in her nightmarish trance. She was in her parent's car, and they were dropping her off at her uncle's house. She could feel her father's accusing eyes looking at her with disgust. Her brother sat next to her, distant and cold. They were all going on vacation, but Summer was not allowed to go with them.

"I don't want to stay, Momma! I wanna go with you! Please let me come!" Summer was too young to understand that she didn't fit into her family's idea of perfect. She was a freak, an accident that had tarnished her family's name and destroyed her father's honor.

Summer's father couldn't look his shameful son in the eye for more than a second or two. Summer's brother was grateful that his family wouldn't have to be seen with what he could only describe as a faggot.

"You can't come to the political convention with us this year. Wait till next year, I promise," her mother, Sandra, said.

"But, Mama!"

"Get out of the car. We have to go!" Summer's father screamed at her. He couldn't take any more of the weakling he had for a son. Summer's mother had tears in her eyes and was afraid of what her husband would think of her if she were to brush the tears from her youngest son's eyes. So, she didn't. She hated the fact that Summer was gay, and she knew her youngest son would never be accepted by their family. It was as if he was a stepchild or a foster kid, as if he wasn't truly their flesh and blood.

It was all the crying Summer could do. He was quickly whisked out of the car into his uncle's arms.

"Bye, baby," Summer's mother said. "Be good, Bobby. Please take care of him, Kevin."

Kevin waved to the car as they sped off, and for each yard they drove away, a tear fell from Summer's eyes.

She couldn't break free as she floated to the room she always stayed in at Uncle Kevin's.

"Sit, Bobby. You know you're safe here. I love you, in more ways than your father ever could." Keven stood before Summer, his large hands undoing the buckle of a tattered brown belt. He lowered his trousers and as he stood up, he tilted Summer's chin back, so she looked him in the eye.

"You're a sweet boy, Bobby. This is how we show each other that we care."

Kevin let out a small gasp as he held Summer's gaze. He could tell that Summer was far, far away. In her mind, she was at an apple orchard, one of the last happy memories she held. The autumnal sun was warm still, and though many of the apples had been plucked from their trees, a butterfly floated from blossom to blossom. Making up for lost time, maybe.

CHAPTER 5
TO THE COMPOUND BUT OF COURSE

SUMMER STILL COULD FEEL the sun on her skin where she had been lying in the orchard during her dream. She awoke to the alarming sound of the trap on the door being yanked open.

"Bobby Moore, get up!" an irritated CO yelled. Summer had to try harder to pull from her sleep. "Bobby Moore, get up now!" the CO screamed again. He was in a rush to get other inmates to wake up, and he didn't want to stand there all day.

Summer turned over in the bed to acknowledge him. "What?"

"You have Team. And Adams, you know I have to cuff you up too. Get up!" the CO yelled.

"Buffy, get up," Summer said, as she shook him. "What, gurl? They need to learn how to talk to a lady," Buffy said, completely frustrated and cranky. "Waking me up with that bull-shit! Hold your horses, cracker!" Buffy directed to the CO.

"They said I'm going to Team. What's that?"

"Don't worry. It's your counselors, so you might be going to the compound today."

Summer was handcuffed through the trap in the cell door and

taken to a room where her counselors were. One was a fat, white, lady with a short hairstyle, and the other was a buff, white guy, who looked as if he had chewing tobacco in his mouth.

"Mr. Moore," the buff man said. They called him Scandal.

"Miss," Summer said as a normal response when referred to as a man.

"We have room on the compound, and we're going to let you out, but the captain sent us down here to browbeat you on our strict policy against any sexual activity between inmates. If you think that's going to be a problem, you should let us know now."

"No, it won't be a problem," Summer said with confidence.

"You don't sound too sure," Ms. Mires spat. Ms. Mires was, of course, the rotund-shaped woman. Summer had to bite her tongue as she tried to hold in a chuckle.

"I'm sure!"

"There's no need to get angry with us; we're just doing our job."

Sure, Summer thought. *That's if being an asshole is your job.* "I'm not angry at you. I'm just tired of everybody making a big deal out of who I am," Summer exclaimed to Ms. Mires.

"This is prison! You do what we say and what we want. You're going to be assigned to Unit 2A, and you better be on your best behavior. If you have any further questions, they'll have to wait until your initial team, or open house, every day during mainline."

My God, Summer thought. *You had to be a rocket scientist to be an inmate, initial team, open house, mainline.* But she was too pissed off to ask the two people in front of her what any of it meant, especially considering how they'd spoken to her so far.

"Fine, bye," Summer said smugly.

The COs took Summer back to her cell to pack her things. On the way, they passed a small room where inmates were getting their hair cut. The barber, Atwater, met eyes with Summer, and they held each other's gaze until she passed the door. When she returned to her cell, Buffy was brushing her teeth. "Gurl, you was on some weird shit last night, let me tell you. You got in the bed with me and curled up and you was holding ya hands against your ears. I thought I was going to have to press the panic button."

"Just had a bad trip," Summer said.

"What unit are you going to?" Buffy asked.

"I think they said 2A."

"Damn, they're sending you over there with Bad Breath Britney. She's okay. But she'll steal ya man as fast as you can blink your eyes, so watch her. I'll be out in three weeks or more."

"There was this guy out there cutting hair. Who's that?"

Buffy had to think for a second, and then he knew instantly. "Atwater? He act like he's all that. He's the Assistant Grand Sheik of the Moors, with his bourgeois ass. Why? Did he say something to you?"

"No, I was just asking."

The COs returned to get Summer. Buffy hugged her before they were placed in handcuffs. "You be careful out there. And I forgot to tell you last night, but don't even think about messing around with Sosa if you don't want a race riot on your hands."

Summer looked frightened. She didn't know what awaited her, and she was scared shitless.

When Summer walked out of the SHU, her eyes had to adjust to the bright sun. It was sunny and hot; her mind and body relaxed in the warmth, if just for a moment.

She was carrying the little belongings she had and was walking with about six other inmates who'd been released with her. All eyes were on her because she was the only gay amongst the guys who surrounded her as they walked down the compound. If she had to compare it to anything, it looked like a college campus. The whole compound was outside, with buildings and corrugated barbed wire atop the fencing.

Summer shuffled down the walkway, amazed at how big the prison was.

Other inmates ogled at her, and she heard all types of stuff. "Damn baby, you need help with that?" and "Just what we need; more fags on the compound."

Summer looked straight ahead, refusing to make eye contact with those cat-calling her. When she finally entered her unit at least a hundred men got up to look at her. She noticed Sosa was in the same unit, which was very reassuring.

The CO came out of his office. "Who are you?"

"Sum- Bobby Moore."

"You're assigned to cell #208 on the top range. Let me know immediately if you need a pillow or a mat."

Summer waited to see if the CO had anything else to say.

"Is that it?"

"Yes," he answered curtly.

Summer looked over at Sosa, who was sitting at a table with three other Mexicans. He didn't hide when he winked at Summer and gave a welcoming smile.

Summer smiled back and almost tripped over her bedroll before she picked it up and headed to her cell. When she got there, she noticed the cell was smaller than the SHU, and it lacked a shower. But it also had personal lockers.

There were pictures of her cellmate with his family on the bulletin board. Her cellmate was white and most definitely gay.

After she arranged her bed, she was startled to see Sosa standing at the door, looking at her with a seductive grin. Whatever fear she felt went away immediately as she heard him say, "Morena deliciosa, you are all mine."

She couldn't help but laugh when he entered the cell.

"And what makes you so sure I'm yours?" she said.

He sat on the toilet while Summer put the finishing touches on her bed. "I was hoping and praying that you would come to this unit. And here you are. It's a sign for me, you know?"

She turned and noticed he had a commissary bag full of stuff. She squinted as a smile spread across her face.

"Sosa, I don't want to cause no problems. I've been told about some racial stuff, and I don't want to be in the middle of it, so there's no way I can take anything from you." Summer didn't know what made her say what she said next. "But I do think you are adorable!"

"Listen, morena deliciosa, I got these things because I want you to have them. What do they say?" He searched his mind for the English phrase. "No strings attached." Sosa got up and gave Summer the overflowing bag.

He walked out of the cell, content with his interaction, but turned around when he heard somebody talking to Summer.

"Home girl, what's up?"

Summer was on guard as the unfamiliar short, acne-faced guy who approached her, carrying another commissary bag of goods in his hands. He was in his mid-thirties, but she couldn't really tell his age. This guy, who Summer had never met, walked up to Sosa as he set the bag down on the ground.

"Sosa, you know how this shit is run. You know the rules, man. She's from D.C., and you respect it or get your people ready."

Sosa stood tall from the affront. "Fraze, when I leave a year back, I no even know you had a voice without Black, E, and Berry with you."

It was clear Fraze didn't want to start anything right here, so he held up the bag to Sosa. "This bag here is from Black."

Sosa waved him off, seeing he didn't want any drama. "I'll see you later, Morena, but don't forget what I told you on the bus," he said, looking at Summer.

Summer was speechless momentarily because this was the time, she needed his guidance and protection, and here he was, walking away to leave her with a man she had not met.

"Fraze," he said to Summer, as if reading her mind. "Black

told the homies that you were here, and he gave me this to give to you. It's a care package."

"What's this for?" Summer asked, somewhat defensively.

"Nothing," Fraze said. "Nothing at all. Whenever a homie from D.C. comes in, we give them something, zu zus, wham whams, and a radio. We's D.C., and we gotta look out for each other. If you wanna catch up with Black, he works in the barbershop. He'll be there tonight after count."

"Catch up with him for what?" Summer was still apprehensive.

"Check this out, champ. A lot of fools are gonna be hounding you around here. Black is good protection. Everybody respects his gangsta; keep that in mind. So, just swing by and say what's up to him. And now is a good time to start looking for a job before they put you in the kitchen or CMS."

"I ain't working for nobody in the kitchen or whatever CMS is."

"Chill out, home girl. Tomorrow, all you have to do is talk to Ms. Mires and tell her to hold down on giving you a job assignment until you find the job you want. Because, trust me, they'll stick you wherever they want. But I gotta run to make a phone call before everybody comes back on recall. I'll holler at you later."

Shit, Summer thought. *Some more language I don't understand.* But if her memory served her right, Buffy explained that recall meant everybody had to return to their units in order to be counted at 4:00 p.m. Whatever he said about CMS had something to do with Compound Maintenance Services, which she read on a wall outside the office upon entering the unit. She knew for a fact she wasn't working for anybody. Lucky enough, her modeling agent had cut her a check for her last gigs, totaling a whopping $6,000, of which, in D.C. jail, she had only spent $600. She was cool on funds. Summer dragged the care package into the cell and tried her best to fit the two bags into her small locker. She was hoping to God that Sosa wouldn't put any money on her inmate account and people would stop bringing her bags of commissary. She really didn't want to be in the middle of other people's shit.

CHAPTER 6
GAY BASH

ATWATER HAD his wife in the palm of his hand. He was speaking with her in the telephone room, and he hated the fact whenever somebody else spoke, there was an echo that bounced off the walls which made it hard for him to hear his wife.

"What? Stop worrying and calm down. Tyler should be over there to speak to you in a second. Everything is under control," he said to his wife, Shonda.

She had always been attractive and still was. She was in her early forties and had two children, aged twenty-one and eighteen. She had them with Atwater before he was arrested eighteen years ago. At the beginning of his bid, things were a little rocky. Eventually, he started listening to the older guys around him, who gave him advice on how to get his wife back like he had her on the streets. Most of the advice consisted of him being understanding and patient when she complained about him being locked up.

"I don't like Tyler coming over here. He ain't ya friend, and I hate when you regard him as one. Because if he was really ya friend, you wouldn't be in prison; he would."

Atwater heard the attitude in her voice. "What I tell you about speaking recklessly over this horn? That's too much

44

information. Baby, to be with a boss you must think bossy without letting your emotions cloud your judgment. So, boss up."

"Atwater," she called him by his first name. "I don't want to hear that or anything about the Prophet Noble Drew Ali. I'm the one out here with these kids. I've raised them all by myself."

That took Atwater by surprise. "Let me address that right quick, so we won't ever have to cross this bridge again. When I met you, you didn't have dreams or ambitions. All you wanted to be was a housewife. Everything about going to school to become an accountant was my idea." Atwater could hear Shonda slamming pots and pans down in the background, but he continued. "It was an idea within a bigger idea."

"Remember when the kids were young, and I suggested we put them in private school, and I paid the tuition? I know you remember. Everything up till this point we've done together. I know you're stressing, but I got ya, baby."

Shonda sighed. All this time waiting had been so tiring on her.

"I didn't mean to say that. I'm sorry."

"Don't worry about it." Atwater believed he understood her more than she understood herself. "I know you're just anxious to get me home."

"That is so true," she laughed, and when she did, the phone beeped to mark the fifteen minutes allowed for each call had come to an end.

"The phone's about to hang up but rest easy knowing I'm on my way home and we're going to be together like I always promised you."

"I love you, Atwater."

"I love you more."

"I'm going to write you an e-mail you tonight. I got some things on my mind that need to be put on paper." She sounded anxious.

"I'm going to write to you too. I'm romancing you, though. I have to get your mind and body ready for when I get out."

"Yeah." She smiled. "What are we going to do when you get out?"

"We're gonna make this hunger disappear."

"I can't wai—" The phone cut off in the middle of their conversation.

Atwater hung up the phone and went to his friend, Jeffrey Bey's cell. Jeffrey was cleaning when Atwater walked up to him.

"Islam Moor," Atwater greeted.

"Islam. What's going good with you?"

"Same ole same ole. It never ceases to amaze me how short-sighted some people can be. I just hung up with Shonda, and she hit me with some 'I've raised the kids all by myself' bullshit."

"She knows that ain't right," Jeffrey Bey added.

"I know," Atwater replied.

"Moor, you're a hustler. You're one of the few that can still send gees home and take care of ya kids and family. There's only a few in federal prison that can do that. Most of us have been washed up by the Feds."

"Real talk," Atwater said,

"And she is always hatin' on Tyler."

"What's that about?" Jeffrey Bey asked as they walked into his cell. Like many, he was serving an unfair 30-year sentence.

"When she went to college, she got all brand new. She thinks that Tyler should have got this beef, but I took the rap for him. And she's been tripping ever since." Tyler was the cause of Atwater getting busted. Atwater was selling drugs too, but he told Tyler to move the drugs from the house they were staying in because he felt like the spot was hot. Tyler lied to Atwater and said he moved everything out of the house. When the Feds kicked in the door and searched the house, they found the drugs and Atwater was charged. Atwater took the rap, never implicating Tyler nor mentioning his involvement. Two brothers locked up is worse than one.

Jeffrey Bey sighed, knowing how hard it was to keep it real and be a stand-up man while the government dangled time over their head.

"Atwater, there ain't too many brothers out there like you no more. You have to catch brothers up to your pedigree."

"Real talk. I wish I felt as confident as you sound. I don't know what the world is like anymore. I've been down practically my whole adult life."

"Trust, you are more than capable."

They were interrupted when they heard the CO yelling for mail call. They walked out of the cell to see if they received any word from outside.

Atwater heard his name being called, and he called down for Craze-zo to get it.

Craze-zo was twenty years old and far away from home. He didn't have many homeboys from Los Angeles, but he had gotten really close to Atwater. After Craze-zo gathered the mail, he walked over to Atwater.

"Islam, cuz. I see you have the pony-express crack-a-lacking."

Atwater laughed. "For sure. The love you get from without demonstrates the love you have within."

"I would get on some die-hard Cali time and express that I don't love them hoes. But I feel like it wouldn't fit in this demonstration we're having."

"It's not that," Atwater laughed. "You're elevating ya game, but what's up with ya fade? I'm used to seeing you look more dapper than that."

Craze-zo was high yellow with freckles and curly hair. Overly conscientious about his pretty boy looks, he felt he had to balance his look by being an over-the-top gangster.

"I'm waiting on you," Craze-zo said.

"You know where I'm at. Meet me at the barbershop this evening after count."

"You heard they got a new punk on the compound? They say he looks like a model," Craze-zo asked.

"No," Atwater said, not really feeling like discussing the fact he had seen Summer in the SHU while he was cutting hair.

"Cuz, on Crip, I can almost guarantee on all my dead homies that that punk is gonna have these niggas fucked up like that Puerto Rican punk did awhile back. But on Crip, if I see one of those fags out of pocket, cuz, I'm trippin' on sight," Craze-zo said as he showed Atwater the handle of his eight-inch steel homemade knife that he always carried with him.

CHAPTER 7
THAT'S WHEN HE FOUND OUT WHERE TRUE POWER LIES

NATHAN HOWARD HAD BEEN CALLED Britney Spears since he got to the compound, even though he hardly bore any resemblance to the pop star. It was a nickname far more in connection with his attitude than with his looks. He introduced himself to Summer as he entered their shared cell. The CO slammed the door behind him.

"Hey, my name is Nathan, but everybody calls me Britney."

They shook hands, and for the first time, Summer understood why everybody called him Bad Breath Britney. One whiff of his breath was enough to make Summer nauseous.

Once Britney took off his uniform and put on his sweat suit, he arranged the medicine cabinet to make room for Summer's things.

"I'm Summer." Summer remembered what Buffy told her.

"Nice to meet you. This cabinet over here is yours. I'll move all those cosmetics on my side. I hope you don't snore or fart in your sleep because I do. I don't have any grippers left, and if the both of us are farting at night, this room will smell worse than Dante's Inferno come morning. And we're ladies, so windows always stay cracked come winter, spring, or fall."

"Do you ever breathe when you talk?" Summer teased.

"Nostrils, baby." Britney rocked his head as if performing oral sex on somebody.

"Top range, stand up count!" a CO screamed as they counted the inmates.

"Stand up or they'll shake our cell down and take all our stuff." Britney and Summer had to stand up quickly before they passed.

After the COs passed, they relaxed. Britney took the time to run everything down to Summer.

"I work at Unicor. My job includes boosting the factory manager's confidence. I literally sit behind a desk and tell Mrs. Bowers how beautiful she is and that her husband's a jerk for banging the pretty little secretary in Unit 3B. The first chance you get, you need to find a job."

"I know. Somebody named Fraze told me already."

"Fraze is all right. But I can help you get a job at Unicor as a production clerk. Mrs. Bowers will hire anybody I suggest. That is, if that's what you want."

"I don't know where I want to work, or if I want to work at all."

"Believe me, you don't want to work in the kitchen. They'll have you serving 1,200 inmates, sometimes twice a day. Talk about draconian measures."

"What?"

Britney waved her off. "Don't worry about it. At Catholic school you get a good education on literature and priests." Britney winked.

"Nuh-hum, Buffy said you were crazy, but I couldn't have imagined that you were this crazy."

"You met Buffy the Vampire?"

Summer looked confused. "I thought his name was Buffy da Body?"

"Not with all the guys he's shredded around here with those horse teeth."

"You're wildin'!"

"You don't have to lie. I know he was back there talking about me. Let me guess: Bad Breath Britney. But he doesn't know that Ray Ray doesn't think my breath stinks, and you bet not say anything."

"I won't. Besides, that's hardly my business, and a closed mouth never tells."

"Goood. Come on, let's go to chow. They're unlocking the doors."

CHAPTER 8
SOSA

"HEY, FOOL, GET UP," Michoacan said to Sosa, who was on the bottom bunk fast asleep. "Tis time to eat."

"I can't eat right now. I'm in love with the pinche Morena deliciosa," Sosa said as he sat up. It was better now to tell his partner how he felt about Summer. Michoacan was a part of the Paisas, which was a loosely translated Spanish word that meant countrymen.

Paisas was probably the biggest prison cartel in the federal system. Their shot callers were called Reps and, because they controlled all the illegal immigrants from Mexico, they generally had numbers on their side. Their numbers included more than fifty percent of those incarcerated. To be as connected as Sosa was in Mexico carried weight, even outside of Mexico.

Michoacan, who was 5'5" tall, dark-skinned with long hair, and somebody Sosa knew he could depend on if he ever needed to make a hit in prison.

Michoacan laughed about Sosa being in love with Summer. "Un culo al ano no hace dano."

"Yeah, but the pinche ruka is a Morena. But I want to fuck her so bad I couldn't sleep for two nights. Fuck the pinche myates. I'm going to get some of that sweet ass; so what if I have to cause a riot." Sosa had tunnel vision when it came to Summer, and Michoacan could not divert his friend from his path.

"No vale la pena," Michoacan said, who loved Sosa because he was the boss, and put plenty of money on his inmate account.

"Fuck it—I don't care. I got to have morena deliciosa."

CHAPTER 9
SHE JUST COULDN'T
KEEP HER EYES OFF HIM

SUMMER FOLLOWED close behind Britney as they walked to the kitchen once their unit was called for chow. It took them a minute to get to the serving line, and once they got there, they immediately regretted coming.

The line server plopped a scoop of runny mashed potatoes on their trays and a beef fritter that hardly looked edible.

"Eat up, baby girl," the server said to Summer, winking at her.

"Shut up, Terrence," Britney said.

They sat down at the table where guys from D.C. sat, and a couple of guys came over to meet Summer. They were all cool. Buffy explained to Summer that D.C. guys were open-minded to having gay homeboys.

Summer couldn't eat the food. It looked disgusting and tasted bland. But Britney ate it as if nothing was wrong.

"What?" Britney asked as Summer looked at him.

"How can you eat this stuff?"

"It takes some getting used to. But if you want to skip it, I have some food in my locker. Actually, you just got here. You can go to the commissary tonight, even though it's not your shopping day. You can get first-time shopper. You have money on your account?"

"Yeah."

"Let's go see if you can shop tonight," Britney said. Summer agreed, even though her locker was already full of the welcome gifts she received earlier.

They went directly to the commissary, crowing in with the other shopping inmates. Britney could hear all the sneers and shit-talking going on as they passed.

Britney asked the CO at the commissary if Summer could shop, and he said yes. They filled out a commissary list of all the things Summer wanted and handed it in. They had to wait a long time before Summer's number came over the display. They filled two laundry bags with food. Summer knew she wasn't going to have anywhere to store all the stuff.

"What kind of ice cream you want?" the CO asked Summer. She wasn't that big on ice cream, so she asked Britney if he wanted one.

"Cherry Garcia," Britney responded. Summer went ahead and ordered two.

Slim stood at the door, waiting to be called for his commissary. He was dressed fly; his clothes were crisply ironed, and his braids were freshly done. He stood tall, and always stayed clean and fresh with new shoes and new clothes that were purchased from the commissary.

"Punk, ya betta stop looking at me, 'for I give you a black eye," Slim said to Britney.

Britney walked over to him, set the commissary bag on the ground, and got in his face.

"You haven't heard what happened to Run when he tried to give me a black eye?"

Slim didn't say anything. Instead, he turned his lips to the side of his face, as if he wasn't hearing it.

"FYI, I dislocated his jaw and broke his arm. Just let me know when you're ready because I love the spousal abuse. Break up to make up."

Everybody laughed, but Summer was getting panicked with everybody gathering around to see if they were about to fight. Summer looked to see if there was any way she could sneak out, but it didn't seem feasible. It was a stroke of luck they didn't fight because if they did, she wouldn't have known what to do. Summer sighed as she grabbed the receipt and signed it. She and Britney exited the same door that Big Franco was entering.

Big Franco let Britney and Summer pass, staring at the latter's backside as she hurried past him. *I ain't no fag*, he thought.

When they walked out, Summer saw the barbershop on the side of the commissary store. She wanted to thank Black before heading back to the unit. She didn't know how all these political factions in jail would play out, but she was sure she didn't want to be on his bad side.

"Is that the barbershop Black works at?"

"Yeah, he should be in there," Britney answered.

There were about a dozen men in the room. For the most part, everybody was getting their hair cut. In one of the chairs, somebody was braiding another's hair. Summer sort of wandered about the room, noticing Atwater at one of the chairs. His back was to her.

"What's up, home girl? What you been up to?" Black asked.

He looked different from how she remembered him from the other day when they both were in the holding tank. His matted afro was now braided, and he wore a gold chain, but he still looked as big as ever.

"I'm okay. I just wanted to say thanks for looking out, and to see how you were doing?" Summer spoke to Black, but her eyes were glued to Atwater, who still hadn't looked up from his work.

"Don't worry about that. You can thank me later. I want you to meet the homies over there. That's E and Berry."

Summer turned to see the two young brothers behind her. They looked like stone-cold killers. Besides E having braids and Berry having a short haircut, they looked like twins. They nodded. "Whenever you have a problem, holler at one of us."

Black turned to face Britney. "Damn, what's up, Britney? You act like you can't talk."

"I can talk, Black. I just didn't want to say nothing because you have his hairline pushed behind his back. That's why I can't let anybody cut my hair."

"Bad Breath Britney always got something slick to say," Berry said as they laughed.

"Ain't nobody going to cut your hair anyways, white boy. I don't even know how to cut white people's hair," Black said as they laughed.

"Those clippers cut my hair like they cut everybody else's, so stop it."

"You a sexy momma, but all that shit you talking is gonna get your ass kicked," E said playfully.

While they were clowning with Britney, Summer kept her eyes on Atwater. Atwater's creamy brown skin and Caesar haircut reminded Summer of how men looked outside of the prison walls: richly toned and handsome. He was not nearly as big as Black, yet he was somehow far more imposing.

Atwater stole another glance at her by keeping his back to her and looking at her in the mirror before him. He could feel his blood rush. He tried to stay focused on Craze-zo's haircut.

"Britney can back her shit up though," Berry said.

"I'd whip Britney's ass," E said.

"Hey, homie, I'm with you. But I seen Britney in action. Believe you me, you don't want to have to live with the reputation of getting beat up by home girl," Black said.

"You mean faggot," Craze-zo interrupted them, tired of

hearing all the gay shit being spoken in his presence. He fingered the knife handle in his pocket. Everybody looked at him questioningly as Britney let the commissary bag fall to the ground again.

"Islam Moor," Atwater said, trying to keep everybody's temper calm. "Sometimes foolishness travels faster than wisdom and sound judgment. Excuse us."

"What! That fool don't want no wax with me!" Craze- zo said, snatching his barber bib off his neck.

"You disrespecting my friend, Cali?" Black said as he put the clippers down.

Craze-zo looked confused for a second, and Atwater came to his aid. "He straight, Black. He's with me. I just need to have a word with him. He's like family to me."

Black was reluctant as he said, "Islam."

Britney picked up the commissary bag and walked out with Summer following.

Black was about to follow them when he stopped and said, "Don't be mad, Britney. Shit! See you later, Summer."

"Bye, Black," Summer said.

Black looked at Craze-zo, who stood there still heated. Atwater shook his head at Black, suggesting he understood his frustrations with Craze-zo.

"I said I got him, Black. Don't trip off that shit."

"What was the disrespect for?" Black still couldn't understand. E and Berry were ready to put in some work anyways, especially on this nigga who was a thousand miles away from home.

"Moor, let that die down. Islam," Atwater bided him. "Islam, but hey, champ, don't be so quick to judge the next man till you've walked a mile in his shoes."

Black recommenced cutting hair, but he was thirsty for blood. To cool everything down, Atwater took Craze-zo outside, and they walked to the other side of the commissary.

"Craze-zo, what kind of idiot shit was that?" Atwater asked once they were by themselves.

"Homie, I ain't tripping or worried about no fag, or no fag-lovers. I hate faggots! And I told you I'm waiting for one of those fags to jump out there."

"It wasn't that fag you would have had to worry about. You would have had to worry about E and Berry, who were strapped to the teeth waiting for you to jump out there. They would have butchered us in there."

"Us?" Craze-zo asked.

"Yes, us, because I would've had to jump in. You're with me. Just like Black couldn't allow you to disrespect his people because they are with him. You gotta step your game up if you're kicking it with me. I can't have you jeopardizing my life with that I don't give a fuck attitude. I've built too much shit in my life to have it torn apart on some bullshit. You could have fucked up all the shit I have going on, and all my plans for the future in just a couple of seconds because you can't control yourself. Now go back in there and apologize to Black."

"What for? I didn't call him a faggot?"

"Craze-zo." Atwater realized it was going to take longer than he thought to make him understand. "It's called finesse. Never, ever allow yourself to use disrespectful words, not even to your enemy, not even if you're going to kill him. If you compliment the man you're going to kill, he'll never put his guard up to you. And trust me, you don't want the likes of Black, E, and Berry sitting around having unresolved issues with you."

It took a minute for Craze-zo to surrender, and it was largely out of the respect he had for Atwater, who he saw as a father.

They went back into the barbershop and Craze-zo approached Black. "Black, I didn't mean to disrespect you. I just called it how I seen it. My bad. I was out of pocket."

"Apology accepted, Cali." Black meant it. "They throw us all together in here, and we have to learn to have respect for people who are different; that's all."

Craze-zo finally understood. "That's real talk."

Atwater looked at Craze-zo through the mirror and smiled. However, he knew his advice was temporary because Craze-zo was hot-headed.

CHAPTER 10
I CRIED MY HEART OUT

"I SHOULD HAVE KICKED his ass in there!" Britney huffed.

"For what?" Summer asked. This was their tenth time going over it.

"So that he'd have to live with getting his ass whipped by somebody gay," Britney said.

Summer sighed. She was attempting to fit all her commissary purchases in her already cluttered locker.

"You're going to have to put some of that stuff in my locker."

Britney helped Summer put some of the things up, and he came across Summer's receipt.

"Damn! You robbed a bank?" Summer snatched the receipt away.

"Everybody in here ain't a flea-rotten prostitute."

"That's true. It's only us gorgeous hos. But you had money out there?" Britney asked, kind of shocked.

"I still do. I'm a model. I've ripped the runway, did the venue of all the Black magazines. I've done commercials and videos. I've done it all."

"How did you manage to get locked up then?"

"I used to cash checks all the time. But soon as I stopped, I got set up, and they busted me on bank fraud and identity theft."

Summer explained that she had stolen other girls' identities only out of necessity, so she could get work without anyone knowing she had been born male. All her illegal activity was ending before Peyton tricked her.

"Damn, that's some shit. But you were never scared that when you were modeling, they would find out that you were a man?"

"Not really. I mean, besides, with this tiny appendage attached to my body, it's impossible to tell."

"I don't know. Your hair is looking a little messed up," Britney laughed.

"That ain't fair. I don't know what to do with my nappy hair without a stylist in sight."

"Why don't you use mayonnaise?"

"Why would I do something stupid like that?"

"I don't know. I thought that was Aunt Jemima's recipe. Plus, a lot of guys in jail do it to get waves."

"I'm not that desperate."

"I'm just teasing. You really are stunning, Summer."

"Thank you. I really needed that. All of this prison stuff can really kill a person's spirit. I don't hate much, but I hate this place."

"Have you been feeling down?"

Summer nodded her head.

"Here, have a seat and tell me all about it."

Summer left the remainder of the commissary to one side of the bed as she recounted the story of how her life had turned into a nightmare. She told Britney about the ordeal with Clayton's family after Peyton exposed the truth about Summer's gender. Clayton had accepted Summer, but his family was adamant that he leave her. When he refused, choosing to move away and live with Summer in Virginia, they cut him off. They never spoke to

Clayton, even when his mother fell ill and died in the hospital. When that news reached him, Clayton took it out on Summer, blaming her for isolating him from his family. She could remember him coming home one night, an open beer bottle in his hand, looking especially angry. She asked him where he had been.

"I don't have to answer to faggots," Clayton said between swigs of his bottle.

"Who the fuck are you to be calling me a fag? We sleep in the same bed. You oughta start calling me mommy with how often my tits are in your mouth," Summer spat, sick of him coming home like this.

That was the night he started beating her; things didn't last long after that. Summer moved out to live on her own, seeing Peyton occasionally even though things were tense. Losing Clayton made things seem so monotonous for Summer. Men loved her until they didn't, and it always seemed to be her fault when they stopped.

Britney helped Summer as she cried, shushing her and saying these low-down men didn't deserve her. It was little consolation for Summer, but it was nice to hear, nonetheless.

CHAPTER 11
SHE COULD NEVER SHAKE THE DEMONS OF HER PAST

THE SKY WAS dark the following day, and the sun was rising behind thick, grey clouds.

Summer needed at least another hour of sleep to feel completely rested. She'd get up, make her bed, and make something to eat because she never wanted to step foot inside the chow hall again. Summer thought they probably fed hogs better than the inmates at Schuylkill were fed.

"Summer, you have to get up. You're on the call-out for an appointment."

Summer awoke to the sound of Britney brushing his teeth and splashing water on his face. She only heard him say she had an appointment, but she didn't know what a call-out was.

"Appointment?"

"They have you for a psych evaluation at 9:00 a.m. They're going to have you running all over the place today and tomorrow, but they'll tell you all the details. I have to go to work. I'll see you later."

"Okay."

Summer prepared some oatmeal, then gathered her things for the shower.

She was about to head out when Sosa popped up at the door.

There were three things Summer liked about him: he was cute, persistent, and he didn't care about the political stuff which frightened Summer, but she found it thrilling and exciting all the more.

"Morena deliciosa, you're going somewhere without me?"

Summer thought he was cute on the bus, but now he looked edible. He had on a creased sweat suit with a gold cross necklace and a gold Rolex watch he smuggled into the jail.

Britney's alarm clock read 7:45 a.m. Summer had an hour and fifteen minutes to kill before she had to be anywhere.

"You're gonna get me in trouble, Sosa," Summer said as she placed her shower stuff on the locker and sat back down on the bed.

"I got something for you, Morena deliciosa. Can I put up the towel on the door?" Sosa asked.

Summer had seen several people put a towel on the door window so nobody could look in while they used the bathroom. Some would knock to make sure the inmate was okay inside, but most respected their need for privacy.

Summer's breath was heavy with lust. She wanted Sosa to spread her ass cheeks and spend his load deep inside her body.

"I don't mind," she said.

He put the towel up on the door, came back, and stood in front of the bed.

"So, what do you have for me?" Summer asked. She could tell they were down to their wit's end.

He threw a cellphone on the bed, and Summer jumped as if it were a snake.

"How did you get this?" Summer was looking at the phone in her hands.

"I tried to tell you, Morena, that I got some good connections. Here, call somebody." He picked up the phone and gave it to Summer. She thought about calling Peyton to curse her out but then thought better of it. So, she called her mother. Her mother answered on the third ring. When Summer heard her voice, she hung up as fast as she could. She couldn't stomach the thought of revealing where she was calling from.

"That was quick, Morena," Sosa said as he stood there. By now his dick was erect and poking out of his sweats.

Summer scooted to the end of the bed. She caressed his dick. "I'm hoping that's not the only reason you're here," she said.

Sosa looked lovingly down at Summer as she pulled his dick from under his sweatpants and placed her lips around the tip. "Mi Dios, Morena!" he gasped, falling back onto the locker for balance as Summer tickled his dick with her swirling tongue. She thought about how she'd been wanting to taste him since they met on the bus and slurped his dick without taking a breath.

"Morena, let me fuck you."

Summer didn't stop. She took his balls in her mouth as she ran her tongue along the bottom of his ass while she jacked his dick with her right hand. When she looked up and saw the expression on his face, she put his dick inside her mouth again until he shot a wad down her throat and collapsed on the bed. Summer kept his dick in her mouth the whole time as she swirled her tongue over the agonizing pleasure zone that had him trembling and pleading for Summer to stop. She wouldn't relent. After the strong pleasure waves passed through his body, his dick stiffened harder than before.

"I gonna fuck you now, Morena deliciosa."

"You gonna fuck me?" Summer asked, lying flat on her stomach after taking off all her clothes.

"Mi Dios, Morena. Tu cuerpo es mejor que jamás imagine."

"Yes, speak Spanish to me while you fuck me!"

"Deja me mirar a ese culo maravilloso."

Summer didn't understand a word he said, but she wiggled her hips side to side. Sosa bit and nibbled on Summer's ass and sucked on her cheeks.

"Grab some Vaseline from the medicine cabinet," she instructed.

He wasn't gone a second, before he was back massaging it into her ass and on his dick. He jammed his dick in so fast and hard, Summer had to bite down on her cellie's pillow to stop herself from crying out.

Right when they were about to get into it, there was a knock on the door. Summer's heart beat out of her chest as she tried to get up, but Sosa held her still.

"Hey, CO, I taking a fuckin' shit!" Sosa hollered, but he wasn't coming out of Summer to save his life.

"Who's in there?" the CO asked. "It's count time."

"What's your last name, Morena?" Sosa whispered. "Moore."

"Moore's in here. Now can I take my shit in peace?"

The CO left the room because it was an unnecessary count anyway. It wasn't an official count, but sometimes they did an extra count after 8:00 a.m.

"Hold on, Sosa," Summer said because now she thought somebody might come in, and she remembered what Attenberger said about sending her to ADX.

Sosa stopped, but only for a moment to explain that the officer wouldn't come back. As he continued, he began to hammer that ass until the speed and forcefulness made them both orgasm at the same time.

Sosa was barely able to drag himself away from Summer, but it was now 8:45, and Summer had to rush to get to her 9:00 appointment.

After her shower, she put on the funny-looking uniform that was mandatory for all inmates and headed outside to see if she could find the psychology building. Every building looked so similar from the outside that she struggled to find it until someone was kind enough to point it out to her. She went inside and told the secretary at the desk her name. Summer was told to sit and wait.

They called her moments later, and she went into the psychiatrist's office. The standoffish attitude of the woman behind the desk gave off every indication she was as much a CO as she was a psych doctor, if not more.

"Well, Ms. Moore, your record is very exciting," the lady said. "My name is Mrs. Salinas, and by what I've read, it seems you've tried to commit suicide more than enough times to be locked up somewhere in a straitjacket. But, since that's not something I can recommend, is there anything else you need?"

"No," Summer said bluntly. She didn't like how long Mrs. Salinas spent studying her file.

"I'm going to keep you on your hormones, as is your right, and I'll prescribe some medicine for your apparent bipolar disorder. Are you having trouble sleeping still?"

Summer didn't want anything from Mrs. Salinas, but she shook her head, affirming the question.

"Very well. I'll prescribe something for that also. That's it for now, and if you ever feel the need to speak about something, you can make a call out."

Summer stepped back into the hall, and when the secretary smiled at her, she was too annoyed to return it. Summer strolled around the building impatiently for a bit, forced to wait until the next controlled movement before she could return to her cell. She sat in the lounge and studied her nails.

Two orderlies were cleaning the area, and when Summer looked up, she realized she was alone with them. The one named Tyrone came and sat at her side. "You from D.C., right?"

"Yes."

"What's up? You wanna party?"

She knew what Tyrone was asking. She was still buzzed from her experience with Sosa that morning and considered his offer, but she just didn't want to give in so easily. "What you mean, 'party'?" she asked, still seated.

"Hold up one second." Tyrone went over to Love, who was in the utility closet putting the mop bucket away.

"You still have those X pills from yesterday?"

"Yeah, nigga, why?" Tyrone gestured toward Summer, then met Love's eye line with a nod.

"Dr. Alonzo's office?"

"Let's go."

Love went to the unoccupied office like he was going to clean it and took out the pill bag he had keistered. The ecstasy was crushed and packaged in paper.

While Love was prepping in Dr. Alonzo's office, Tyrone went back to get Summer. He hadn't seen someone so attractive since he had been locked up.

"Summer, right? I'm Tyrone, and my dude going in that room is Love. He's good people. Look, I have some ecstasy. I'll hook you up if you wanna party."

Summer looked into his adventurous eyes, and she made the decision that whatever he meant, she was down.

"Where are they?" she asked.

"We got them. You down?"

"Yes," she easily replied

"Come on."

Tyrone led her back to Dr. Alonzo's office and locked the door behind them.

"Ooh-child, you fine as fuck." Love helped himself to her busty breasts.

"Thanks," Summer said coyly, loving the attention they gave her. They couldn't keep their hands off her. They groped her ass and Love went as far as to kiss her neck.

"Damn, Summer. You're so fine, I'd suck on your daddy's dick!" Love said, completely taken.

"You won't have to, nigga. You can suck on my dick," Tyrone said as they laughed.

"Where the shit at?" asked Summer.

"Right here," Love made a kingly display of the lines of the X he had under a paper on the desk.

"Snort it, baby," Tyrone said.

When Summer went down to take the straw and snort the fine powder, she felt Tyrone's dick grinding on her ass.

"God damn, baby, you're a real muthafuckin' girl. I thank the US Marshals for sending you here."

Summer snorted more than three lines of ecstasy leaving very little for them. But they were too busy fighting over the privilege of grinding on her ass to notice. Even through the khakis, her plump ass and coke-bottle shape were easily discernable. She had the kind of body that got men in trouble.

Summer gasped pleasurably, suddenly feeling the two dicks against her body. She wanted to be ravished on the spot.

Love was already feeling the line he did moments before and began kissing all over her. Tyrone kept his eyes on Summer's pretty face, afraid to look down. He took his dick out and pulled Summer from Love. He had to get his before he overthought things and lost his erection. Summer was too focused to see the way his eyes drifted across her body, only to dart away.

It was the best head he'd ever had, despite Love biting and gnawing on Summer's ass. Tyrone would have laughed if the head wasn't so powerfully occupying.

It felt good to Summer too. Her ass was getting ate through her pants, and the more he ruffled her cheeks with his tongue and his face, the more she wanted to be fucked. She gobbled Tyrone's dick during the exchange and gave his dick her special. She sucked it like she truly loved dick and he nutted quickly. While humming a lullaby, she drank it down and swallowed his dick without gagging.

"Love." Tyrone trembled. He almost passed out. Love

jumped up and saw how Tyrone looked as if he'd died a heavenly death, and Love knew he had missed something grand.

Summer pushed Tyrone out of the way and massaged Love's dick through his pants.

"Take it out, baby," Summer begged, as she gently bit on the bottom of his hard dick. He collapsed against the table.

"I think I'm falling in love." He watched Summer take his dick out of his pants and sucked it as if he had juice inside of him. She slurped and twirled her juicy red lips around the helmet of his dick, then dropped her mouth all the way down to swallow him whole. He would have sworn she was the prettiest girl he had ever been with.

Tyrone gathered himself as Summer worked her magic on Love. He was so cum drained that he didn't have enough vigor to fuck Summer who was by now wagging her sexy ass like a bitch in heat!

"You wanna fuck me?" Summer asked Love with her golden, sex-hungry eyes sparkling. But he was too far gone. And when she felt his helmet flare, she slurped his nut down her throat relishing the taste. She pulled her face away and asked for some water, which Love promptly delivered. As she rested her mouth with the cool drink, Love spoke to Tyrone in the corner of the office.

"Tyrone, I ain't never had head like that, and she pretty enough to tongue kiss. I think I'm in love."

"Hold up, Love. Fall back," Tyrone said. "Summer, I know we ain't finished yet?"

Summer sat up. She was still hot and horny as hell.

"What else you got in mind?" she asked, grabbing Love's dick again. He groped her ass in return.

"Shit, we got smoke, drink, and plenty more dick in my unit. You down?" Tyrone asked. On the sly, Tyrone rubbed his fingers together, making sure Love caught the gesture.

"I'm down for whatever, as long as your friend fucks me." At this point, Summer felt so good and high, she didn't care about all the gangs, territories, and turfs. She just wanted to continue having a good time.

As promised, Tyrone snuck Summer in Unit-4B disguised with a low cap on her head and a big jacket. Tyrone brought out lots of hooch and weed and arranged for a few paying patrons to get a piece of her fine ass.

Love was first, and it took everything Tyrone had to pull him out of the cell after he finished. Others had gone in, and Summer serviced them all, something she had never done before. She continued to drink and smoke as men came and left the cell. Her vision became foggy and even though she could feel the men entering and leaving her body, they all began to meld together. Summer was having a hard time keeping track of her visitors, and the space around her seemed to shift. Eventually someone pulled her pants back up around her waist and she was led back to her unit.

A teenage Summer stood before the mirror in her room. Her face was gently made up with brown mascara and pink lip gloss. She had taken it from her mother's makeup bag and, in doing so, Summer crafted a look that resembled her mother's. She'd always thought her mother was the prettiest woman she had ever seen. Yet, she couldn't remember the last time her mother had received a compliment. Summer sat on the edge of her bed, moving the flesh of her thighs out from under her to amplify the curve from waist to hips, and she was pleased with the result. Then, her father stormed into her room without knocking.

"Did you steal your mother's makeup? What the fuck do you think you're doing, Bobby?!" He barked, leaping to grab Summer by the face before she could hide herself. Summer jerked her head away from him, but he caught her by the hair, forcing her eyes to meet his. He studied her, silent for a moment, before he threw her onto the floor. Summer tried to stand, but her father hit her again. Fist closed and knuckles white, he refused to let her get up.

"Get out my house. If I ever see you again, I'll kill you. I swear to God, I'll kill you . . . Get out!"

Summer ran from the house, her lip bleeding onto her shirt. She didn't know where to go, but she ran anyway. The image of her mother hysterically crying, trying to pull her father off her, replayed in her mind. She hadn't noticed, but her brother had seen what happened. He stood watch, silently approving of his father's measures to keep his house in check.

She tossed and kicked in her sleep until Britney woke her for the 4 p.m. count. Britney had just returned from work to find Summer strung across his bed with vomit everywhere. He just laughed until Summer started screaming from her hellish night-mares, which was around the same time the COs were counting. Britney cleaned the mess while Summer tried to get on her bunk at the top, but it proved too difficult, and she collapsed on the chair.

"You gutter mouth slut. You need to get your smelly ass in your bed. You're a mess, and I know your ass is soiled with nut."

"Leave me alone," Summer said pitifully. Her head was pounding, her ass was sore, and it took all she had not to vomit again from the sour taste she had in her mouth.

"Not ever. You have the whole compound talking about you, and you were probably too wasted to even remember it. Lucky girl."

After Britney changed his bedsheets and cover, and sprayed disinfectant, he laid Summer back in his bed. He grabbed a bagel from her locker, spread cream cheese and honey over it, then gave her aspirin. "Eat this," Britney said as he coddled Summer and fed her. "You'll be all right, don't worry. A couple of more crashes like that, and you'll be fine. I'm here for you."

Chapter Thirteen Dreamy Eyes and Passion

Summer and Sosa fucked every chance they got. They used the showers, cells, and restrooms while Sosa's crew kept watch for them. They knew they had to keep the boss protected while he spent time with his little Morena.

Unfortunately, Black caught wind of what was going on between them.

It had been a few days since Summer's ordeal in 4B, and Black had sent word through Fraze for her to meet him in the chapel so they could speak. Her days in the unit with Sosa were wearing her out, but the chapel promised solitude. She thought about how even if she did run into one of the men she had been with in 4B, she wouldn't recognize them.

The air was crisp and cold, sending a chilling shiver through her. She pulled her jacket tight and picked up her pace. She was surprised when guys were saying, "What's up?" to her and greeting her like never before. *They must have heard about 4B*, she thought. She even saw Love and Tyrone walking to the gym.

When she went inside the chapel, it was nothing like she imagined. A hallway led to the main sanctuary and along the hallway were other rooms for different religious groups to congregate and hold services.

Black was the Grand Sheik for the Moorish Science Temple of America, outranking Atwater, who was the Assistant Sheik. They were both a part of the same faith, but they never formed a tight friendship.

Inside the main chapel, the Moors were arrayed in their attire with red fezzes on their heads, Moorish pendulums, and shiny shoes. They had paintings of Noble Drew Ali on a chair, Marcus Garvey on another, an American flag at one corner of the chapel, and a Moroccan flag on the other side.

Atwater stood at the podium, and it drew Summer to the door that was guarded by two doormen. When they went to open it, Summer waved them off.

She couldn't hear anything Atwater was saying, but she could hear the applause. She stayed there for a minute, watching him until someone tapped her on the shoulder.

"Excuse me. Can I be of some assistance?" an inmate named Lazy Eyes asked. As his name suggested, he had dreamy bedroom eyes that would make one feel intoxicated when gazing into them.

Summer had to snap out of it. Lazy Eyes was most definitely good looking to say the least, and he'd caught her off guard completely.

"I . . ." Summer was lost for words, and Lazy Eyes, who was from Baltimore, wore a knowing smile.

"My name is Lazy Eyes," he said, drawing more attention to his dreamy eyes. "I'm the chapel's librarian. I know you're new in the system, but if you want, I can give you a quick rundown of the chapel's services." He was the perfect gentleman, nothing like Love and Tyrone.

"I'm not religious. I don't really believe in God," Summer said, and she wasn't completely lying, but she didn't want to run him off either. Nevertheless, she was there to meet Black.

"That's alright. Tell me are you Wicca or Santamaria? Because you look like you have some Latin in you."

Summer ignored the fact he was playing in an effort to converse with her.

"I haven't even heard of any of that stuff."

"Okay, do you like music?"

"Yeah."

"Right this way. Ladies first," he pointed straight ahead. At first, she was reluctant, but then she followed.

"I'm going to hip you to some good music." Lazy Eyes took her to a corner where a CD player was. He went into a closet, grabbed a couple of CDs, and brought them back. He put on dancehall and reggae music because it was the only music they had besides gospel.

Summer shook her head to the reggae music inside the headphones. Lazy Eyes kept smiling and licking his lips at her. He mumbled something, but she couldn't hear him.

When she removed the headphones, he said, "You like that?"

"Yeah, but I liked the Dancehall better."

"So, you can move those wide hips?" Lazy Eyes laughed. "I'll order some more for you. Can I let you in on a little secret?"

Summer shook her head.

"I think you are most definitely sexy, and I ain't never swung like that, but since you came on the compound, I've been wanting to get my hands on you."

Summer didn't wait for him to say anything else. She slid her hands between his legs and was satisfied with what she felt. She smiled seductively and said, "We can do something."

"When? Right now?" It was too much for Lazy Eyes to believe, and his dreamy eyes twinkled like shooting stars.

"Whenever."

"Go to the restroom, and I'll be in there when the coast is clear."

"Where's the restroom?" She knew she was pressing her luck with her timing, but Lazy Eyes was too irresistible to pass on, and she could already taste him in her mouth.

"Over there in the corner."

She took her jacket off and left it in the chair. As she headed toward the restroom and passed some guys in other rooms, everybody turned to look at her phat ass. She had on her tight sweats that pulled in the crack of her ass.

Minutes after she had gone into the restroom, Lazy Eyes arrived and shut the door. He stopped for a minute to take her in. She looked like the devil from his wet dreams. Summer giggled lightly, loving how hungry he looked. He grabbed her tits and fondled them.

"Damn, baby, these are real?"

Summer took one of his hands off her tit and put it on her ass. "This is real too," she said, kissing him on the lips. He tasted like peppermint candy. She slurped his tongue and took his dick out of his pants.

"God damn . . . shit!" he muttered, along with a bunch of gibberish that got lost at her mind-boggling skills. She felt the rumbling, and his semen sluice forth. And when she gurgled the tender head of his dick in the pit of her throat, he thought he might die because it felt so good!

She disappeared before he could realize he wasn't sleep-walking . . .

CHAPTER 12
THE MAKING OF
GREATNESS

WOULD you like to share the meat and mead of an old man, young black scholar?" Old School asked Atwater as he was heading to his unit.

Shonda was expecting a call from Atwater at this time, but he couldn't pass up a chance to receive Old School's attention.

"You're going to break bread with me?"

"The breaking of bread is for Lords and disciples, while the sharing of meat and mead is for friends and family. Come on and take a lap with me."

Atwater told Old School about his conversation with Shonda, still hung up on her claim about raising their children alone. Old School laughed and attributed Shonda's statement to the unique station of a woman, their frailty. Atwater couldn't help but laugh at how Old School could explain so much with so few words. Although Old School was fifty-seven years old, he seemed far beyond his years.

They got to the yard and walked down the track. The setting sun cast little warmth upon the men's faces. In the cool breeze, they walked with their hands behind their backs and their chins level with the horizon. Very few people were out and about. This was usually the time Old School took advantage of the peace and tranquility of the yard. He'd come out every night around this time to walk, think, and plan.

"Do I see a worry crook in your forehead?" Old School asked.

"What?"

"That wasn't there when I saw you yesterday. You're letting Shonda stress you out?"

"No, Old School," Atwater laughed. "You know the youngster I'm always with? Craze- zo? He got into it with the homosexual, Britney Spears. He called him a faggot, and Black, E, and Berry were going to back Britney up."

Old School paused before he spoke. People usually gave bad advice, not because they couldn't give good advice, but because they didn't fully apprise a situation before speaking.

"Why would Black back the homosexual?"

"Because he came to see Black, and Craze-zo butted into their conversation and called him out his name."

"I see. Being a young man is very hard. We both were there, and it always seemed like we had to prove ourselves in an effort to become our own men. Being Black and young and in prison, we think the only way to prove ourselves is by hitting or stabbing somebody. How many of these brothers do you remember writing a national best-seller, or did some Don King moves once he got out of jail? You see, it's hard to think of that, but I'm sure you can think of more than enough examples of when somebody stabbed or hit somebody upside the head."

"You're right about that."

"You're about to go home, Atwater. I don't want you to go to the streets and drown in a sea of economic crisis. But to leave here and go out there with no plans or saving grace would mean that the eighteen years you've spent inside here were all for naught. And when you go back, remember this: a man who fails to plan, plans to fail."

"I got some plans, Old School, but they're scattered in my head."

"I know you have that partner of yours out there and he's still selling drugs, and he's probably knee-deep in the streets. So do you know what that means for you?"

"No."

"It means that that's all he can offer you, a spot in his dope territory. And believe me, he'll share it reluctantly. It's cool to send some funds and take care of your wife, but he's been out there practically surviving by keeping people out of his game. Nobody likes to share. If you're just a pawn, they'll have you caught and brought right back to me. The crackers have set this game up for us to lose, and the more we try to get over, the deeper the shit gets."

Atwater listened intently. He was waiting for Old School to get to the point, knowing Shonda was probably getting anxious about his being late for their call. However, Atwater wouldn't rush Old School.

"It all comes down to power, son. You have to seek out those in high places and knock them down. You are tasked with turning pimps into tricks.

The power lies in knowing your trick and exploiting them for all that they are." Old School brought their stroll to a stop as something became clear to him. He hoped what he said next would help Atwater throughout his life. "When you get out, make sure you do what all great people do: build yourself an intelligence-base and get you a think tank that keeps you informed."

This was the beginning of all Atwater's scattered plans coming together.

CHAPTER 13
BLACK OUT

SUMMER WIPED the saline taste from her mouth and went to get her jacket. She headed for a bench that was on the outside of the main chapel. Moments later, the Moors had ended their service.

As they stalked out, Atwater emerged, trailed by other Moors. When he looked over and saw Summer, they locked eyes. He couldn't hide the hunger rising in his throat. He felt an urge so strong that his heart pounded violently in his chest, making him uncomfortable.

Black came out seconds later and took the empty seat on the bench where she sat.

"What up, home girl? How you doing?"

"I'm fine," Summer said truthfully. It would have been a lie if she hadn't encountered Lazy Eyes and Atwater before he arrived.

"I told Fraze to tell you to meet me because I heard about what you did."

Summer didn't know where this would lead. She looked off to the side and saw Lazy Eyes making pleading fuck faces at her. She had to stop herself from smiling and keep her eyes on Black so that she wouldn't give him away.

"You trying to play me, muthafucka?" The easygoing Black

melted under a disguising mask of an easily triggered temper when he had the feeling that Summer was up to something.

"I don't know what you're talking about."

"You know what the fuck I'm talking about!" Black's whisper might as well have been a scream because it was just as threatening.

Summer held her hands in submission, expecting a blow. "What did I do wrong?" she asked nervously noticing E and Berry standing nearby.

"You know you my bitch, right?"

"W-w-what?"

Black looked around to make sure nobody in the vicinity was looking. Then he grabbed Summer by her scruffy afro-tail. Tears welled in Summer's eyes from the searing pain.

"Yes, ok!" It felt like her hair was being ripped from its roots, then she felt his other hand wrap tightly around her throat.

"We 'bout to find out. You gonna give me some of that bussy tonight! Bitch, I got all this time and you giving my bussy away in your unit and 4B. I'll fuck around and kill all these niggas. I'm taking care of that right now as we speak. Now get your ass in the bathroom!"

CHAPTER 14
WAR ON THE DOWN

SOSA HAD a pit in his stomach from the vibes in his unit. He was sitting at the table with Michoacán and a couple other Paisas. He grabbed his knife from his cell, then rushed back to the table keeping the weapon well-concealed in his sweatpants.

"Sosa, why you look paranoid? Pinche Morena leaves five minutes, and you can't keep your ass still in the seat."

"No me mames," Sosa said, knowing why he felt alert.

"I wouldn't bullshit you," Michoacán said.

Where the fuck is that pinche myate, Fraze? Sosa thought. He didn't trust Fraze at all.

Without warning, a team of six officers stormed into the unit and ran straight to Sosa's cell. Sosa thought of the cell phone and Rolex that he'd left in plain sight. He'd paid $200 for someone from CMS to put a stash spot in the wall so he could hide stuff but had completely forgotten to put them in there.

Five minutes later, a CO came out of the cell holding his cell phone and watch in the air. "Sosa!" the CO hollered.

Sosa stepped up to the CO with Michoacán at his side.

"I'm Sosa, but that's not mine," he said as

Michoacán came forward. He already knew to claim ownership if Sosa were to get caught.

"It's me," Michoacán added.

"Nice try," the CO, whom they'd never seen before said. "That's not what our informant said." The other COs gathered around Sosa and put him in handcuffs. Sosa knew he would never see his Morena deliciosa again, and he was furious.

As the COs escorted him out of the unit, he looked back and yelled to Michoacán. "Mata el pinche Moreno Fraze y el Negro!"

Sosa knew nobody other than Black and Fraze would want him out of the picture. He'd paid COs to give him a heads up if they were on to him, so somebody had to drop a kite. A kite was a confidential letter to staff. Sosa wanted the pinche morenos to pay dearly. Sosa didn't have to even be in the same prison to prepare the Paisas, they were already strapped with knives from CMS. It was going to be a bloodbath.

CHAPTER 15
KNIGHT WITH SHINING KNIVES

BLACK GAVE E and Berry the nod. Mysteriously enough, nobody in the chapel noticed what was happening.

Summer looked for Lazy Eyes, but he was nowhere to be found. Black pushed her into the bathroom and shoved her face first into the wall once the door was closed. Summer trembled with fear as her pants were pulled down. Then they heard the commotion outside. Summer collapsed into the corner of the bathroom.

Black pulled his pants back up and opened the door to see what was going on.

"What the fuck you want, pretty boy?" Black lurched toward Lazy Eyes, who had a knife drawn on E and Berry. He wasn't alone either. His closest homie, Raheem, also held a knife in each hand. They'd ambushed Black, E, and Berry, neither of them having knives of their own.

"You trying to rape a man and you the Grand Sheik?" Lazy Eyes asked. When he saw Summer in the corner, he wanted to stab Black in the throat.

"Mind your fuckin' business!" Black said, knowing he was outmatched by the look on Berry and E's faces.

"Nigga, I oughta kill you!" Lazy Eyes put his knife to Black's neck as the overhead speaker announced the ten-minute movement. "Get the fuck out of here before I change my mind!"

Black and his crew got out of there as fast as they could, but everybody in there knew it wasn't over.

When Black and his crew left, Lazy Eyes made sure the only CO in the chapel was the Chaplain himself. It was clear the Chaplain hadn't seen anything because he was in his office, busy with something on his desk. Lazy Eyes looked at Raheem and told him to give him a couple of minutes.

When Lazy Eyes went into the bathroom and shut the door, Summer jumped up and ran to him. She thought she was afraid before she entered the prison, but she was a hundred times more afraid now. And to make matters worse, Lazy Eyes was in her mess now. She didn't know what to do.

"Stop crying, baby," Lazy Eyes said.

"No, it's all my fault," Summer said, with her head on his shoulder.

"It ain't your fault." Lazy Eyes grabbed Summer's chin so he could look her in the eyes. "I saw what that fool was doing, and I grabbed my knife and got my boy Raheem to watch my back." He kept spare knives hidden in the chapel for times like this. It was just sheer luck Raheem dropped by. "Don't ever say a nigga tryna rape you is your fault."

Lazy Eyes' words were comforting. Out of everybody she had screwed since she'd arrived, she could see herself falling head over heels for him.

"But he's gonna come back and get me!" The realization of Summer's words scared her more than anything.

"Yo, fuck that nigga. I got you, baby. That's my word. I'd kill that nigga or get rid of him before I let him touch you. Now, let me taste that sweet tongue of yours." They kissed passionately, like teenagers in love, until Lazy Eyes led her back into the chapel's lobby area. He made sure Raheem sat with Summer until the yard closed. Then they returned to their units on high alert.

CHAPTER 16
PRISON DREAMS

SUMMER HAD FOUND out Sosa had been taken to the SHU. That Sunday morning, she discovered he'd put six thousand dollars on her inmate account. When Britney saw that, he just shook his head and laughed.

Love was hanging around Summer's cell while Britney threw together a microwave-cooked meal. He was hoping to get some time alone with Summer, but she was unresponsive to his advances. Black had scared the living God out of her, and despite the protection of Lazy Eyes, she wanted to stay put in the unit. Not even Britney had been able to convince Summer to leave the unit, and Love finally bounced once he realized Summer wouldn't be putting out for him, at least not today.

Once he left, Britney tried again to get out of the unit.

He was drunk off some hooch that Love had brought, and he wanted to go to the gym.

"Come on, girl, please. Let's get out of this unit."

"Ain't nothing to do out there. And you know Black wants to kill me." Summer told Britney everything about that night.

"So what? You can't hide from him. Get your drunk ass up and let's go."

It was Summer's first time going to the gym. She didn't know the prison housed so many people. She thought she saw almost everyone during chow, but there were tons of inmates she had yet to see.

When she walked into the gym, every eye turned on her. The sexual tension was so thick she could choke on it. A group playing basketball got distracted by Summer's shorts that were pulled tight into the crevice of her ass. The T-shirt she wore went above her belly button and was knotted at one side of her waist.

"If that's a man, I'm gay, my nigga, 'cause I'd fuck the shit out of that bitch!" somebody yelled.

"We already ran a train on that muthafucka, and the pussy and the head were the bomb!" someone from 4B responded.

"You punk muthafucka. Why you ain't come get me?"

"Nigga, you was too busy working for Mr. Charlie."

Summer couldn't help but feel uneasy, and when she heard them calling the ten-minute move, she begged Britney to take her back to the unit. All she could think of was Black lurking in some dark corner, ready to jump out at any time. When she turned around, Lazy Eyes bumped into her and quickly whispered in her ear to go to the library's bathroom immediately.

Summer acted normal and held her poise as if he hadn't said anything to her. She grabbed Britney's hand and told him to take her to the library.

Once she was in the library, she headed straight to the bathroom, where she waited. Britney sat at a table and kept watch.

Moments later, Lazy Eyes came in primped and preened. His cologne could be smelled from afar.

He took a minute to look at the tasty treat who was smiling from ear to ear. Lazy Eyes was definitely her type, as she couldn't help blushing as he approached her.

"Why you haven't been coming out? I've been trying to get at you for a minute," Lazy Eyes asked, sweating her.

Summer loved it a little too much. "I've been thinking about you too, baby," she said as she ran into his arms and ran her tongue over his lips. Lazy Eyes acted as if he was still mad. He hadn't seen her for what felt like a year of endless longing.

"I had a fool clean this bathroom, scrub the fuck out of this shit, and the chapel bathroom, waiting for you to come back and see me. So, when we finally were together, we'd be in a clean ass place."

"I'm here," Summer said, grabbing his dick and massaging it. If he was mad before, he was hot and horny now.

She kept kissing him, knowing that would make him happy. "I want you to fuck me, baby," she whispered, kissing his ear and neck while massaging his dick.

Lazy Eyes could think of little else but Summer when he wasn't with her. No girl had ever had him fucked up in the head like Summer did, and he couldn't tell if it was just because he was in jail or not. He dreamed of her, woke up thinking about her, and could smell her scent everywhere he walked. He wanted to fuck her so badly that his head was throbbing.

"I don't want to fuck you," he said, but it was a lie. His face had betrayed him. Shit, he already put his life on the line for her.

Summer turned and brushed her ass against his stiff penis. She rocked back and forth while asking, "You sure you don't want to be inside this ass? It's cold outside baby, and I'm so hot for you right now."

Lazy Eyes knew if he fucked Summer, he would be head over heels. It didn't make sense, for her being placed in this facility. He wondered how people could possibly allow Summer to be in there, surrounded by all these men. He pulled her closer, thinking about what would happen to her if he wasn't around. When he looked down, his dick was already head over toes.

He grabbed her perfect 36C breasts from the back and pulled her to him. "You want me to fuck you?" He grinded his dick on her ass. She moaned pleasurably and smiled seductively.

"I want you to fuck me until you nut inside my tender ass. Butter my guts, baby." Summer pulled her sweats down so Lazy

Eyes could see what he was about to sink his teeth in. Her ass was perfect! Heart-shaped, full, and not a blemish in sight. Her pronounced arch tapered into the small of her back. Her teeny-tiny waist and the composition of her body would make Melissa Ford envious. Lazy Eyes had to bite his bottom lip in disbelief!

"You like what you see, baby?" Summer sounded like a nympho. She knew what she was working with, conceit in her question and thirst in her eyes.

"Hell muthafuckin' yeah!"

Lazy Eyes was prepared. He squirted Vaseline in his hands from a tube he brought with him, massaged it onto his dick, and some into her ass. She wiggled into his hand as he slipped two fingers in. When he heard her moan, he couldn't wait any longer. He slammed his dick inside her as she reached around and assisted him.

"Go deep, baby. I can take all ten inches." Summer opened her legs more and guided him deeper by pressing against him.

He groped her titties and became scatterbrained as she crashed into his mid-section with her soft ass. When she knew he was about to cum, she turned her head to the side and passionately kissed him as he drained his contents inside her and fell limp.

With all the madness that was going on at that prison, being with Lazy Eyes made things a little easier. He made her feel completely secure, and his fuck game was bananas! Summer thought being with Lazy Eyes would bring security and, for that, she was grateful.

CHAPTER 17
RENDEZVOUS GONE WILD

SUMMER and Lazy Eyes kept up their secret rendezvous every day for three weeks straight. He met her every night at the same spot, and sometimes they would meet earlier in the day at the chapel. Then they'd go back to the library at night to finish off their incessant deeds.

On one of these nights, after they left the bathroom, he sat down and explained why he had to keep everything with her on the down-low. There was something Lazy eyes had been wanting to say since they'd started messing around, but it was hard for him to say it.

"Look, we ain't got a lot of time, but let me put everything out there so you'll know where my heart is."

Summer was still sucking on Lazy Eyes' neck. "Damn, you listening or what? And stop fucking with my dick."

"I can't. I love that big fat dick."

"Hold up. I'm tryna come clean." Lazy Eyes gripped Summer's ass and sat her on the bathroom counter. "I ain't like none of these 'ho ass niggas. Whatever I do, I put my heart into it. I don't like this coward down-low shit."

"You coming out, baby?" Summer chuckled.

Lazy Eyes smirked. "That mean I'm a homo-thug. But it

don't matter, 'cause whatever I do, I stamp it with my thug insignia. But for real for real, my shit is complicated. My wife's father is here."

"What?!"

"I know. But when she be coming to visit me, all I can do is think about hugging, fucking, and kissing your fluffy ass lips." By now, Lazy Eyes was smooching all over Summer's face while she giggled and welcomed the wet nothings.

What he told her was the truth. He was married, and his father-in-law was in the same compound with them. He hated the fact he had to keep things on the down-low because he wanted everybody to know that Summer was his. At this stage in the game, he honestly didn't give a fuck who knew. But out of respect for his family, he tried to keep it from being known.

Meanwhile Summer was doing a different kind of creeping, trying to avoid Black. Whenever he sent Fraze to get her, she acted like she was sick with the flu or indisposed. And she was lucky enough not to have to go to commissary the past three weeks, or he would make it known that he still intended on making Summer his property.

By now, Summer was in love, and the love was mutually shared by Lazy Eyes. Unlike many, he was a real nigga and didn't give a fuck if she was born a man. She had the best pussy and head game he ever had, and she looked as good as his finest hoes. *Fuck what a nigga thought*, he reasoned. But secrets were seldomly held.

On one pleasant night, Lazy Eyes was eating Summer's ass out. She had bought some X lines from Tyrone, and she and Lazy Eyes did more than enough X lines to take their already heightened sexual experience far higher. He slivered his tongue in and out of her sweet-smelling ass and nibbled all around it. He grouped four of his fingers together and ass screwed her.

She loved it, but she preferred his big dick over his tongue. She turned around on the sink to face him with her ass on the edge of the counter. She wanted him to fuck her from the front. He stuck his jellied tongue in her mouth while he fucked her brains out. His pounding was so mesmerizing she had an orgasm, and then another a minute later as Lazy Eyes jammed faster inside of her.

Lazy Eyes was hitting her ass hard while they thought Britney to be vigilant and watchful. Meanwhile, a brother from the Nation of Islam had slipped by him as he flirted with somebody at the copy machine.

He opened the bathroom door and switched on the lights. Summer's bare ass was in the air, with ten inches pumping in and out of it.

"What the fuck, nigga!" the brother from the Nation asked.

"Shut the fucking door, muthafucka!" Lazy Eyes said, but he didn't dare pull out of that sweet ass.

The brother from the Nation of Islam looked at the filth before him and slammed the door behind him on his way out! Over Summer's protest, Lazy Eyes wouldn't stop until he had finished.

Chapter Twenty Visitation, Meaning Family Feud and Love!

The next day, Atwater went to work out with Craze-zo. While they were working out, they heard the talk on the compound about Lazy Eyes getting caught fucking the punk in the library bathroom. The brother had spread his discovery and demanded the Baltimore Cart, which was a gang Lazy Eyes ran with, checked him into the SHU. However, Lazy Eyes' troubles weren't so easy to resolve. He had a peculiar situation with his father-in-law being on the compound with him. The news was sure to travel fast.

When Atwater and Craze-zo heard the details of Summer's tryst, Craze-zo felt that he was right for wanting to beat up

Britney that night at the barbershop. Of course, Atwater agreed, not wanting to appear suspicious.

While Atwater was working out with Craze-zo, he heard his name called over the loudspeaker. He went to the CO and was told that he had a visitor.

He had to run back to the unit, shower and put on his visiting clothes. He knew Shonda was on some surprise shit, but he didn't care.

When he went out to the visiting area, there she was: fine, fresh, and fabulous. She wore a zesty orange Stella McCartney ankle-length dress and off-white YSL platform pumps that set out her 36-22-38 bust, bends, and curves. Her naturally black long and curly hair was in a flat twist-out much like Corinne Bailey Rae's coif.

When Atwater saw her, he laughed, knowing she had scored a low blow on him for her to surprise him with the visit and looking zesty, tasty, and relishing. In her eyes was an apology for saying she was raising the kids all by herself. This impromptu visit was more than warranted. They talked about everything, and she loved Atwater all the more. She shared with him how she had made dinner for the kids, and they didn't show. They were young adults who didn't have time for their mother.

When Shonda saw Summer enter the visiting room, and sit across from them, she couldn't believe her eyes! It wasn't possible for them to have women in jail. The only explanation was even more maddening. She became jealous and preoccupied with a thousand thoughts. She watched Atwater's eyes closely. She immediately took to comparing herself with the other feminine body in the room when she noticed Atwater purposefully averting his gaze.

"What is that!" Shonda asked, livid and beside herself, as she nodded over to Summer.

Atwater wished she hadn't seen her. "What?"

"You know what I'm talking about!"

"Shonda, don't start that bullshit. How can I stop who they bring in here?"

"Is it a girl?"

"It can't be a girl and be in here," Atwater said. "You should watch your mouth when people are in ear-shot of us."

———

Summer couldn't keep her placement in prison a secret forever. Eventually, her mother found out and demanded to see her. Peyton had been telling anyone that would listen about Summer's crime; Sandra was told while she was grocery shopping, pulled aside by a family friend. It had been said without sympathy, maybe even with a bit of light-hearted relief.

"Sandra," the friend took her hand in theirs, "you can finally rest easy knowing that God has taken that foul boy of yours out of your life."

Sandra simply nodded then, going about her shopping as if she hadn't been told some of the worst news a mother could receive.

Summer hadn't seen her mother in years, ever since her father ran her out of the house. Her mother entered the visiting room, looking as beautiful as ever. When Sandra saw her son sitting there as a woman, she couldn't help but cry.

"Momma, I don't need you to be here if you're going to be crying."

"Bobby, I'm sorry." She hugged her son, and it was too hard for her. "I miss you, baby. No matter what, you're still my baby boy."

Summer leaned away. None of this would've happened if

Summer hadn't been kicked out of her father's house when she was a teenager. She was forced to make it on her own; how could she have possibly survived otherwise? The things her mother allowed had led to her current situation; she had almost been raped! And as always, with everything bad that accompanied her life, her parents had something to do with it; one, indirectly, for being weak and the other, directly, for being hateful.

"I'm not your baby boy. I'm a grown woman, and you're either going to accept it or you can leave." Summer crossed her arms in front of her. It was as hard for her as it must have been for her mother. But she wouldn't apologize any longer. She was who she was and that was final! Summer looked Sandra directly in the eyes as she waited for a response, tears already beginning to fall.

Her mother took a second to weigh what she was being offered. She missed her baby boy. She missed the . . . daughter she never had.

"I missed you, Bobby. I know it's been hard on you because of your father and brother, but I never knew what to do."

"You should have left him, Momma." And even though it sounded crazy, Summer really felt that way. She knew her mother always contemplated it; she wasn't sure why she never went through with it.

"You don't understand," her mother said. "I didn't know what to do."

Seeing her mother like that hurt her to the core.

"I'll never talk to them again," Summer said, referring to her father and brother. "They tried to make me hate myself, and they almost succeeded." Now Summer was the one crying in her mother's arms. She didn't know she had all that hurt and pain inside of her, and in fact, still longed to be loved and accepted by her mother.

"I love you, Bobby, and I'll always be here for you even though I never knew how to handle the situation."

"I love you too, Momma, and if you really love me, then call me Summer."

Sandra knew what it would take to have her child back in her life, and that was all that mattered. "I love you, Summer."

They had an emotional hug, but only time would tell if her mother would tuck tail and desert Summer again.

CHAPTER 18
TROUBLE IN THE CAMP

B-ROD WAS LAZY EYES' father-in-law. He was in his mid-fifties, and he was the official shot caller for Baltimore.

B-Rod was big, and the strength he looked to possess belied his advanced age. He didn't have a lot of patience for bullshit, and as soon as the issue with Summer and Lazy Eyes was brought to his attention, he was all over it.

He was coming from outside, looking for Lazy Eyes. When he passed the kitchen, he saw Lazy Eyes heading the other way.

"Lonny!" he called him by his first name. "Come over here!"

When Lazy Eyes saw who it was, he knew it was going to be some bullshit.

"Tell me about this rumor going around that you got caught fucking a boy in the library restroom." B-Rod wasted no time with formalities.

Lazy Eyes dropped his head because he wasn't going to lie to any man! A man only lied to a person he was intimidated by or scared of; he wasn't scared of anybody!

"Lonny, this is not the type of shit you do being married to my daughter!" B-Rod could have smacked his son-in-law. "Have you forgotten about your kids with Brandy?" B-Rod took a minute to calm down because he loved his grandchildren, and he didn't want to let one mistake define an individual whom he respected. When it dawned on him what that meant, he calmed down. "I won't mention it to Brandy, but I bet not hear about you being with that boy no more, all right?"

Lazy Eyes just shook his head because he wasn't going to lie to the OG.

"You don't understand. I'm in love with her."

"Her—who the hell is her? Brandy?"

"No, I'm talking about Summer."

B-Rod snatched up Lazy Eyes by the collar. "This is my daughter we're talking about! You leave that boy alone, or I'm going to check you in." Checking in was the shot caller of the group forcing someone to tell the authorities that they needed administrative segregation because they couldn't live on the compound.

"Yo, take your hands off my shirt!" Lazy eyes said as he pushed B-Rod's hands off him.

B-Rod looked around and, seeing that he was about to get them sent to the SHU, he walked off.

Lazy Eyes was going to meet Raheem by the commissary, but they already ended the move, and it wasn't many people on the compound.

As he came around the corner, Berry grabbed him, and E punched him in the throat. They backed him into a corner and were about to poke holes in him with ice picks.

"Hold up! Lieutenant Muncy coming! But hold that bitch nigga's mouth and keep him still!" Black said as he kept a lookout.

While they were watching for Lt. Muncy, Lazy Eyes broke their grips off his shirt and walked away calmly. He was shaken up a little, but Muncy didn't even notice anything out of the norm.

"What are you doing outside and there's no move?" Lt. Muncy asked Lazy Eyes.

"I'm coming from outside. I forgot my ID, and I was trying to go back to the unit to take a shower."

"Go straight to your unit. And the next time I see you out of bounds, I'm going to write you an incident report."

"Yes, sir," Lazy Eyes said. Lt. Muncy didn't know he just saved his life. Lazy Eyes scurried off to his unit, almost skipping.

Black, E, and Berry went into the barbershop, which was accidentally left unlocked by the compound officer in charge of securing the compound's buildings. They didn't know that Atwater was in the cleaning room wringing out the mop when he overheard them come in.

"Black, we have to alert the homies and let them know this shit is about to go down, because I know that nigga is going to get all those niggas from B- more," E said, mad he didn't get to kill Lazy Eyes.

"Damn! The fucking lieutenant picked the perfect time to be walking around!" Black said.

"And that bitch ass nigga squirmed away," Berry added.

"I swear by the end of tonight, that's a dead nigga," Black said. Even with what he was making off the heroin, he couldn't continue to let the threat that Lazy

Eyes presented go unchecked. The botched ambush was going to cause a war between D.C. and Baltimore.

―――――――

Lazy Eyes went straight to his cell, crawled under his bed, and busted a hole in the wall, extracting three long knives from his stash spot. He placed them on his bed, and for a minute, he looked long and hard at them.

If he was to go to war with D.C. niggas, they'd just put him in the SHU and ship him off to another joint. He'd be fucked because he wouldn't see Summer, and now that he had that heaven-ass, he couldn't live without it. It'd be unbearable. He returned the knives back to his hiding place, grabbed a sheet of paper out of his drawer, and scribbled something on the paper. It is always good to have something on somebody, he thought. He went downstairs, and when nobody was looking, he kicked the small paper underneath the CO's door, then walked off to wait and see how his plot would hatch.

He really thought that would be the end of all his troubles.

Atwater returned from his lovely visit with his wife. He washed his face while his cellmate, Thompson Bey, read a book.

Atwater heard the front door to the unit open. COs marched in, and he didn't know what to think.

"Damn, about ten COs just came into the unit," Thompson Bey said. "They must have found some wine."

"No, I think they're getting somebody."

"Who?" Thompson Bey asked, crouching over on his top bunk to see over Atwater's head.

"They're taking Black, E, and Berry out," Atwater said, considering what he had heard in the barbershop.

CHAPTER 19
WHY DOES EVERYBODY DIE OF HIV IN THIS BOOK?!

SUMMER WAS READING a book Britney gave her called *Convict's Candy* by Amin Meadows.

The CO just cleared count and popped the door when Fraze came charging into their cell.

"They just took Black, Berry, and E to the SHU."

"What?" Britney and Summer said at the same time. It was the biggest relief they didn't expect.

"Yes, and word is that Lazy Eyes did some hot shit and dropped a kite on them. Tonight, we're going to have a meeting. So be careful around here because the shit can go up any minute now."

When Fraze left, Britney couldn't stop laughing. "Summer, you have this place going up in smoke because of that good pussy of yours."

"Shut up!" Summer snapped as she climbed on her bunk to lean over and see if she could see Unit 4B from her bed. She couldn't see anything, and she didn't know if they made the ten-minute move yet, or if Lazy Eyes would go to the gym during the chow move.

"Give me a mirror." Britney handed her a mirror, but she still couldn't see shit from her angle.

"I'm going to the gym on the move," Summer said.

"Stay out of it, Summer," Britney advised.

"I can't," Summer said.

Since Summer wouldn't listen, Britney reminded her to be careful. "He just told you something was about to happen."

"I know, but I'm gonna go out on the rec and come back when they open for mainline."

"Just be careful."

Lazy Eyes was already in the gym plotting with Raheem. Nobody came out yet because they still hadn't called all the units for evening chow.

Even though Raheem never agreed with Lazy Eyes messing around with Summer, he'd die at his homeboy's side.

Lazy Eyes had his sweats turned inside out, and his pockets hung like rabbit's ears at his side. He brought his knives because he wanted to make sure anybody from D.C. walked a tight rope around him.

"Are the homies coming or what?" Lazy Eyes asked briskly.

"Yeah, nigga. Calm down. They're going to be here after dinner. Yo, shit is fucked up. They're saying you dropped a kite on Black and them."

Lazy Eyes didn't lie to anybody for nothing. "So, what! Yo, between me and you, I did that shit. I let them know where them niggas's heroin stash spot at. Them D.C. niggas are bitches without them three. What? You think they'll send scary ass Tyrone or Fraze? Them niggas is through."

"Yo, word up, dog," Raheem said as they slapped hands and laughed.

"Word up, I wouldn't even worry about them no more. They'll send some kites out da SHU suggesting I did it, and I'll just deny it. It ain't like they can prove I done it. Them niggas are through!"

"What about B-Rod? He's trying to get the homies to check you in."

"Fuck that. I'm uncheckable. B-Rod could be trouble. But he's family, and I don't think he wants to see me fucked up. He's just mad."

Right then, Summer walked in, looking a bit pale. It was truly feminine, and Lazy Eyes's heart poured out to his beauty.

Summer went to the bathroom, and that was his cue. "There she goes. Watch out for me," Lazy Eyes told Raheem.

"A'ight," Raheem said as Lazy Eyes disappeared into the bathroom.

Summer was in the last stall, which was the biggest. The bathroom was filthy, but it offered them the privacy they needed. Outside, people would be coming to the gym after evening chow, and whatever they had to say, they would have to make it quick.

"You alright?" Summer asked, looking as if she'd been crying. She had on a big t-shirt and her tight sweats. She looked like she hopped out of bed and came out to meet him.

"Told you I'd get rid of that nigga for you. Now it's just me and you. I love you to death." They kissed, and he could taste the salt of her tears and feel the love in her heart.

"I don't want you to get hurt, baby," Summer said. She could feel Lazy Eyes fondling her tits because there was always a strong sense of lust, urge, passion, and hunger that went before the perils hovering overhead. "Everybody from D.C. is supposed to meet up tonight. What's going to happen, baby?"

"Nothing ain't gonna happen. Them niggas are bitches without Black and them. Don't worry about nothing. I got every-thing under control. I'ma wife you, baby. We can be the first to get officially married. Obama back this shit now. You gonna be my Mrs.?"

"Forever, baby." And Summer meant it as she grabbed Lazy Eyes' dick. "Let me suck it, baby."

"Not right now."

"Fuck that. Let me suck it," Summer insisted.

Lazy Eyes' dick was harder than Damascus steel, and Summer went to relieve him of that aching madness. With Summer giving him the best head ever, it was moments before Lazy Eyes shot a load off, and Summer had her supper.

"Yo, Lazy. B-Rod is coming with the homies!" Raheem shouted into the bathroom.

"What?"

"Come 'ere."

Lazy Eyes fixed his pants, still lusting. He pulled away from Summer, who started crying again. She followed him out of the bathroom.

B-Rod had a squad of eight homies from Baltimore with him, but Fraze was with them too.

"What y'all got that D.C. nigga with y'all for? Them niggas tried to kill me today!" As Lazy Eyes spoke, Raheem stood at his side, ready for whatever.

"Lonny, you gotta check in."

"No, nigga, y'all gotta check me in. I'm uncheckable." Lazy Eyes pulled out his knife and handed one to Raheem. Lazy Eyes looked over at

Summer. "Watch out, baby."

"No, I'm going with you!" Summer cried out.

"Get your homeboy, Fraze," B-Rod said. But to

Fraze, it didn't matter if they fucked Summer up too.

"Summer, get out of the way," Fraze said, but he didn't move to go over and get her.

"No!" she said, still really scared.

After B-Rod, and the other Baltimore guys took out knives that were just as big, she saw it was going to be worse than she imagined.

"Summer, get out of the way!" Fraze screamed.

"I said no!" Summer had the nerve to reach for the other knife Lazy Eyes had in his pants.

"Just grab him!" B-Rod ordered.

"I'll stab a muthafucka if you touch my girl!"

"Get his ass!" B-Rod commanded.

They converged on Lazy Eyes and Raheem, and Lazy Eyes shot out like a soldier and stabbed one of them in the throat. One went to stick him in the side, but Raheem stuck the guy first, and they swarmed on Raheem, who was jabbing his knife as he took two hits for everyone he swung.

Lazy Eyes took out his other knife and had a knife in each hand. He went to get them off Raheem and they scattered when he came from behind them, sticking them like a madman. "'Ho-ass niggas! Fuck you, nigga!" he screamed and stuck. When B-Rod came from his blindside and hit him in the chin, Lazy Eyes became dizzy.

Summer tried to run to his aid, but Fraze jumped on her and held her down while she watched them butcher Raheem and Lazy Eyes until the COs came in and broke up the melee.

CHAPTER 20
SURPRISE, SURPRISE

FRAZE RUSHED Summer out of the gym, so they both wouldn't be sent to the SHU with the rest of them. She could barely walk back to the unit as her mind replayed Lazy Eyes getting butchered like that. It was too much to see.

Once Fraze managed to get Summer back to the unit, she was hysterical. Fraze wanted some get back on Summer for getting Black, E, and Berry sent to the SHU. He just always had the feeling Summer was tied to the three being sent to the SHU somehow.

The COs were responding to the commotion going down in the gym. Fraze left Summer to collect herself in her cell. He was walking away when he turned to see Michoacán and Ramirez coming up behind him.

"My friend, what happened out there?" Michoacán asked with a smiling face.

"It ain't nothing, amigo. Just some shit between them Baltimore niggas." Fraze was too busy talking to see Michoacán slip a knife out of his pants. He jammed the sharp pointy end into Fraze's neck while Ramirez started to jug holes in his side.

"HELP!" Fraze screamed as he tried to get away. He couldn't

go anywhere because Ramirez delivered a solid blow to Fraze's chin that leveled him to the ground. Once he hit the ground, they continued butchering him.

Summer heard the commotion going on outside her cell as she was about to tell Britney what happened. When they heard the cries for help and heard the screaming, they ran to the door to look.

"Stop! You're gonna kill him!" Britney screamed as Summer fainted.

Michoacán and Ramirez kept on, knowing full well there were no COs to respond to their vicious attack.

The Paisas had the attack planned out so well that at the same moment they were going in, the Blacks were being attacked in all the other units. Tyrone was butchered while he was talking on the phone, being that they couldn't kill Black for snitching Sosa out. They killed another one of Black's homies from D.C.

It took the Blacks in all the units to realize they were being surprise-attacked. But once they did, they started targeting the Mexican inmates without further discretion.

When the COs saw they had a riot on their hands, it was too out of control for them to do anything about it. They went to a secure place and called for back-up from local police and nearby jails. They put on riot gear and returned with a superior fighting force. They shot rubber bullets that stung like hell and shot tear gas all over the compound until they gained control of the prison.

When the smoke cleared, three Blacks were dead, twenty were injured, while four Paisas were killed, and thirty injured.

The administration locked down the joint because at least a hundred inmates involved in causing the riot would be prosecuted federally and shipped across the country. The lockdown lasted for three weeks until the administration felt the inmates no longer posed a threat to themselves.

Raheem and Lazy Eyes almost died during their scuffle with

B-Rod and his men. They were rushed to the hospital in a heli-
copter and they both survived. Nearly everyone involved in
inciting the riot was shipped to another prison, including Black,
E, and Berry. Sosa, Ramirez, and Michoacán were also relocated.
The riot went down in prison history.

CHAPTER 21
WINGS OF WIND

ONCE THE ADMINISTRATION deemed the inmates no longer presented a threat to one another, they let everybody off lockdown. But being that the SHU was then full; they had to let out some people, and Buffy's time had come. He thought he would have gotten out sooner, but he was wrong.

As always, he came out talking boss shit, and everybody was mad they had put him in their Unit 2A, where his girls were. He dropped his belongings in front of the CO's office as Summer ran up to him and gave him a hug.

"I thought you wasn't ever gonna get out," Summer said.

"You've been here a little over two months, and I hear the compound went up in smoke because of you." He smacked his lips. "Bitch, ya poison ivy. I gotta talk to you, miss thing"

"Adams, get in here!" the CO said from his office. "You're in cell #216. Try to stay under the radar this time."

"Okay, cutie pie."

Summer helped him take his bags up to his cell. And when they got there, and dropped everything on the floor, Buffy unpacked his things.

"Has Funky Breath Britney been messing with my man?"

"No, not that I know of," Summer said unconvincingly.

"Bitch, ya lying. But anyways, Black was mad about you trying to defend Lazy Eyes' fine ass. His feelings were more hurt than anything, but he told the homies not to touch you. Gurl, you must got some good pussy."

They laughed.

"And Lazy Eyes . . . out of all people. I didn't even know he was going. He got a wife and kids, and he was willing to leave them for you, let me tell you. They're gonna start calling you Sunshine like the chick in the movie *Harlem Nights*. Remember that Italian guy left his wife and kids?" Buffy smacked her lips again.

Summer was glad to know that Buffy had no indication the Paisas's ambush of the Blacks was because she was fucking Sosa. Even though she fainted when the riot began, somehow, she knew it was because of her. The thought of people being dead all because of her made her sick to her stomach. The three weeks on lockdown were good for her to get needed sleep and emotional support from Britney.

"What are they saying about Lazy Eyes?" Summer asked. Now she was sad again. She was prettiest when lost in her sadness, and it made Buffy love her all the more.

"Don't worry about him. They're back there selling death threats, door-banging to the fullest. Let me tell you." They laughed because they knew door banging was threatening another inmate while you were locked in a cell, meaning you really didn't pose a threat.

"When is he gonna get out the SHU?"

"Bitch, are you crazy! He's getting transferred somewhere across the planet, let me tell you. Black, E, and Berry too, and all those idiots that were in that race riot. I'm just glad I wasn't here because somebody would have tried to kill me. Forget about them. Tonight, I'm going to get my hair cut, and we're going to party! We're going unit to unit: dick-a-treat, let me tell you."

They both laughed.

"You just keep that good pussy of yours away from mine, and we won't have no qualms. A man get a taste of that sweet ass of yours, and he thinks he can do supernatural things, like fly, or stab eight people to death, let me tell you. Bitch, I gotta go and wash my sexy ass. See you in a minute."

Summer was sick Lazy Eyes was no longer there. Even with him gone, she felt a great weight lifted off her chest, knowing she wasn't going to have to worry about Black, E, Berry, Fraze, or Tyrone.

It was nighttime outside, and it looked peaceful. Three weeks after the racial riot, peace settled over the jail. Everybody that was left behind had pretty much done some dirt and got away with it. Nobody could hold bad blood against the other because they had to live with one another in close quarters. So, they had to make the best of an impossible situation. Fresh off lockdown brought genuine respect and a calm that seemed beguiling.

CHAPTER 22
BLOSSOMING CALM

ABOUT EIGHT PEOPLE were in the barbershop waiting to get their hair cut. They were talking about all the stuff going on.

"What high-power forces ail you to patronize this humble establishment?" Atwater asked Old School, who picked the closest chair by the door to seat himself. He knew Old School would have some deep thoughts about the race riot, even if he didn't voice them now.

"I saw a light on a hill, and I ascended."

Everybody laughed.

"Riddle me that," Atwater responded.

"There's no riddle to my old fables. I just came to see how you were getting along in this place of constant madness."

"You see what I'm doing. I'm in here perfecting my craft. Besides that, I'm putting my plans together. Planning far and beyond."

"Don't try and sell me nothing. I ain't buying."

"It's more than one way to skin a cat." When Atwater said that Britney, Summer, and Buffy walked in, laughing and giggling. They wore tight clothes and looked primped and preen.

Old School tipped his hat. "Good evening, ladies." He was always the perfect gentleman, no matter how he felt.

"Hey, Old School," Buffy said dismissively, knowing he was being sarcastic.

"Tone or Atwater, can one of y'all cut my hair?"

"Sorry, mami. I got a couple of heads to cut that been here at the move. Come back manana." Tone was Puerto Rican and his accent said it best. Being that he was Puerto Rican, he wasn't involved in the race riot because Puerto Ricans didn't run with the Paisas or Blacks.

"Dang! Atwater, ya gotta help me out." Buffy wouldn't take no for an answer.

"I got you. Let me finish this head."

After that, Buffy was fussing with Britney for whatever trivial qualms he had against him. Although Summer was in mourning over being separated from Lazy Eyes, she still couldn't keep her eyes off Atwater. When she came into the barbershop or wherever else she chanced to see Atwater, her eyes belonged to him.

"I know you were fucking Ray Ray," Buffy fussed, trying to keep his tone low, but that was like pulling teeth.

"No, I wouldn't do that. Not to you, girl," Britney said, lying through his teeth.

"Bitch, please!"

Their conversation was a bit tart for Old School's delicate ears, so he asked Atwater, "Where's your shadow at?"

"Craze-zo went to commissary. He's supposed to be bringing me an ice cream in a couple of minutes. Why? You wanted to holla at him?"

"No, I was just asking. I always see y'all together."

"He's like my brother."

"Brother from another mother?"

Atwater finished cutting the guy's head in his chair. While the dude was checking out his haircut, Atwater brushed off his chair and made eye contact with Summer on the low. She smiled at him because she couldn't possibly contain it. She was melting.

"All right, young blood. I'll see you later," Old School said, and Atwater thought he'd been caught.

"Love, Old School."

Buffy went to get in his chair. "Two with the grain. Caesar all the way around."

"What? No taper fade?" Atwater asked, which was Buffy's usual.

She gave him her signature smack. "I ain't got time for all that. I just got out of the SHU, and I have to make my rounds."

"Excuse me." Atwater laughed playfully.

"How's your wife?" Buffy asked. He had seen Atwater's wife several times during a visit.

"She's chilling. She was just up here last weekend."

"The same one I seen when we were on the visit together?"

"The one and only."

"You've been down for a while, haven't you?"

"This will be eighteen years."

"And your wife's been with you the whole time?" Buffy sounded shocked. Atwater zipped the clippers over her raga-muffin naps that snapped back into a smooth surface.

"Yes."

"I don't know how she's doing it. I couldn't imagine going on dick celibacy for eighteen days."

Everybody in the barbershop laughed.

"Eighteen minutes," Britney added.

Atwater held the clippers and thought about how to handle that. "Y'all wrong for that."

Tone laughed with them. "Mami, y'all foul."

"Just keeping it real, sugar, let me tell you. So, what's your secret?" Buffy asked Atwater, who was focused on Buffy's hair-cut. But Summer was focused on him!

"It ain't really a secret." He looked up into Summer's

dazzling eyes that were fountains of immeasurable love and the promise of creamy dreams.

"Sometimes people don't know what to do with themselves, and when you give them purpose, they'll run after you."

"That's whas' up. Didn't she move from St. Louis to be closer to you?"

"How you know all the details?"

"Everybody knows the details of romance in paradise. You're a good guy."

As Atwater finished, he brushed his chair off. Summer was too shy and abashed to do anything but look at him. And when he looked at her, she couldn't hide the smile or the incredible speed of her racing heart.

Buffy had other plans for them, and they headed to Unit 1B, where Ray Ray lived. And now Buffy could fuss at Britney, but only if Summer would shut up about her crush!

"Damn, he's fine. I have to have him!" Summer said.

"Who?" Britney asked.

"The barber," Summer said.

"Tone?" asked Buffy confused.

"No, Atwater. Didn't you see how he looked at me?"

"Bitch, worry about Lazy Eyes. He's a married man," she smacked her lips. "But I guess that never stopped you before."

"Oh, that was clever," Britney said. "But I did see him staring at her."

"He must've heard that all he'd have to do was say hello to her, and she'd give him a mind-boggling orgasm with her fast, good pussy having ass."

"You're hating, ho," Summer said, and they all laughed.

"Ain't that the truth," Britney added.

"Bitch, you got your nerve. We about to go in here and confront Ray Ray. It's Buffy the Body or Toilet Face Britney."

"I got your toilet face, stank bitch."

"You impotent, dick-sucking harlot," Buffy shot back.

"Ya momma's a strumpet on Planet of the Apes."

"With your herpes in the mouth and gonorrhea in your ass."

The three of them couldn't help but laugh at the back and forth between them. As they neared unit 1B, Franco and Slim stood outside in the front of the unit where they lived.

"Look at Franco," Buffy said.

By now, everybody had heard about how Franco and Slim put in work during the riot, and it was sheer luck they weren't being shipped to another prison.

"He ain't never got on drawls," Britney said.

"Dick just a swinging back and forth. And I know he has a foot of dick his big strong ass. It'd a be like fucking a gorilla on Viagra, let me tell you," Buffy said.

And as they approached, Franco said, "What the fuck y'all bitches laughing at?"

"Shut up and shave your hairy chest, you gorilla-looking mutha fucka," Buffy snapped and smacked her lips.

"Fuck them punks," Slim said, who was always super fly, sly, and cool. This time, Britney didn't pay him any mind because he was on his way to get higher than a kite.

They snuck into the unit and went straight to Ray Ray's cell on the second floor. He was a tall, light-skinned guy with ruffled braids and a shaggy and sparse beard. He had just gotten out of the shower and was drying his toes with a towel when Buffy and his gang barged into his cell. "What up, Ray Ray? What's this I hear about you and Britney?"

"Damn, you could at least see how I'm doing."

"I told her nothing happened between us," Britney said defensively, trying to lead him.

"I ain't trying to hear that shit right now," Ray Ray said.

"Oh, ya not? Don't make me set it off in this bitch."

Ray Ray's friend, L, came to the door and knocked. He was making his rounds in the units, selling his wares when he happened to see them in Ray Ray's cell.

"What up, L?" Ray Ray said.

"Nothing. I just came to say what's up to the home girls," L said. He had taken over supplying the joint with drugs from where Tyrone left off.

"Hey, L," they said together, having met him on another occasion.

"I got some Bang Bang. Y'all trying to hit that joint or what?" L asked because he wanted to party after coming off lockdown.

"Probably, but we not trying to get stuck on the move," Britney said, knowing it was getting late and they had to leave on the 7:30 p.m. move, or they'd be shit out of luck.

"Y'all can leave at pill line at 8:00 p.m. The CO working is cool as a fan," L said, taking his wares from his pocket.

"What's that?" Buffy asked. "Sex'stacy."

Enough fa' all of us?" Buffy asked.

"Chill out. I got you."

L spread lines on the table, and they blasted off.

Summer floated back to the unit in a trance. Her feet moved, but she didn't feel like she was really walking. When she got to her bed, she passed out. It was as if the last dream she had not too long ago was still in progress.

She was running from whom or from what, she couldn't say. She just knew her father had just kicked her ass. Her clothes were ripped, and her face felt shattered in two.

But as she ran, she saw the headlights of a car ahead, and she was blinded by the dazzling lights. She tried to cover her eyes, but when she did, she uncovered her eyes and she was on a runway, modeling clothes.

She strutted down the runway as cameras whipped and flashed away, and she felt as if she was on top of the world. But,

but . . . she almost tripped and fell. When she reached out to grab for balance, she was suddenly shaking the extended hand of her business manager.

"We're going to make a lot of money off you," the manager said with a cunning smile that read dollar signs.

More lights flashed, and she covered her eyes from the brilliance of the light snaps, but she saw her face spread across magazine covers like *King*, *XXL*, *Essence*, and *Ebony*.

But the blinding light she covered her eyes from was her father pummeling her to the ground with hateful fists.

"You'll never amount to anything, you faggot! Get out!" her father screamed with phlegm pouring from his mouth.

Summer was fleeing her father as much as she was in her dreams, nightmares, her fears. She was dressed in drag, and she knew the woman's clothes on her body were supposed to be there. And when she looked down at the gash on her wrist, she was in the back of a car and her hand was holding a small straw, and there were lines of cocaine before her. She snorted them and felt the charge instantly. When she leaned back in the seat, she felt the sun's rays resting on her skin. When she opened her eyes, she lay in her special orchard with butterflies drifting poetically on the wings of wind.

CHAPTER 23
I HAVE TO HAVE HIM

TWO DAYS HAD PASSED, Buffy was settled back in, and the compound returned to normal.

They headed to the gym where a basketball game was in progress, and it looked like a riot. The guys threw elbows and tripped one another. Bystanders and homeboys kept their hands on the hilt of their sharpened knives, waiting for something to pop off. Murderball was in full swing.

L and Ray Ray were playing on the same team while Buffy and Britney were cheering away. It was so loud in the gym that it did them no justice to scream and act a fool.

Atwater was in a group of Moors, and his cellmate, Thompson Bey, sat at his side.

"Stop staring at him. You might offend him," Buffy warned Summer, but the bitch was on her scent.

"I can't keep my eyes off him." Summer had puppy-eyes. It was sick and cute at the same time.

"You can't stop talking about him neither. I feel bad for Lazy Eyes."

"Out of sight, out of mind. Cupid done shot that bitch with a new dick," Britney said.

"Straight in the ass," Buffy added as they laughed. Summer gave them the finger.

Atwater got up and raced to the restroom, so he wouldn't miss that much of the game.

"There he goes, horny ho," Buffy said. "You better skedaddle if ya want to catch him."

"Right now?" Summer asked as if she was a dimwit.

"No, bitch, when a full moon comes out and turns Britney into a werewolf," Buffy responded.

"I probably still could give better head than you, vampire."

Summer summoned her courage and went to the bathroom. When she went in, she saw Atwater at the urinal. She went straight to the handicap urinal in the back and acted as if she had to piss. She waited for a second, and when she came out, there was a short line of guys waiting to wash their hands at the sink which had a mirror over it. Summer was lucky enough to stand right behind Atwater.

When the guy at the sink left, Atwater offered Summer to go before him. She washed her hands, but she was looking at him on the sly through the mirror. They held eye contact, which seemed like forever, and it silently communicated that they were feeling each other.

She walked back into the gym now certain Atwater felt the same way she felt about him. She just didn't know how to make the first move.

They finished watching the game and the ten-minute move was called at 7:30 p.m. Summer went to the library because Buffy thought Ray Ray wanted to meet him there. When they got there, Ray Ray didn't even show up. So, they were stuck on the move. When Summer looked up, she saw Atwater was there watching videos.

She couldn't contain herself, and she let Buffy and Britney know. "Atwater is in the library now. What should I do? Should I just go in there?" Summer asked, fidgeting with her shirt.

Buffy said, "Calm down, bitch."

Atwater emerged from the room and headed for the bathroom.

It's now or never, Summer thought. Buffy was going to be on watch because Britney already proved to be useless.

When Summer went into the bathroom, Atwater wasn't pissing. He just stood there. "I've been waiting on you." A sure smile framed his mouth.

It was music to Summer's ears. "I can't keep my eyes off you."

"You're going to get me in trouble." Atwater knew it! But he was too far gone to give a fuck.

"How so?" Summer asked, narrowing their distance until she stood right in front of him.

Atwater felt his dick lurch in his pants. He didn't think Summer saw it, but her hand dashed out to grab it. He couldn't stop her from massaging his dick.

"I know you want me. I see how you look at me." It was the moment of truth, and as Atwater stared into Summer's eyes, he felt like he was looking into the face of Rihanna.

"I want to fuck you so bad; I don't know what to do," the words trailed off Atwater's tongue before he could stop them.

"You wanna fuck me?" Summer asked senselessly; she already knew the answer. She took Atwater's dick from his pants and sucked it on the spot. Atwater flung his arms back to close the bathroom door, but Summer stopped him.

"Leave it open."

Atwater looked confused, but Summer peeped down the hallway to make sure Buffy was watching out for them.

"I had to make sure my girl was watching."

"Damn, I wanna fuck you bad!" Atwater said as if he was lust drunk. The little game of eye tag was coming to an end, and they both were about to wind up the winner.

Summer pulled down her shorts and bid him on. "Fuck me

then," she said as she leaned over the sink. Their encounter reminded her of when she was with Lazy Eyes, and he'd pound ten inches in her. She felt a fever in the night.

"I ain't got no protection," Atwater said in a serious tone. He wasn't the one. Fuck no! Not after doing eighteen years would he come home with HIV or worse! He had heard all the stories, and he wasn't the one, not today or ever. Atwater would have never thought about having sex with a man until he saw Summer, who didn't resemble one at all. But one thing he wasn't going to do was fuck that man raw.

Summer pulled her pants back up because the mood was hampered. She knew they were going to meet back up again.

"What sign are you?" she asked.

Atwater thought it was funny that she had asked. "I'm an Atwater."

She remembered it. "When are we going to meet back up?"

Atwater rearranged his pants. "Meet me at the gym tomorrow night."

The rendezvous for the next night was music to Summer's ear. She was going to have him in every way possible.

CHAPTER 24
CAN'T GET YOU OUT OF MY MIND

ATWATER NEEDED a walk to clear his head because he didn't know what the hell just happened back there. He went back to his unit from the library, knowing he was overly attracted to Summer. He even thought about the things he would do to her if nobody knew. But he never thought he would act on it.

Damn me! He knew the urge was beyond him when he took the image of Summer back to the unit with him: her soft neck, her high and soft cheeks, and those fluffy lips. He knew he was damned! He couldn't wait to get his big dick in her sugar buns and wax-wane until he spazzed out. He would hold her hips and shatter her spine with his diesel load.

Fuck! He had to get control of his thoughts. The whole time he was thinking about nutting so hard in Summer, his cellmate was talking about miscellaneous things. He could have been talking about hidden treasure, but it still would have been miscellaneous. Shit! Atwater felt all hot and bothered in the cold and unnerving air.

He went straight to the shower, took a cold shower, and thought about his fine wife and beautiful children. The cold shower cleared his throbbing mind. He just couldn't do it. He couldn't drive headfirst, speeding into a head-on collision that would end with a plummet off a mountain peak. But that was exactly what it was if he made love to Summer. Oh, my God! Make love?

Atwater soaped his dick up and started to jerk it as fast as he could. He knew if he shot off a wad, he'd gain some semblance of control. But as he stroked his dick, he felt every callous on his palm, and he was just tired of jacking his dick. It had been eighteen years of fucking his hand. Plus, he was taking a cold shower, so his hands felt like fucking an empty soda can.

He dried off and went to his cell. Atwater slammed the door behind him, and Thompson Bey looked up at him like he was crazy.

"What's up?"

"Nothing really, just got something on my mind," he said. After he brushed his teeth, he grabbed Robert Greene's *33 Strategies of War*. He read it but still had the same thought of Summer's lips sliding up and down his shaft until he nutted down her throat. Frustrated, he slammed his book closed.

And it was as if his cellmate knew the content of his mind.

"Atwater, these brothers are a trip. The homies are talking about checking Love in. They said that fool was in a homo-orgy a few weeks ago."

"He from St. Louis?" Atwater asked, feeling like Thompson Bey had to know what he was going through.

"That's the only Love the homies would be concerned with. But Moor, I find it impossible that a man could come in here and get turned out." A shadow of guilt shaded over Atwater's face. "And it's always them D.C. niggas that got all those fags."

"Must be something in the water out there," Atwater said, and he could have punched himself.

"I don't really agree with checking Love in though because I know T got personal issues with him, and he's just trying to use this as an excuse. You know Love be into everything, and I know it's some ulterior motives. Really, who's checking brothers in for fucking punks?"

Atwater sighed. "Hardly ever."

"I think the only reason the B-More Cart checked Lazy Eyes in was because he was married to B-Rod's daughter."

"You're bullshittin'!" It was the first time Atwater heard that.

"The truth is far from bullshit. I feel B-Rod too. That boy Lazy Eyes was fucking probably got the package; he's always at pill line. I saw him head for pill line tonight when we were leaving the law library. You know them D.C. niggas be having that shit. HIV in D.C. is as high and as worse as places in Africa."

"But what trips me out, even more, is the whole time Lazy Eyes was fucking that boy, he'd be out there on the visit tongue kissing his wife. I always say if you pitch, you'll eventually catch."

They laughed together. Even though Atwater was thinking about pitching only hours before.

"That's foul." Atwater brushed the light perspiration from his brow.

"I heard they ran a train on Lazy Eyes' boy, who they call Summer in 4B when he first got here. I can't even front; I ain't never seen men react to nobody like that. When that punk came into the gym tonight, it got so quiet I could hear hearts beating," Thompson Bey laughed to himself. "Real talk, in my pimp days, I would have had to put that punk to work."

"Islam Moor," Atwater said, which was supposed to instill value in the conversation they were having. It was improper to talk about things that were debasing to men and Atwater knew he was fronting to the max.

"Islam Moor," Thompson Bey started laughing. "I'm just keeping it real."

"No, I understand. I think it's just the novelty of having somebody on the pound that looks like a girl."

"Yeah, Moor, and not just any girl; that fool looks like Rihanna," Thompson Bey laughed harder. "But you're missing what I'm saying. I guarantee that even on the streets, that boy got dudes going. I think women would even be curious. It's a live wire in the human psyche to marvel at anything exotic. And he fits the bill. Pure psychology."

Atwater was relieved Summer had affected his cellmate too. "You may need to stay away from that boy talking like that."

"Islam Moor. I'm going to bed. I've got to go to the plantation tomorrow."

Thomson Bey turned the lights off, and Atwater was left to his thoughts. His mind went to the conversation he had with Old School when they walked the track.

His thinking was that there were only three divisions of people: pimps, hoes, and tricks. He had to keep his mind above the water and seize the opportunity of the prospects Summer had. It was chancy, risky, even dangerous, but he still had the semblance of a plan forming in his mind of how he could take pimping to another level. If what he thought could work, he could get Old School out of prison. He laughed and was too excited to go to sleep. He tossed and turned, thinking about his plans, his future, and the egging thought he couldn't get out of his mind: the touch of Summer's soft ass, which he thought about thrice as much!

CHAPTER 25
THE FANTASY

UNLIKE ALL THE other images and nightmares that passed through Summer's mind while she slept, for the first time, she had a lovely dream.

She was laid out in an orchard of soft red roses and Atwater had her legs straight up, ramming his dick inside her. He moaned, and she felt as if she had a g-spot that he was hitting. The head of his helmet flared, and she knew he was buttering her buttermilk biscuits as she took his sugar tongue into her mouth while he released his motherlode.

His eyes were doting as he peered into her eyes, and she loved the feeling of having power over him. His massive member was wedged between her cheeks, still hard, and he fucked her with the most passion ever. She had completely surrendered, relinquished to his strong arms locked on her hips and his manly prowess, selfishly seeking its climax as she welcomed his toll. His dick felt like pure fire, and it was the most warming, satisfying, and soothing feeling she ever had.

Summer awoke as her evanescent dreams fled. And for once, she woke with a smile on her face.

Britney had already left for work at her job in Unicor, so Summer got up and refreshed herself. She threw the towel over the door's window so she could have some privacy. Summer stripped naked and did a once over in the mirror.

It was so rewarding for her to look at her shapely body in the mirror. It was perfect! Everything was sleek, smooth, and firm. She clasped her tits to her chest, and the cleavage looked sexy and appealing. She twirled on her heels and looked at the arch in her back and her phat butt and she celebrated! Oh, but for her hair and lack of makeup and clothes!

She shaved her legs, armpits, and pubic hairs and she felt her comfort zone return. She made something to eat because later that night she knew she was going to need all her energy for her amazing tryst.

That dreary turquoise evening, Atwater and Craze-zo went to work out in the weight room. It was always crowded with people. The good thing was there were two weightlifting areas, outdoor and indoor. They went to the indoor. Everybody was in there since it was cold outside.

They were on the incline bench and Atwater was lifting while Craze-zo spotted him.

"One more. Push!"

When Atwater finished, a Mexican came over to ask if he could have the bench next, which was always the case. You had to call the weights and wait in a long line for the group to finish to have a turn.

"We have two more sets," Atwater responded to the Mexican as Craze-zo went to do his set.

While Craze-zo was getting ready to do his set, Summer and Buffy came to the door to peek into the weight room. Summer shot Atwater a quick knowing-eye, and Atwater felt his heart leap. Craze-zo gave Summer and Buffy the evil eye and they took off.

Atwater laughed. "You're a funny dude."

"No, man, those faggots is vicious. They got this whole compound off balance. What kind of shit is this? Niggas are going. And from what I hear, the Rihanna punk got trained in 4B, was fucking Black, Lazy Eyes, and that Mexican, Sosa. Word is before the orgy in 4B went down, Love and Tyrone— rest in piss, were fucking that faggot. On my hood, had you let me stab that one punk that night in the barbershop, them faggots wouldn't be so bogus right now."

"You can't stab somebody up because they're gay," Atwater said. He didn't know Summer was tossed around like that. He was just happy he didn't slip up and fuck the punk. The head was cool because it wasn't like you could get HIV or AIDS from a blow job.

"Why not?" Craze-zo asked, his face completely blank of understanding Atwater's statement. "Me and my homies from my hood used to fuck punks up in Hollywood all the time. Shit, every prison I've ever been to, them faggots have some shit in a twist. Look at these clowns around here. All of them fools went to the SHU, and I know that race riot had something to do with the punk because all the key characters were fucking him. To add to that, one of them niggas was ready to leave his wife for that punk! Mark ass niggas! Cuz, they got to get me out of this region before I put a plug in one of these busters!"

Atwater laughed because he had his doubts. If the power of temptation was so strong, how could he resist it? "Your set, Moor."

While Atwater and Craze-zo were lifting weights, Summer and Buffy stood in the entranceway of the gym, which was right next to the restroom. Summer was having a fit because Atwater hadn't already come out to meet her. She had been thinking about him all day, and it was just too bad he had his evil and hateful friend with him. She hated him! But she kept it courteous and spoke to some of the guys who passed by on their way to the weight room.

"Damn, what is taking him so long?" Summer asked.

"Calm down, bitch. You probably about to get the best dick

on the compound, let me tell you," Buffy said playfully.

"I've been thinking about him all day. Every time he's with his friend, he never even makes eye contact with me," Summer fussed.

"He's probably fucking him."

"Shut up, bitch. He ain't gay!"

Franco and Slim came into the gym like they owned the place. Franco's chest and chin were to the sky.

"Look at Franco," Buffy said, looking at his log poking out of his shorts. "Hello, Franco."

"You better stop talking to me, faggot, before I beat you up," Franco threatened.

Summer and Buffy laughed.

After Franco and Slim went into the weight room, Summer started to stress again.

"Where is he?"

"Calm your hot ass panties down, bitch!" she smacked.

"There he goes," Summer said, finally relieved.

As by design, Atwater headed straight toward the bathroom and went to the handicap stall.

When Summer entered the restroom, somebody was in there, so she acted like she was using the urinal until he disappeared. She stole the chance to go to Atwater. She went into the handicap stall and closed the distance between them in seconds. Atwater was so hungry and lust-dumb; he welcomed the grand gesture. She melted under his kiss and fell listlessly into his arms.

For a moment, he kissed her until she was dizzy. But she wanted to feel her dreams from this morning resurge!

Summer dropped to her knees and yanked his massive dick from his pants and gave him mega head! She took his sex lever into her mouth. When his dick was deep in her throat, she gurgled. He thought Summer must have known sorcery! Never in a million years could something feel so good! She whirled her mouth around his dick and slurped the pre-cum dribble and jacked her head back and forth. And he knew she was a genius. When he nutted in her mouth, he grabbed her arms so hard she thought he would snatch them out the sockets. She gurgled deeply in the back of her throat. The whole time, his orgasm was in a twist!

Atwater shivered like a man being pulled out of an iceberg. Summer loved pleasuring him! She nibbled on his pulsating helmet and slurped at it. On a rare occasion, his dick responded to the sapping slurps, and he got hard again. Atwater began sweating. Her head was so supernatural he could have easily mistaken her for a snake charmer par excellence. He shot another wad down her gurgling throat and almost collapsed to his knees. If she continued, he knew he would need a gurney to carry him back to the unit.

She licked her lips like a demonic nympho that just feasted on its prey. "You alright?" she asked.

Atwater was momentarily motionless from pleasure. "I think so."

Summer laughed. She didn't need anybody telling her the full merit of her skills.

They heard somebody enter the restroom, and their spell broke. Summer helped Atwater up, and his color returned to his face.

"When am I going to see you again?" she whispered in his ear, gently grabbing his pulsating dick.

"Whenever," Atwater said.

They heard the guy leave, and it was Summer's chance to exit. "I'll see you later." She pecked him on his cheek, leaving abruptly.

Moments later, he was about to leave. When he looked down, he saw her ID on the ground. Atwater picked it up and placed it in his front pocket.

That was the best head ever!

CHAPTER 26
RENDEZVOUS POINT

SHONDA CAME RIGHT BACK to visit Atwater again. This time, she brought their children, Mason and Macy.

Mason didn't look anything like his father, but Macy was a blend of her mother and father's good looks.

"What up, Pops!" Mason said as he hugged his dad, standing an inch taller.

"Daddy!" Macy said. She hugged her father, and she didn't want to let him go because she missed him like crazy.

Shonda looked completely mouthwatering with her pendants, jewels, snug-fitting dress and, superbly whipped hairstyle. She kissed him like it was their last kiss.

When they sat down, Shonda was first to speak. "We have some good news to tell you, and that's why we came up here because they wanted to tell you in person."

Atwater smiled. "What good news?"

"You sure you don't want to eat first?" Shonda asked.

"We can wait. I want the news first."

They all looked at Mason, who was smiling from ear to ear.

"You know how you've always been talking about getting into positions of power, networking, and strategizing success? Guess what? I've been accepted into West Point."

Atwater was speechless. He couldn't believe it! He knew such a position meant power, connections, and, above all else, influence.

"That's what I'm talking about! Give me a hug! Damn you make me proud!" Atwater yelled.

"Hold it down, Atwater," the CO said, who sat across from them.

"My apologies. My son just hit me with some good news."

"I understand," the CO said and went back to monitoring the visitors.

Atwater had to know everything. "How did you get in? Doesn't a senator have to refer you?"

"That's why I have you to thank. You were so instrumental in getting me accepted; you just don't know. To keep it real, when you told mom to put me in military boarding school, I hated you. But now I understand why you did it. That's where I met Timothy Hathaway, and his father's a senator out of Maine. His father wanted to refer a minority to West Point, and he immediately thought of me."

"My son is going to be a Five-Star General."

"And an engineer," Mason added.

"Damn—you make me proud!" Atwater couldn't have been happier. Everything that Old School drilled into his head was coming to fruition. Everything was owed to Old School's thoughts and ideas, and Atwater felt as if he owed the old man a prince's boon.

Shonda was in tears. "All of this machismo is making me cry." But it wasn't the machismo. It was seeing her husband with their son and seeing the love everybody had for Atwater that made her happy.

Seeing her mother crying tears of joy, Macy was also choked up.

"Macy, tell him your good news," Shonda said.

"There's more?" Atwater asked shockingly.

"Daddy, I'm going overseas to get an education. I'm going to Oxford, and I have a full scholarship because I'm a Rhodes Scholar. I'm going to the same college that so many powerful people went to -- like Bill Clinton."

Atwater was choked up. "I need a minute to get my head together. This is too much," he said as he dropped his head to cherish the moment. Macy hugged him.

"You were right about strategizing success," Shonda added.

"I love y'all," Atwater said. They had a family hug, and the CO didn't say anything.

"You just make sure you come home soon. Stay safe," Shonda said. They ate lunch and talked about everything until the visit ended. What tripped him out was he kept thinking about Summer while he was with his family. And he didn't know what it meant.

Jealous passion perhaps...

The next evening, Summer raced out of the unit to meet Atwater. It was 8:05 p.m. and the pill line was just called.

Atwater was already up the walkway when Summer left the unit. He took a detour toward the automated machine by the commissary and barbershop, waiting for Summer to catch up with him.

She came up behind him, wearing a cap on her head. Her face looked luscious with those rosy, red lips, and her ass looked full and wide. And with those thoughts, Atwater could forget everything.

"Where have you been? I thought you were going to meet me last night?" Summer asked, sounding hurt. It made Atwater laugh because this was really a woman! He hadn't been possessed by a woman in a long time. It was different with Shonda. She'd always been there.

But before Atwater could respond, Summer said, "You were with your girlfriend?"

Atwater didn't know who she was talking about. She couldn't

have been talking about Shonda. How could she have known about their visit?

"Who are you talking about?"

"Your friend."

"Craze-zo?" Atwater could have guffawed. "That's like my little brother."

Summer softened at the yearning in his eyes feasting on her busty breasts and wide hips. She knew if she had been a piece of candy, she would've dissolved!

"I've been checking up on you. I know you're from Virginia, you and the guy you're in the cell with."

Atwater laughed.

"Somebody's been feeding you bad information. I ain't from Virginia."

Atwater was talking to her, but at the same time, he was still trying to be discreet. He could tell Summer didn't give a fuck who saw or listened. She could have tongue kissed him in front of everybody with a middle finger to them.

"If this is going to be too much for you, you need to let me know right now. I'm falling in love with you. I just can't stop thinking about you." Summer had been wanting to get that off her chest all day, and she finally said it.

"Calm down. You're alright." Atwater's sheltering voice and soft words were assuring.

He tapped the automated machine, and the screen went back to its entry page, and they started to walk off side by side. Summer, anxious to be with him the past couple of days, was now settled and calm.

"When I'ma see you again?" she asked with hidden promise in her eyes.

"Tomorrow night," Atwater promised. He knew he needed her again. Her mouth was a honeycomb. By now, he ruled out the possibility of ever fucking Summer because there was no way he would get a condom.

"Why don't you come out during the daytime? That would be good too."

"I'll keep that in mind," Atwater said with a sly smile. His smile was powerful and magnetic, and Summer couldn't keep from smiling herself.

"I'll see you then."

CHAPTER 27
TRUE LOVE NEVER DIES

BOBBY MOORE!"

The following afternoon, during mail call, Summer heard her name called. She shot down the steps and grabbed her letters. Some were from her mother, who was probably the only person that knew she was in jail. But the other was from somebody with a return address she didn't recognize.

When she opened the letter, she knew exactly who the letter was from. It was from Lazy Eyes, and he sent the letter to somebody on the streets to send to Summer. When she opened it, she smelled his potent scent, and it reminded her she really missed him.

Buffy came over to her and asked her who it was from. They ran to her room so she could read him the contents.

Summer,

I'm fucked up back here. They're talking about sending me to USP Florence in Colorado. I can't stop thinking about you. I broke my fist against the wall because I can't be out there without you with that good pussy of yours. The best ever! Hands down . . .

My wife wants a divorce because her dad told her about us. But fuck that bitch. I'm in love with you! I swear I'm going to wife you when I get out in 3 years. I've been thinking a lot about that, and if you steal a woman's identity, we can get married! Real talk, you look better than my bitch anyways. Shit, you look better than all my baby mommas put together. Lol Yo, check your account. I had my homie put $10k there. And you better get a job before they stick your ass in the kitchen. Go and talk to the secretary at the chapel where I used to work. She'll look out for you because I told her about us. I got you, baby. Forever, my lady. Love you. Oh yeah, when you get out of jail, I'll have you a spot, clothes, and everything you need.

Love you.

After Summer read the letter, she and Buffy fell out on the bed, laughing.

"Bitch, you got some good pussy!"

Chapter Thirty-One Where Is He?...

The next day, Atwater came to chill with Craze-zo. They were walking the yard and talking about what Atwater was going to do when he got out in a couple of months. Atwater had so many ideas since he met Summer and it seemed crazy. He couldn't tell Craze-zo, but he kept his youngster in suspense by telling him how he would be living, traveling, and doing it real big.

Summer and Buffy were also walking on the track, and Summer just needed Atwater to steal a minute away with her. She knew he was on the down-low, but damn, how down-low did he have to be? It was frustrating, and she had too many options to be tripping off him; she knew she deserved better.

Buffy was even tripping. "He should have been gone to the bathroom."

"He knows I'm here waiting for him. Every time he gets around that idiot, he acts like he don't know me," Summer fussed. It was so unlike her to be so uptight all the time.

"I told you they're probably fucking, let me tell you."

"I told you he ain't gay," Summer said, knowing if she didn't look like a girl, he wouldn't be fooling around with her.

"Shut up, gurl. He ain't all that. Lazy Eyes looks better than him."

"Shut up."

Summer was furious when she was unsuccessful meeting up with Atwater. She had to take a walk of shame back to the unit. She fumed and fussed the whole way back, driving Buffy crazy.

She couldn't wait until they called pill line because she wanted to see Atwater. When Britney came back from work, she fussed and fumed some more.

Pill line was finally called, and Atwater was at the automated machine. Summer walked as fast as she could to give him a piece of her mind.

When she walked up to him, she got a whiff of his cologne, and she wasn't as mad anymore.

"I'm so tired of you and your shadow. Y'all must have something going on I don't know about. You didn't even try to go to the bathroom earlier."

"Chill out," Atwater said. He liked that shit, but everything was difficult for him. "At least say what's up first."

"You know how I feel about you. I'm falling in love with you. You need to let me know how you feel."

Atwater backed up from the machine, and Summer went up to the machine like she was checking her account.

"I like you. What are you tripping about?"

"Everything is going to smooth out."

"I ain't trippin'. I just can't take having these feelings for you and being completely ignored. It would be easy for me to fall deeply in love with you. You stirred me up." Summer kept tapping the machine, but she couldn't stop thinking about the last time she brought Atwater to his knees, in the velvet clutches of her gurgling throat. She smiled and faced him. "You tasted so good the last time."

Atwater laughed. Damn, he was so fond of her.

They traipsed toward the walkway. "You mind if I write you a kite?" Summer asked.

"No, I'd like that."

"I have to ask you something. When are you going to stop being scared and fuck me?"

Atwater couldn't believe the question. "Real soon," he lied. "That's my word. I'm going to take my time with that ass," Atwater eyed her ass mischievously.

"I'ma see you tomorrow," Summer said. She could've skipped to pill line as good as she felt.

CHAPTER 28
IF TRUTH BE TOLD...

ATWATER WAS in the band room listening to live musicians. They sounded so good, he thought he was at a concert. The guitarist plucked and strummed the guitar so skillfully that Atwater felt his neck hairs ruffle.

Outside the music room, it was nighttime. The sky was filled with smoky clouds, and the trees from far off whipped freely in the wind.

Atwater saw Summer coming down the walkway, and he thought this would be a good chance to give back her ID. Over the past few days, he didn't know where the budding relationship would lead, but he felt they would be lifetime friends. She was tied to a lot of his plans for the future, and that's why he wasn't just fucking her. He wanted to develop her mind better, and he thought there was no better way than to seem preoccupied with other things. For her to understand him, she had to understand that he handled business first, and pleasure was a product of success and not vice versa.

He headed straight to the restroom, and Summer saw him when she entered the yard. He was waiting for her in the handicap stall when she entered. She melted in his arms, and for a minute, she didn't say anything.

"Missed me?" Atwater smiled.

She looked up and kissed him. "Yes, I've missed you. And I've missed this." She brushed his dick. "I'm going to make this mine and mine only."

"You wouldn't know what to do with all that," Atwater teased.

"I'm sure I could put it to use." They laughed and Summer slipped her note into his pocket.

"I'm going to read it before I go to bed. And here's your ID."

"You had my ID? I was looking all over the place for it."

"You dropped it."

She kissed him again. "I'll see you later."

"Alright."

Atwater left the bathroom first this time, and Summer followed closely behind him.

Summer went to the entranceway where Buffy and Britney were waiting for her.

Atwater was about to leave, but he held Summer's gaze for seconds until he heard his name called. He turned and Old School was sitting, unbeknownst to him, in the basketball bleachers checking out the exchange between him and Summer.

"Atwater, one second. Hit a couple of laps with me on the basketball court," Old School said. The gym was empty, and they'd be alone. "I'm not interrupting you, am I?"

"No, I was about to get my stuff. I was over in the band room listening to Jeffrey Bey and his group."

They started making their laps, and Old School set out at a brisk pace. He was never one to beat around the bush.

"The Greeks used to say women are for childbearing and boys are for fun."

Atwater was aghast! Old School just couldn't have known about him and Summer.

"Come again?" Atwater said wanly.

"The deaf and foolish shout and scream because they don't understand that signs and symbols are for the conscious mind. Riddle me that. A wise man could decipher dark sayings, break down enigmas, and put the pieces of puzzles together. Have you heard about King David and Prince Jonathan from the Bible?"

Atwater didn't dare answer that question. Even if he knew the answer, he wouldn't have said anything. Old School was on a spiel. "King David wrote the dead Prince a eulogy. He said, 'the love I had for him surpassed the love of any woman.'"

"Islam Moor. What are you trying to imply?" Atwater was a bit offended, and he didn't like the fact that Old School could read him so easily, bare him so shamefully.

But Old School kept digging. "You ever read the book of Psalms about King David getting persecuted? They say it's a prophesy for Jesus Christ. But I say King David got persecuted because of his affair with Prince Jonathan."

"Old School, I don't know where you're going with this."

"You haven't read about Alexander and Hephaestion, or Set and Heru, or the Sacred Band, or Sulla of Rome, or at least 80% of Hollywood's major actors?" Atwater shook his head and was about to drop his head to the ground, but Old School brought Atwater's attention to Summer, who was still standing in the entranceway, laughing with Britney and Buffy. "Look at him. He has the silhouette of a woman. His whole body, spirit, and manners are that of a woman. He's far prettier than any lady CO on this compound, or any I've ever been to."

"You think I'm judging you?" Old School leveled the question at him, and it was then that Atwater looked up at him. But that was it! He felt that Old School, who had been his counselor, his mentor, in short, a father to him, had judged him, and it was more than he could take. But the more he looked at Old School, his eyes had understanding, sympathy, and empathy even.

"No, I don't think you're judging me." Atwater was certain of it now, and he had to come clean. "I fell into my low. I've been down eighteen years without the merest touch of a woman. I've missed the banter of a woman's laughter, her frailty, the lyric of her walk, and the taste between her sweet thighs. And when I saw Summer, she gave me some of that. I knew I was too far gone when I used to take her image back to the unit with me, and I didn't have anybody to talk to about it. I let Summer get into my head, and I started feeling like one of those tricks you were talking about the other day. She has the softest lips, and her ass feels soft, and she gives the best head I've ever had. But I ain't trying to be another Lazy Eyes, and I most definitely ain't trying to take nothing home to wifey."

Old School was the perfect listener, and it was as if he understood what Atwater was going through. "Did you kiss him?" Old School asked.

Atwater just told him she had the softest lips in the world. He shook his head.

"You got it bad. What's your ulterior motive with him? You ain't tender dick, are you?"

"Hell no!" Atwater said emphatically. Of course, he had ulterior motives that would help him and Old School. "I'm most definitely going to get some money."

"What's your angle?"

"I'm putting that pretty thing on the internet. Get a couple of tricks to contribute to his legal aid. When I was at Terre Haute, a cat from Atlanta was getting plenty of money like that." Atwater couldn't tell Old School his real plan. It was to be kept a surprise.

"What's plenty of money?"

"How much a high-profile attorney cost? What $60k to $90k, and they were getting a lot of different Johns," Atwater answered.

"Strategizing success," Old School added.

When Old School said that, Atwater told him about his son

and his daughter and the good tidings they had brought him. Old School truly felt a part of Atwater's family.

At that minute, the ten-minute move was called over the loudspeaker. To that, Old School said, "Young Blood, I'm going to always trust and roll with your judgment call. But remember, amongst all the emotions you'll have with him/her, keep the presence of your mind."

Atwater looked at Old School as if he knew that already. "Come on now, this is me you're talking to. That's why I like this chase because I have to struggle with temptation. I like living on the edge a little bit."

Old School laughed. "What happens when he gets possessive and starts demanding more and more of your time? Young Blood, don't get emotionally attached. Don't be like Lazy Eyes. You have too much to lose."

"Never that," Atwater said as they headed toward the exit. "You're like a father to me. I'm hearing you on everything you're saying, but I have to take this ride and see where it leads."

"You better. How else would a man test his mettle and wits? Iron sharpens iron and man sharpens man, no homo."

Atwater went straight to the unit. He brushed his teeth, washed his face, and got his clothes out for tomorrow.

His cellmate jumped on his bunk, and once he saw that his cellmate was occupied reading a book, he hopped on his bunk and read Summer's letter.

Atwater,

I'm trying my hardest to be patient. I know you're on the down-low, but how down-low do you have to be? You have me waiting outside, walking the yard, trying to get your attention, and sometimes you don't even go to meet me. I just be giving you a hard time when I talk about you and your shadow because I know y'all don't have nothing going on. But I hate the way he looks at me. My brother and my father used to look at me the same way. It's a long story.

If this is too much for you, please let me know because I wouldn't play you like this. What's worse is you keep kissing me and holding me tight, as if this is something that you want. I'm confused! Let me know what's on your mind.

Distant whisper . . .

Atwater smiled. She was too much.

CHAPTER 29
I'M TIRED OF PRISON

MRS. MIRES WAS the wicked bitch of the prison. If she could be nasty, she'd spite herself to be even nastier. She had no sense of being cordial. Being decent never crossed her mind. It made her little stump legs and fat body seem grotesque. She wore her blue CO uniform, and it became her personality as if her blue uniform and badge could compensate for her foul mouth, nasty manners, and her ugly, shapeless body. With her short hairstyle, she looked like a short-stop who should be spitting chew with a horse stuck between her legs and a straw in her mouth.

That morning, Mrs. Mires called Summer to her office, which was in a hallway between two units. Summer did as she was told. There was nobody back there with Mrs. Mires except the secretary and an orderly who was emptying the trash cans.

"Princess, go to the chapel when you hear the call for the ten-minute move," Mrs. Mires told Summer.

"For what?" Summer asked. She didn't like the sneer in Mrs. Mire's eyes.

"Because I said so. And also, put on your boots and take off those tight pants. And if I see that you've altered another shirt, I'm going to write you an incident report."

"What's that?"

"You'll find out when I write one. Now get out of my office and put your uniform and boots on."

Summer padded out of her office and went to change her clothes, as she was told. When she put on the two-piece uniform and the gangly boots, she felt like the horse-bitch Mrs. Mires truly was.

They called the ten-minute move, and Summer marshaled out with the other inmates. She went to the chapel, and it was quiet and empty inside. It was nothing like how she remembered the last time she was there.

When she went into the Chaplain's office, a sharply dressed white lady in her early forties, clad in D&G transitional frames and a body that looked like she never missed a workout day, greeted her. Summer knew this must've been the lady the inmates would line up outside of her office to ask her meaning-less questions, just to get a sneak preview of her jazzy attire.

"Hello," Mrs. Hoover said, starkly differently from Mrs. Mires. She seemed urbane and cordial.

"My counselor, Mrs. Mires, told me to come down here," Summer said, using her kitten voice because she liked the lady at first sight.

"Hello again, Summer," she smiled and winked an eye. "You'll be taking over Lonny's old job as a library clerk. He sent me a kite and told me to give you his old job and to look out for you." She squeezed Summer's hand over the counter between them.

"He told me a lot about you, too," she shook her head. "And you are every bit as pretty as he said.

"Wow!" thought Summer not thinking that Lazy Eyes would actually do as he said.

The phone rang. She told Summer to give her a second and she would show her around. So, Summer stepped out of her office and looked around the chapel. She walked by the bathroom and remembered that was the first time she had made out with Lazy Eyes. Yes, the library had a wealth of memories with him. If she sniffed the air, she could still smell his musk; his cologne scent and feel his thrust in her lubricated bend. It was a pleasing thought she was suddenly pulled from when the lady emerged from the office.

"Sorry about that," she giggled.

"You're going to basically do everything Lonny was doing. Your job is very simple, and I'm sure we're going to get along just fine. You'll hand out books, CDs, videos, and any other religious apparel needed. Those lockers are where we keep everything, and I'll unlock it as need be."

"You have the Sunnis's locker there, the FOI there, and the Rastafarians's over there, too. On the other side are the Hebrew Israelites, who share the same locker with the Jews, Wicca, and Santamaria. The Jehovah Witness and Protestant's lockers are there. And, of course, the last locker in the corner is for the Catholics."

Summer laughed because it was a lot to remember. "I'll try to get it remembered."

"You will. I'll show you the library where you'll spend most of your time."

They walked to the room that Lazy Eyes came out of the night Summer met him. It was diagonal to the main chapel.

When they walked in, it was just as Mrs. Hoover said: spacious, relaxing, and private.

"We have books on every religion, no matter what it is. Here's a religious catalog." Mrs. Hoover held up a Yellow Pages-sized book. "The CDs and videos are in that drawer. They have to fill out this sheet and give you their ID to rent them.

"Now that that is all done, I want you to tell me about you and Lonny. He's already told me so much about you."

Summer smiled sheepishly. But she still hadn't warmed up to Mrs. Hoover yet.

"I understand. I want you to call me Kathy, okay? You don't have to call me Mrs. Hoover and be all official," she laughed. "I'm not all gung ho. I'm only a secretary. I collect my check and that's it. I'm here to be your friend. You understand? And I was friends with Lonny. That boy is crazy!" she laughed. "He talked so much about you. I feel like I know you already."

That loosened Summer's tongue, and as first sight impressions went, Summer knew she'd like her.

"What did he used to say?" Summer asked. And that's how their friendship began.

CHAPTER 30
LOVE'S LIKE A ROLLERCOASTER...

ATWATER AND CRAZE-ZO listened intently to the music Jeffrey Bey and his band played in the band room, but Atwater's mind was on Summer. He needed to see her tonight to ease his mind. He had been uptight lately about getting out. It wasn't easy for a person to do eighteen years and then get released, and responsibility hit them all at once. He held everything down from jail and that was his comfort zone; he knew it would be different. Everything would be different. *Don't fret*, he told himself.

He saw Summer sauntering those juicy thighs up the walkway, and her hair was disheveled. It was obvious she didn't know what to do with her hair. He thought she probably was the type that figured beauty and body overcompensated for anything as trivial as a hot comb and some hair gel.

She saw him and headed to their honeycomb hideout. He appeared instantly into her arms.

"What kind of letter was that?" he asked.

"A *truth be told* letter."

Summer wanted to suck his fruit dry of its succulent juice, but he pulled away and handed her a letter. "Read this. I'll meet you tonight at pill line. I have to get back to the music room."

"Is that it?" Summer asked. She wanted much more. "You ain't gonna let me get any nourishment."

"If you keep drinking this bull's milk, you're going to lose that pretty figure of yours."

They laughed.

"Do you even like me, Atwater?"

He laughed. Up until that point, she had never called him by his name.

"Hell yeah! Let me feel that ass. Damn!" he said as she brushed her ass against his dick and pushed it against his mid-section.

"What?" she asked skeptically. "Let me guess. Feels like a woman's ass is what you're thinking?" she asked sarcastically, shameful she had to go through this with him. But how was he to know?

He shook his head affirmatively.

"When will you accept the fact that I'm a 100 percent black woman?"

"I'm a 100 percent convinced now. That's on the prophet!" Atwater added, exasperated.

"I'll see you at the pill line. I'm gonna read the letter right now."

Chapter Thirty-Five Testing The Water...

The moon cast a pale silvery glow over the night, and Atwater had to put his jacket on against the chill in the wind as he made his way to the pill line. He saw Summer walking up the walkway at a fast pace, and he had to damn near trot to catch up with her.

She slowed down when she saw him coming. When he saw her face, she looked like she'd been crying.

"What's up with you?" he asked.

"I've never been more insulted in all my life! I don't need a pimp. Everything you put in that letter just says that you want to use me like my manager did. I'm already on the internet. Here's my Facebook picture." She gave him her profile picture that was on the internet, and damn was she even prettier! "That's how I look when I have a stylist and a make-up artist."

"Why are you surprised? I hope you didn't think I walked around the streets with my hair like this. I'm a model."

"Calm down," Atwater said. At least until they were able to walk to the automated machine, he couldn't keep his eyes off the picture she handed him.

"I have plenty of money," she continued to fuss in her hushed tone. "I don't need a pimp. Here's my commissary receipt. I always keep three zeroes on my account. If I love somebody, Atwater, I'll give them whatever they want. But those were hurtful things you said in that letter. Asking me why I go to pill line. I'm bipolar! But you don't listen to me," Summer said in a desperate and hurt tone. She threw the letter back at Atwater and disappeared into the night.

Atwater smiled. He had done what he had wanted, to shake up her foundation. She gave him the key he needed to get her to do what he wanted her to do. What did she say, "if I love somebody, Atwater, I'll give them whatever they want?" How relishing. *The key to unlock her had come to him so easily* he thought to himself.

CHAPTER 31
MAKE-UP TO ... BUSTED

SUMMER WOKE up different than she had in the past two weeks, and she felt sluggish.

Summer dragged herself from the bed. Britney was already gone and left a note on her bed saying he was going to whip them up a meal that night and for her not to eat anything until he returned from work.

She had to put on her gawky uniform and gangly boots and trudged to work, feeling uncomfortable in the men's clothes.

When she went into Kathy's office, after the chaplain left to attend a meeting up front, Kathy made Summer a refreshing cup of coffee that snapped her back instantly; she was as giddy and graceful as ever.

When the chaplain returned, Summer headed for what would now be her office. She went inside to clean and arrange everything to her liking. She had to give the place a woman's touch and knew if she could appreciate it, so would Kathy.

But while she was cleaning up, Atwater stumbled in without as much as knocking.

"You got some trash in here that needs to be emptied?"

When Atwater looked up, he couldn't believe it was Summer

sitting behind the desk watching TV. She just rolled her eyes at him.

Atwater went to empty the trashcans, but an awkward moment passed, and when it had, he didn't feel like letting Summer off the hook that easily.

"So, you still following me around I see," she said with disdain in her voice.

"I didn't know you worked here," Summer said with an attitude without looking back.

"I find that hard to believe. I thought you had your informers who told you that me and my cellie were from Virginia and blah blah blah. I distinctly remember you saying that." Atwater had a smile that read victory.

"You know what? Fuck you!" Summer added. She didn't want to look at him because she wanted to stay mad at him.

"Was that Bobby or Summer talking? I did hear you last night when you said you were bipolar. I read your real name on your ID."

"Keep on," Summer said. Finally, she looked up at him, and she was glad she did.

Atwater set the bag in his hand on the ground. He was enjoying himself too much to leave.

"Check this out. I didn't completely accept in my mind that you were a real woman till last night, as crazy as that sounds. This is all new to me. When I wrote you, I thought I was being helpful. I didn't mean to hurt you. And plus, I didn't know you were laid like that out there. But I respect that."

"What led you to believe otherwise?" she asked curtly as Atwater pulled the door closed.

"Don't even go there."

"Don't go where?"

"You don't think I know about what you did in 4B with Tyrone and Love? I know the details of how you let them get you high and drunk. I know about Sosa, Lazy Eyes, and Black."

"You sound jealous," Summer leveled. "Fuck you. You must wanna meet Bobby, talking to me like that."

Atwater loved this shit. He got two inches from her face as she sat in the chair. "Yeah, show me Bobby."

Summer grabbed his arms. He wiggled away, and she jumped up to grab him again. He bear-hugged her and trapped her, planting kisses on her gorgeous face as she kissed him back. Kathy came in.

"Bobby . . ." She was shocked to see them hugged up together, and she smiled as Atwater jumped back. "I didn't see anything." Kathy smiled mischievously. "Excuse me, Bobby. We need you to put the new items in the lockers when you're finished in here. I'm sorry, that's all I wanted."

Kathy pulled the door tight this time. When she left, Atwater picked his bag up to leave.

"Thought you were busted, huh? With your '*keep it on the down-low* ass.'" Summer couldn't stop laughing.

"Islam Moor." Atwater said and then exited.

Once Atwater left, Kathy ran back into the room when she saw he went to the bathroom.

"You got you a cute one!" Kathy said, all smiles. "But be a little more discreet. Next time, put up this TV sign here. See this side: 'Do Not Disturb.' And keep the door locked."

Summer smiled. She had her a friend. "And hide these." Kathy had handed her a fistful of condoms, and Summer couldn't believe it. "I have plenty whenever you need them. Just let me know. But don't tell anybody I gave them to you. Nobody."

Summer placed her left hand over her heart and swore. It was the only hand she had free. "I can't say thank you enough."

"A singular thanks would be plenty. Now I have to get back to work, and you have to think about what you're going to do with those."

. . .

Chapter Thirty-Seven Make-up Tips...

After work, Summer floated back to her unit as if she had wings. She now had a job where she could have privacy, and her boss was the coolest in the world.

When Britney came back from work, Summer told him and Buffy everything about her day, and they couldn't stop laughing.

"Bitch, you got to be the luckiest ugly duckling in the pond," Britney said.

"Let me tell you," Buffy added.

"Whatever. Tomorrow we're going to make love."

"Go on and give him that worn-out pussy," Buffy said.

"Ain't that the truth." Britney slapped hands with Buffy. "She lost all her grippers in 4B." They laughed.

"You guys have to help me get ready for tomorrow. I can't go in there with my hair all over the place." Summer wanted to look irresistible.

"It never stopped you before," Britney said.

"Shut up, funky breath." She smacked her lips as always. "I got you, gurl."

Up until that point, Summer didn't know Buffy possessed any skills. However, Buffy shampooed her hair in the sink, braided it tight in cornrows, put on a do rag, and a tied a shirt around her head. He waited forty minutes until they opened the cells after 4:00 p.m. count and unwrapped her head. He took it out of the corn rows and wet her hair again. He took Murray's wave grease and put her hair in a silky, wavy bun at the back of her head. Buffy then made lipstick with Kool-Aid, used a pencil and petroleum jelly as eyeliner, and hooked Summer's face up.

That was the look she wanted, but she wouldn't see Atwater until the next morning, so this process would have to be repeated the following day.

The next day, when Summer woke up, Buffy was the first at the door when the CO unlocked the cells.

"Get up, bitches," he said, but Britney had already stirred.

"I have to get ready for work," Britney said as he got up and arranged his bed.

"'Hoe, please, we about to give the finishing touches." Buffy went over to Summer to shake her. "Get up, bitch. You have to get ready for work call."

"Just give me five more seconds."

"Get up, bitch," Britney said.

Buffy laughed as Summer stirred. "Please, Britney, I got her from here. Just brush your goddamn breath," she smacked.

"It's teeth, bitch, not breath," Britney said, making sure he blew as much of his breath on Buffy as possible.

"I don't even think I should ever breathe again," Buffy said as Summer laughed.

"'Hoe, it is too early."

Britney went to freshen up while Buffy had given Summer the altered pants of her old uniform back to her. "I hooked your uniform up. Wait till you put it on."

"Na-hum, you're going to get that bitch sent back to the SHU altering her clothes," Britney said with toothpaste suds all over his mouth.

Buffy just gave him the stop sign with his hands.

"Damn, bitch. What did you do to them?" Summer asked as she held them out in front of her. They looked to be skintight, and they were tapered at the bottom.

"I hooked them up. Now get your ass up. We have to douche you, let me tell you."

"I'm not doing that with y'all in the cell."

"I don't know why not." Smack. "It ain't like you know what you're doing anyways. It ain't like the streets, bitch. You have to use this shampoo bottle."

Buffy held up a shampoo bottle in his hands. "Come on, bitch, and Britney get the fuck out of the way."

"Hoe, I'm almost finished anyways."

"Good, because after I douche her ass, I'm going to douche your mouth, let me tell you."

They laughed.

Summer took off her shorts that she slept in and went over to sit on the toilet. And that was the first time the two of them saw her penis. They both laughed.

"What?"

"Bitch, you know what. What the hell is that? You sure you're supposed to be in a men's prison?" Britney asked.

"That's not even possible to be that small," Buffy said, slapping hands with Britney.

"Charming. Can we get on with this?"

Buffy gave Summer the shampoo bottle and Summer douched right in front of them while Britney got dressed for work. When Summer flushed the toilet, the smell was horrible!

"Damn girl, you smell like a dinosaur decomposed inside of you eons ago," Britney said.

"'Hoe, it's no worse than your breath,"

Buffy said. "I got bad breath from sucking your daddy's dick."

"You sure it wasn't from sucking the puss from his ingrown toenails?"

"I wish the both of y'all would shut up. I'm trying to concentrate," Summer said.

"Please, like you need to concentrate to flush your ass," Buffy said.

"Some people do. All ass and no brains."

Summer gave them the finger. When they finished, Summer looked better than she did the day before. Her hair was whipped back in a nifty and wavy bun. The button-down shirt was altered by Buffy, as were her pants. He tied a knot on the side, and it showed her belly button.

Her pants were skintight. She would have to put another uniform on top of her sexy clothes in order to go to work. She also had to hide her make-up by putting a cap on her head. But the good thing was that it was cold outside, and she could put her big jacket on and blend in with everybody else.

Summer went to work, and when she got there, she called Kathy into her office.

"What are you doing?" Kathy asked with a smile as Summer took off the uniform she had on top of her sexy apparel.

"If I tell you, then you're going to have to write me an incident report." They laughed.

"That is too nice, especially considering what you have to work with. How did you put that together?" Kathy thought it was too cute the way Summer's ass was hiked up in her skinny pants, and the shirt tied to the side and the belly button for all to see.

"Tricks of the trade."

"I'll tell you one thing. I'll make sure you're not disturbed," Kathy said as she walked over to grab the *Do Not Disturb* sign. "Just promise me you'll tell me details when you're through."

"Cross my heart and hope to have some wild and savage sex."

Kathy laughed at that. "Just be sure to use the condoms, and nobody should be able to hear you." Kathy was about to walk out the door, and then she turned back around. "You have a hot ass and a hot body."

"Thank you."

When Kathy closed the door, Summer twirled around in a celebratory circle.

Then she turned on the radio to soft jazz, lit candles, and turned off the lights. She didn't know what she could use on the floor, which would be their temporary bed. Summer couldn't find anything, so she laid out her uniform on the ground neatly and waited for what seemed like forever! Where is he?

Chapter Thirty-Eight Creamy Dreams

When Atwater got to work, the first thing he always did was make sure all the trashcans were empty, and then he'd clean the bathroom. But as soon as he went into Kathy's office, she was very direct and even rude, which was unlike her.

"Atwater, go and clean up the chapel's library."

"Okay, Mrs. Hoover. I'll go over there as soon as I'm done here."

"I said now!" she said, and she was stern about it.

He looked at her for a moment. She didn't give him any clue what she was up to.

When he left out of her office, he saw the *Do Not Disturb* sign on the door and returned to let Kathy know.

She told him she put the sign up because the place was so dirty, and she was disappointed by his work performance. He was stung because nothing seemed right with her this morning. Atwater hunched his shoulders, completely confused about everything. He went inside the library, and when he went in, he couldn't believe his eyes!

Summer was lying on the ground; her lips red, her hair whipped up in waves and pulled into a neat bun, and her eyes were shaded and lined.

She had on footsy socks and her ass looked like it would bust out the seams of the skinny pants that Buffy made for her.

Atwater dropped the bag in his hands and wiped his brow. "Get the fuck out of here!" He was lost in her awesome beauty, and for a minute, when he thought that he might have been tripping to have wanted to fuck her, he knew he was right on point!

As of late, he had been second guessing everything. He questioned his sexuality. He didn't understand what was wrong with him. But now that he saw her sprawled out on the ground and her lust-ridden eyes, he knew it was the fact that she was a woman!

There was nothing that told him otherwise, but he knew he could never fuck her because there was no way in hell he was going to raw dog her. He could never live with himself if he carried something home to Shonda, and he was so close to going home.

"Damn. All this for me?" he asked dubious and unsure of how much control he had over this situation.

"And much more." Summer displayed the condoms.

"Where did you…" he was about to ask, and then it all made sense to him. Kathy's strange behavior, the candles, the soft jazz music . . . it was all Mrs. Hoover's doing!

"Don't ask," Summer responded.

He gave her a knowing smile, and the talking came to an end. Summer was undressing him with her eyes, and she couldn't wait to deep throat him and fuck him reverse cowgirl style.

He looked kind of indecisive and skittish. She got up with graceful, seductive movements and brushed her ass against the bulge in his pants. Summer danced and unbuttoned one of the buttons on her shirt and swung her ass, and then backed onto the desk. She made her ass clap, and he touched her soft ass to make sure it was real.

He grabbed her up and kissed her from behind. She stuck her tongue into his mouth, and she moaned deeply because she wanted to feel his full measure.

He groped her breasts and dug his crotch into her full ass. He could have lost his mind!

Summer turned and unbuttoned his uniform, one button at a time, as she looked him in his eyes and placed her lips against his. She took his shirt off to see a well-developed chest and broad shoulders. She kissed every tattoo on them until she made her way down to his pants.

She unbuckled his pants, and then she sucked on his dick. He thought he would bust wild, unchallenged in her throat amongst her gurgles of pleasure, but she stopped and sucked on his balls and kissed his thighs until his passion was raw and gripping; he couldn't take anymore! He tried to take over the intermission, but she stopped him with a commanding finger to suggest she was in control.

"You ain't gonna fuck me until I ride the pony."

His face was drawn up in anguish. The more he heard her soft, gentle, and sexy voice, the more he wanted to nut hard inside of her.

"Ride the pony then."

"I want you to talk to me the whole time that fat dick is in my ass," she said, taking off her shirt slowly. Her tits sprang forth, and he hadn't seen real tits in eighteen years. Atwater groped and sucked on them.

Summer pulled down her pants, and when she did, she pushed Atwater into the chair. She kissed his thighs again, and then slurped the full scale of his dick and put a condom over it. She then greased her butt.

She turned, and when Atwater tried to guide his dick into her ass, she slapped his hands away and did the guiding. She put the helmet of his dick into her ass and twirled her hips without dropping down.

"I got plenty of this for you," Atwater promised.

"Do you?" Summer moaned.

"Yeah, baby, dick and butterscotch."

"Oh, you wanna tease me?"

"You're teasing me. Go on and let that thing drop before I pull you down."

"No, you might hurt me with all that dick."

Summer slowly wiggled her hips and took each inch slowly. His dick was as long as Lazy Eyes's but much fatter; she knew she was going to be in for one.

"I'm gonna let you ride this pony, but when it's my turn, I'm gonna fuck you so hard," he gnarled like a wolf.

"How that feel, baby?"

"Feel like you need to stop fucking around."

Summer slammed down on his dick and took him all the way

in, smashing down hard on his midsection. *FUCK!* she wanted to scream, feeling his massive member in her stomach.

She balanced her weight on his knees and popped her ass into his dick. He couldn't take anymore. He pushed her on all fours and pounded in and out of her as hard as he could. She wanted to scream with pleasure as he bit down on her shoulder when he nutted inside her.

"Ahhhh . . ." she gasped. What more did Atwater have in store for her? She'd have to find out.

CHAPTER 32
FLIGHT...

THEY PASSED two weeks after that, inseparable. Whenever they closed the chapel's library door, they were in a world of their own. In the chapel, they could share intimate conversations, have sex, and get away from being judged.

When Summer thought about how she had been deeply in love with Clayton, lying on the floor with Atwater made her think she had never known what true love was. There was something about Atwater that took her breath away.

"There's nothing I wouldn't do to make you happy," Summer told Atwater with a mist of admiration and deep love in her eyes.

She had not changed at all since the first day of her makeover. She lay there naked, and the candlelight's shadow danced on the walls. The air from the air conditioner was cool, and she had goosebumps all over her skin. She wrapped up in Atwater's big arms and pulled tight against him.

"Is that right?" Atwater said, and he had to know. He knew the way to her heart, and he was fast on the trail. She had told him that she'd do anything once she was in love, and only time would tell.

"If you still want me to get on the internet for you, I'll do it."

Atwater didn't even have to game for it. "When?"

"Whenever you want. I love you." Summer didn't look into his eyes when she said that. She didn't want to see if his eyes would read other than how she felt. Because she wanted to have his love.

Atwater said nothing. His heart was split. Shonda most definitely came first, and he didn't know if he had taken this fling too far. It was supposed to be about money and nothing else. But he had gone tender dick, and he knew that Old School better not find out.

"How did you get these scars?" Atwater asked, touching the scars on her wrist. He noticed them a long time ago but never wanted to ask because he didn't want to pry into her personal business like that.

"I tried to kill myself." Summer was disappointed that he didn't say anything about her love for him, but if he wanted to be hushed about it, so would she.

"Why did you try to kill yourself?"

"It's a long story."

"And we have all day. You're gonna hold it back from me when you just told me you'd do anything for me."

Summer had to think. He was kissing her earlobe, but she wanted to look at him while she told him what he should know. So, she turned around to face him.

"Men only love me when it's easy for them. When they have to go through what I've always had to go through, they leave me."

"What did you have to go through?"

Summer looked at him like it was obvious.

"You'd never ever understand."

"Try me."

"Imagine being disowned by your family. When my mother came up here to see me, that was the first time

I'd seen her in years. And she still doesn't want to accept the fact that I'm a woman. She still sees me as her little Bobby. She writes to me, but I just don't trust her. Plus, my father and brother have always looked at me as if they hated me or as if I disgusted them.

Summer was choked up, and tears formed in her eyes.

"That's okay. You don't have to tell me if it makes you mad."

"No, I'm going to tell you. My father and brother treated me as if I wasn't there. Whenever my family would go on fishing trips, vacations, or outings, they wouldn't take me. And since I didn't have my father's love, my mother had always kept me at bay."

"That's fucked up, baby."

"I know it is. And I haven't always been honest about who I am or what I am. I've lied so much about it. Being that I can pass as a woman, I don't always tell people otherwise, like I was born . . ." She let the moment pass. "I guess Clayton was shocked at first, but he left it at that. But somehow his family found out and his cousin Peyton blamed me for everything because she hooked us up. And that's why I'm in jail: vengeful justice."

"What?"

"Peyton set me up. She had some guys act like she owed them some money, and they said they'd kill me if she didn't pay them. So, I did the only thing I knew how to do to get that much money on such short notice. I started busting checks. And the whole time it had been a setup."

"We gotta get that bitch back," Atwater said, and he meant it.

"No, we don't. It's my fault. She's right. I should have said that everything about me is complicated. I should have said that I don't want people to know I was born a man because I love them and I want them to love me as who I am, not what I am. And if that sounds complicated, there's no better way to explain it.

And that's why I said that when somebody has to face what I've faced my whole life, they'll leave me. They'll end up blaming me for being who I am. But this is who I'll always be. I can't change."

"Have you ever felt like you should have never come out of the closet?"

"Of course, I do. I regret that I am who I am every day of my life. But it's pretty obvious. It's not like I can hide this woman inside of me. It's who I am, and the sooner people realize it, the better off the world will be. People act like somebody gay would go through all this discrimination and hate for some excitement. But this is who we are.

I think—" Summer couldn't bring herself to say it because it would shatter her dreams.

"You think what?"

"I think you're gonna leave me too when you're faced with the reality of what you're doing . . . watch and see."

"I ain't going nowhere. Don't even think like that. I'll never abandon you. That's my word . . ."

"That's my word . . . That's my word . . ." The words waded through Summer's mind that night when she went to sleep. His voice was so settling, and she almost got lost in the words. The words were so comforting that she felt herself drift off into her favorite place in the world.

She was in an orchard. The sun was warm, and the sky was clear. She was running, and she felt her adolescence. She was a kid again, seven to be exact, and she was flying fast across the orchards.

"I'm a Summer! I can fly!"

She twirled in a spot as the sun shone on her face. She spun and did a dance with a Summer that waddled by and whispered love to it.

She didn't know, but her Uncle Kevin was standing by a tree, watching her with a smile on his face. He thought his young nephew was so beautiful, and it took all his power not to get excited every time he saw him.

"Bobby, come here."

When Summer heard her uncle's voice, her sunny day had

instantly become gloomy, and dark clouds hovered overhead. The sky passed, suddenly becoming eerie and dreary, and she was transported back to her uncle's study in his big mansion.

She was crying, and her uncle was pulling down her pants as she stood stark still. She couldn't move because her uncle forbid her to.

"I love you more than your own dad," her uncle said, and it was true, but it was a love that was tainted by perversion, and his eyes were crazed with lust.

"Please don't, Uncle Kevin! Not again!" Little Bobby's pleas were sincere, his cries piercing. But his uncle didn't yield to his pleas.

His uncle kissed him, and Little Bobby hated it. His uncle made him get on his knees and instructed Bobby on how to put his mouth on his penis and suck it. Bobby did as he was told because . . . because . . . his uncle was the only one in this whole wide world who cared about him or ever showed him any affection. Bobby knew what they were doing was wrong, but who could he tell? His father already hated him, and his mother was scared of her husband, so there was nothing to do but comply.

Little Bobby's uncle turned him around, and he felt his uncle thrusting inside of him while he felt the searing pain. Sweat poured out of Little Bobby's pores, and he was drenched in water. He felt like he had been dunked in a tank that was filled with water.

He was drowning, and a hand held his head down under the water. He fought against the water with his hands splashing back and forth as he tried to breathe, but he only sucked up more water. Then he felt his head yanked out of the water, and he was in his uncle's hands.

They were at his uncle's church and his uncle was baptizing him!

"He's reborn again, Lord Jesus. He's renewed in your Holy

Spirit! He'll never be the same again because he was born to you!
He's yours! He's yours!"

Bobby was Summer now and her uncle tried to dunk her in
the water again, but it was as if time had stood still. She could
feel his hand on the back of her head, but when her face was
about to hit the motionless water, she could see her face on the
surface as if she was looking into a mirror.

Her face had changed from that of a youthful boy to that of a
teenage girl. Her lips were full, she had on make-up, and her hair
was flat ironed. She was beautiful and she had gotten lost in the
image. Her beauty was dreamy, and she loved what stared back
at her. This was her. She knew then that she had found herself.
She had been lost up until this point. The only things that were
missing were breasts and wide hips, but everything else was all
she could have ever wanted.

Being lost in her beauty, she had also lost track of time whem
seconds later she heard her father enter her room and everything
went into chaos.

"GET OUT MY HOUSE! I DON'T EVER WANT TO SEE
YOU AGAIN WHILE I'M ALIVE!"

Summer felt her father's hate unleashed, and his fists were
his vengeance. He tried to kill her, and he would have had her
mother not come to her aid. Her brother just watched. He just
stood there to let his mother struggle to decrease their father's
strength. He just stood there as if he had no love for her. He
enjoyed it as much as her father hated it. When she ran away
from her home, she knew that that home had never been home.
And now, she knew that she didn't have any place to go. She
didn't belong to anyone. She was in this world all alone!

Summer stumbled through the streets, and she couldn't help
but think that her mother wouldn't come looking for her. The
thought hurt her terribly because she didn't know if her mother
had ever loved her. She ran even faster, and blood leaked from
her face. Her hair was now disheveled, and she was nothing like

the beautiful girl who had just found herself. She didn't know where to go, but there was only one place in the world where she knew she'd always be welcomed.

"Don't worry. I'll take care of you. Come and sit on my lap while I nurse your wounds. You look really nice dressed like this." Her uncle was sick—she knew! While she hated her life, herself, she was confused about everything. She pitied her uncle and his love but accepted it because he had the only love that she had ever known.

Uncle Kevin led her to the top of the house where his wife couldn't find them. He led her to the third story, and when Summer walked to the top and stared down the steps, it was as if death was calling her. Death seemed so cozy and welcoming. She wondered if death's love would be as queer as her uncle's. But she felt tired, and death looked like a good bed to rest in. She felt the warmth of it, and it reminded her of her orchards filled with butterflies.

She saw the butterflies waffling around in the wind, and she knew that she could fly too, if only she stepped forward.

"I can fly . . . I'm a Summer. I can really fly!" her mouth uttered in a sort of distant jubilation, and she would have taken the step to meet death had her uncle's beckoning arm not grasped her back. Bobby . . . Bobby.

. . Bobby . . .

CHAPTER 33
CAN I FORGIVE HIM?

"BOBBY MOORE! Wake up. You have a visitor," the CO said, and Summer was pulled from her dreams.

She thought her mother had made another impromptu visit, and she dressed casually in the uniform that she must wear.

Summer went through the usual, being strip-searched before she could go out to the visiting room. Then she walked out to the visiting room, and the first persons she laid eyes on were Atwater and his wife. Summer had to walk past them to go to the CO's desk in front of the visiting room.

"You have any picture tickets?" the CO asked.

"No," Summer answered, hating that the COs were always mean and rude.

"You may be seated."

Summer found herself an empty seat, but she sat at an angle where she could keep her eyes on Atwater. She thought Shonda was cute, but to be honest, the bitch was barking up the wrong tree. *Atwater would be Summer's one day* she kept saying to herself. And she dreaded the truth behind it. Just when she was lost in endless thoughts, her uncle, whom she had been having nightmare after nightmare about, came out to pay her a visit.

He had the nerve to smile!

Uncle Kevin always looked good. He was dressed in a beige Brioni suit with a sky-blue tie and handkerchief. He had waves, and he was 6'3". His demeanor was warm and friendly, but this same demeanor had a way of making Summer's skin feel like bugs were crawling on it.

"Have you been here all along? I've been worried sick about you." Her uncle looked worried. For the most part of her past, her uncle would drape her in fine linen, and buy, or give her anything and everything she had ever wanted. He was totally against her modeling because modeling meant that she would have her own money, and she wouldn't have to depend on him.

Summer didn't answer him because she had ice in her eyes, and it had always been that way. She never showed love or kindness to him, and when he fucked her, she was stiff. She would lie still, and he would pour his seed in her while grunting over her. It was nasty to think about!

"I've been calling all over the place looking for you. I thought you were dead. But your mother happened to call me, and she slipped up and said that she had been writing you. And I pressed the issue, and she finally told me the truth. How could you do this to me?" His eyes were pathetic, and as always, he looked sick or ill. When he looked that way, Summer felt sorry for him! Imagine that: the prey feeling sorry for the predator's hunger, knowing that it was at the destruction of its own life that the predator could feel happy and whole.

Summer was so mad and indisposed that she didn't recognize until after a second that Atwater had been watching her secretly for a while. Was that jealousy in his eyes? Because he wouldn't have known the relation between her and her uncle.

"What family? Have you forgotten that my father disowned me?" Tears welled in Summer's eyes, and she hated that he had come to visit her.

"I've never disowned you. I don't care what your father did. I've always been here for you. I've always loved you unconditionally."

"Why are you here?" Summer couldn't take any more. "Do you want me to sit on your lap?" Summer said seductively, but she still had ice in her eyes.

He was embarrassed. "This is the wrong place to discuss or say something like that." He looked around to see if anybody was looking, and Atwater was looking right at him. "You know better than to put family business out in the public like that. Did you check your institutional trust fund account? I put money on your account."

"I have plenty of money, and I don't need yours." As usual, her uncle would pour gifts and money on her to get her to accept the fact that he would always be her benefactor.

"Why are you so evil-spirited? I've only raised you to love the Lord and do God's will."

"Don't come back here anymore. If you do, I don't know what I might do to you." Summer gave him a look that could kill, and for the first time, her uncle realized that she wasn't a kid anymore.

Summer got up and ran to the back to end her visit. She was crying, and she didn't want anybody to see her cry. She just ran.

"There that boy is again," Shonda said, who had been eating lunch with Atwater. For some reason, she felt her life was tied to Summer's, but she could never understand what the feeling meant.

Atwater was worried about Summer, but he didn't give himself away. "What?"

"Turn around and look before it leaves."

Atwater turned to see who he knew was there. He played it off. "What? It's just a fag. What you tripping for?"

"I didn't like the look he gave me."

Shonda knew something.

CHAPTER 34
IT STARTS OUT GOOD

SUMMER AND ATWATER signaled to each other when they left the visiting room that they would meet each other at the automatic machine at the pill line.

Since it was the weekend, they wouldn't be able to have privacy.

Atwater was there before Summer had arrived. The night was chilly, but spring was setting in. Summer had on a jacket that made her look flimsy and little. She had gained back her color from when she had run out of the visit, and the thought of seeing her run out of the visit had been egging at Atwater all day.

This time Summer didn't stand behind Atwater in the line as she usually did, but she stood at his side.

"So that's your wife?" Summer knew the answer because this was the second time she had seen them together.

"What I tell you about not saying hello and seeing how I'm doing first before you start getting all crazy and shit? But yeah, that's my wife."

"You look happy with her. You sure you got time for me?"

"Yo, real talk. I'm trying to get back to the unit so that I can handle the business at hand. Did you get the pictures I told you to bring?"

Summer took out six pictures and handed them to him.

"That's my baby girl. These are perfect."

"Perfect for you. Ya already with somebody else."

Summer's admission was a slip, but on too many occasions she had let him know that she loved him and wanted to be with him.

Atwater studied her for a while. "Come on, I'm gonna walk with you to pill line. What's really on your mind? I'm a little amped up about all this, and I forgot to ask you about your visit. Who was that that came to visit you today? And why did you run out?"

"That's my uncle, and it's a long story. And don't change the subject. I said you're already with somebody."

"Don't start tripping on me now. This is a complicated and complex situation as it is, but Shonda got twenty-two years with me. But she ain't no threat to you when it comes to my heart. I got a big piece cut out just for you. But I'm not trying to crash twenty-two years of being with her over two months of being with you.

"I'm throwing this ad on the net to see how we handle challenges together. Shonda, on the other hand, is tried and tested. I just need you to trust me. Keep your head clear and stress free. You're with me?"

Summer waited before she answered his question.

She nodded.

"You're gonna let me hit that tomorrow."

Summer smiled, and they walked to the pill line.

After they left the pill line, Atwater hurried back to call his homeboy, Tyler. He had to stand in line to wait for a phone to become available. The unit was as loud as ever, and he was just anxious to speak with his partner.

Tyler's phone rang twice before he answered it, and after the automated operator said the call was from jail, Tyler pressed five to accept the phone call. "What's up?" Tyler said.

"I'm chilling. What's going on with you?" Atwater asked.

"Apple snacks and money stacks. What's on your mind? I sent that money to Shonda."

"Good look. I got some pictures, and I want you to start a website. You could either do a Facebook, but I don't know none of that shit."

"Dog, you already got enough flicks of yourself to last you a lifetime on your Facebook."

"It ain't for me. It's for a boy. I'm trying to get paid. So, when you put him on, make sure you put out an All-Points Bulletin for all tricks and johns."

It was making sense to Tyler what Atwater was talking about, but it took a minute to dawn on him.

"Atwater, you coming out of the closet on me?"

He didn't know whether to laugh or cry. "Fuck no! But even if I were, after eighteen years, I'd deserve to indulge. But real talk, I got this boy in here who looks better than Rihanna. You'll see in a couple of days. Put the pictures on the net and in a couple of weeks I'll send you a list of johns who I want you to request as friends."

"Nigga, you done lost your mind in ther," Tyler laughed. "How the boy look?"

"I just told you as pretty as a little girl." They laughed. Atwater knew he could tell Tyler anything, and Tyler would never judge him.

"Don't be bringing nothing to the streets. They'll have your ass sucked up looking like ET on crack."

"Don't worry about that. I got a hefty supply of jimmies, provided by the BOP."

"Don't let me find out you're catching as well as pitching."

"Ah, that's some shit, nigga! Fuck you . . . I got to go. I'll send the flicks."

"Love," Tyler said, as he ended the call.

Atwater was feeling himself; he knew he was about to get paid off Summer.

Chapter Forty-Two The Plan Unleashed . . . Phase One...

The next morning, Atwater had gone to work and when he got there, Summer didn't want to do anything else but suck on his dick. She had been adamant, and once they shut the door, she pushed him on the ground and sucked his dick until he was cumming back-to-back.

He had to talk to her, but he kept nutting so hard as she gurgled his tender dick in the back of her throat that his orgasm balled up and shot out in loads. When he pleaded for her to stop, she laughed because she knew nobody could compare to the head and satisfaction that she gave. She knew she would make it impossible for his wife to ever be able to please him truly as she had, and that was the thought that kept his dick in her mouth for hours on end.

She then dressed his dick with a condom, and she shoved it up her ass. She rode his pony like a sex-crazed girl, and when he thought he couldn't nut anymore, she had him begging her to stop. She couldn't because his dick was hard as steel, and she loved the feel of it barreling down into her stomach. It took her breath away, and she had gotten so much pleasure by pleasing him.

"I can't take anymore." It didn't sound like something a man who had just done eighteen years would say, but Summer had a way of making a person feel like he was exhausted.

She laughed. "You don't want no more of this soft ass?"

He cried because the sound of her voice made his dick stiffen again. She got on all fours, purred like a cat, and wiggled her ass and giggled, blinking her eyes at him.

"Fuck!" He had to hit that. He stood up and kneeled enough to slide his dick inside of her and went all the way to the hilt. He dug inside her, and she pulled his arms tight around her. He held her breasts and fucked her good. She gave it back to him and snarled at him, "Fuck me harder, faster!"

"What that dick feel like?"

"Feels like thunder is rumbling in my stomach and a jack-hammer smashing into my ass."

But Summer would feel her orgasm rising by the incessant pounding, and she tried to give as much of her ass to him until she felt it building. She released it on to the floor as she cried. He placed his hand on her mouth because she was going to give them away. But she couldn't help it. His dick was so hard in her, and her body melted under him. She cried and sucked on his fingers, and he pounded until his charge had shot forth and he collapsed on her back.

"I could fuck you all day," Summer said when she came to.

He sighed, "I don't have any energy to get off the ground. Damn, I wish you were here my whole bid. It wouldn't even have felt like I was in jail."

Summer laughed, "This is like cheating them out of the time they gave us. Sometimes when I'm in here with you, I don't even feel like I'm doing time. I feel like I'm just away on vacation. Take it out," Summer said as she wiggled her hips and he slipped out of her with a moan.

"How you know I was finished?"

"You are because if you weren't, I'd finish you off with my mouth."

"I could take another hour."

"I bet you could," She laughed.

"Turn around so I can look at you." It was Atwater's first time saying that. Although she lay naked in front of him many times before, he had never asked her to look at her whole body.

"For what?" She was still apprehensive. "Turn around."

She turned. "What is that?" He laughed because it didn't look like much of a penis.

"It's a dick," Summer said with an attitude.

"A baby's dick, if that."

"Go ahead and lick it then."

They laughed.

When they were finished clowning around, Atwater looked at Summer for who she was. It didn't make sense, but this was a human being with fears and a love for life. A being who wanted to be loved and cherished and who, as with everybody else, hated to be judged.

Atwater had been raised to hate gays. It was taught to him by his friends, family, and everywhere else he went. He had remembered when he was young, and he would tease certain boys because they acted like girls.

But now that he was here with Summer, he couldn't explain what he had felt for her. He had to question everything. Why would God create gay people? And if it was so bad to be gay or if it was a defect, the defect was none other than God's defect himself.

He kissed Summer passionately, and he thought if he could love her stronger than he did his wife. When he thought of that, he laughed to himself. It was a trip, but he wanted to know more about her, something that went beyond their fuck-crazed days together.

"That day at the visit, why did you run out of there like that?"

By now, Summer was snuggled in his arms. If jail was supposed to be a punishment, she'd take this form of punishment over having liberty.

"I told you it was a long story."

Atwater looked her in her eyes. "I want to know everything about you."

When he said that, Summer couldn't think of anything else but when Clayton had said that to her also when he had fallen head over heels for her and chose her over his family. If it was up to her, she would have never made him choose between her and his family. Love shouldn't be based on a condition of entanglement and choosing between other people. Love should be free and for all. It was a feeling that made her emotional. As she looked into Atwater's eyes, she felt that this was going to end the same way her relationship with Clayton did because people would never let them be them. It would be different had Atwater been gay, but it wasn't the case. The only reason she felt like he was with her was because she looked like a girl.

She loved the musk of a man, the hardness of their bodies, and she wasn't fooling anybody to believe that Atwater would ever accept in his mind that he was gay. It was far from the truth, and she couldn't blame him because she'd never date a gay man. She had slept with Buffy and Britney, but not sexually, because there was nothing that turned her on about them. They were bitches too, and that was it. She couldn't date a gay man any more than he could, and by the grace of her womanly fortune, she had Atwater's love.

"Why are you ignoring my question?"

"I don't know?" She brushed away a tear, and he wiped it away. "I just don't like talking about when I was a kid. I have a lot of nightmares about being young. I'm looking at myself for the first time dressed as a woman, and my father comes in and busts me and he beats me senseless. But the nightmare isn't a dream. It really happened to me."

Atwater didn't want to rush her. He wanted her to come clean in her own time.

"My uncle is a pastor of a famous church. When I was seven years old, he molested me."

"That punk ass nigga!" Atwater said, angry. "Mutha fuckas like that should be killed."

"I know. But the sad thing is that he was the only one who ever showed me genuine love. I took the abuse to win his affection because I didn't feel like I was worth receiving love from anybody else."

"Damn, I'd never know it was that fucked up for being you. I can't imagine because the first time I saw you I thought you were a woman, and it took me a second to realize that this is a men's jail."

"That's my blessing and my curse at the same time. If people could just tell I was born a man, they'd know, and they wouldn't get close enough to me if they didn't like the idea. But because I look so much like a woman, people get close and when they find out—"

"I know. But fuck that shit. Fuck your uncle. He was fucking a seven-year-old boy," Atwater sighed. He wanted to murder him. It hurt him to his core.

"I hate my uncle and love him at the same time. It hurts when I hear you say "fuck him". I don't know—it's just how I feel. He'd make me suck his dick, and then he'd fuck me in the ass. I guess he regretted it because he'd always spoil me with all kinds of presents.

"I know his wife, Debra, knew, but she acted like she didn't. They could never have kids, and I was the closest thing to their child."

"Like I said, fuck him and her. There's only one way for us to get back at the mutha fuckas who raped us. We have to get power. We have to use wealth to increase our power, and we have to use our power to get back at all the people who did us wrong."

"Babe, what are you talking about? Who did you wrong?"

"I just did eighteen years, and you're going to ask me that question? The system did me wrong! This shit is bullshit! They found me in a house with drugs that weren't mine and, because they didn't have anybody to put it on, they put it on me. But instead of them saying that it was a possession charge, they put me on some big conspiracy and fucked me over."

"And you're gonna help me get them back."

Summer lightened to the idea. She'd help him any way he needed.

"What do I have to do?"

"First, we're going to get a decent savings of money. I'm going to request some tricks and johns to your web page, and when they come up here to visit you, you're going to run game on them."

"How? What am I going to tell them?"

"You see how you're excited now? I want you to act just like that when they come and see you. You have to be very flirtatious, and touchy, and they have to be the only ones who exist in this world. I have a list of johns who are millionaires."

"Where did you get the list from?"

"Don't worry about that. I have my means. But when you go out there, you have to be assertive, and you can't ever give them time to think and place details together. You have to control the conversation and always keep the topic on sex. And this is what you're going to tell them."

CHAPTER 35
DEAR JOHN

SUMMER HAD BEEN KIND OF nervous because she didn't know what to expect. Atwater told her that the Johns had responded to her ad as he had expected they would. When Atwater had spoken to Tyler, Tyler couldn't believe that Summer was the boy that he was talking about on the phone.

Summer had her first visit two weeks later. Summer wore skintight pants with a shirt that made her breast look full. Her hair and make-up were nice.

She entered the visiting room and waited in a chair in a corner by the vending machine. When the middle-aged black man came in, she didn't know if he was the trick until he looked directly at her. The lust in his eyes said it all.

A chubby man who dressed nicely wore wire-framed glasses.

"You're prettier in person than in your picture.

You're beautiful," he said.

She could tell that he was nervous by the way he kept looking all over the place.

As Atwater had instructed, she was as flirtatious as ever. "I couldn't wait to see you. Your letters got me so hot and horny." She brushed against his dick as she hugged him, and they sat down.

"Here, let me see you without your glasses," Summer said, and he took them off. "My God! Now I can imagine you fucking me." Summer was doing her job all too well, and she had him stumbling for words. She led the conversation from the minute they sat down!

"When? When can I fuck you? I wanted you the minute I saw your picture. When are you going to get out? I keep asking you, and you keep avoiding my question."

Summer slid her hand between his legs and felt his snub dick that was hard in his britches. "I'm scared to tell you the truth. If I tell you, promise me you won't leave me?" Summer's eyes sparkled, and she massaged his dick in his pants.

"I swear to God! Just tell me when!" He felt he would nut in his pants as he pictured her mouth wrapped around his dick, and he felt sick.

"I have eight more years to do."

"What?" His shock was apparent.

"See, you lied! That's why I didn't want to tell you in the first place. Now you hate me." Summer took her hand off his pulsating dick. He felt like she had shattered his heart. He was minutes away from nutting right there on the spot, and Summer knew it!

"I don't hate you. I'm a bit shocked, that's all. I just want to know if I could do anything to get you out sooner, I mean, anything?" His passion was real, and he had desperation written in his eyes.

"There's an attorney that keeps promising me that he can get me out, but I'm a foster kid. It's not like I have a family who'd pay him. Nobody loves me enough to help me." Summer then brushed her lips against his. Her seductive and blatant behavior should have compelled the COs to have ended their visit a long time ago, but the COs sat there and watched because they got a laugh from it.

"Are you sure he can do what he promises? How much time did he say he could get you?"

"I'm sure. He's the best, and he promised me that he could get me out in under six months."

"Give me his info, and I'll arrange everything."

It was just as Atwater had said he would do, and Atwater already had all the information she would need to give him to send the money and set everything up. This excited Summer all the more.

"You don't understand. He's a high-profile attorney, and he's very expensive."

The John smirked. No money was too much for him. "What's expensive?"

"He told me to give him $25k just to retain him. That doesn't include all the legal papers and process after that." By now, Summer had her hand on his dick again, massaging it. His eyes fluttered. She couldn't tell if he had nutted in his pants or if he was about to.

"As I said," he composed himself, "just give me his info. I want you home, and I'll do anything to that end."

"When I come home, Daddy, are you going to pull my hair when you fuck me?"

He was choked up. He never wanted to fuck anybody in his life more! "I'd love to."

"I can't wait! You'll do all that for me?" She kissed him on his lips, and his mind was gone.

Later on, that night, Summer met Atwater at the money machine, and she couldn't wait to tell him how much of a success she had been. She told him everything that had happened, and he let her know that he had a different John coming the following day. It was all too fun for her, and she was happy she could help him out with whatever he was doing. The only apprehension she had was any of the Johns finding out it was a scam and doing something to her.

. . .

Chapter Forty-Four Those Who Accomplish to Plan, Plan to Accomplish...

Several weeks had passed, and everything that Atwater had said was happening. He had arranged for somebody on the streets to act as an attorney, and the money poured in. Summer was juggling six multi-millionaires. It was funny because to give one-hundred thousand dollars to her legal fund presented no problem to them. She had begged Atwater over the weeks that followed to tell her where he had gotten the list of the rich tricks, but Atwater wouldn't relent! It drove her crazy because she felt like she didn't have power in the situation except to be a ploy in his game, but she loved him all the more for it.

Summer thought she had been doing well for herself while modeling, but the most she had ever made was two thousand dollars at any one gig, and usually she never made that much. She wasn't really a big spender, and her uncle had always bought the big items she wanted, like cars.

He paid her rent and had given her plenty of plastic. But now, the bank account that Atwater had set up for her on the streets had almost two hundred thousand dollars, and she knew that he had stashed away another three hundred thousand dollars for himself. It just seemed unreal that she didn't have to have sex with these guys or go out with them. She just had to go on a visit and give them the impression that she would rock their worlds once she was out. This was the easiest money ever. She didn't even have to read or respond to the letters they sent because Atwater had paid a few people who wrote the guys back around the clock. The letters were always sex-charged undertones that kept the guys in a trance and on her trail.

She and Atwater had accomplished something, and their relationship became more than just sex. They would sit up all day and talk about how she should go to the next visit and what she should say and do. She loved the way his mind worked. He was never conquered, not by his situation or any circumstance. He just saw past everybody and focused on what he should do. He was a very special person.

Atwater had money that he stashed in a bank under an alias. He didn't want to get released on supervised release so his probation officer could track his movement by tracking his money. He wanted to do a lot with that money, and he had to be discreet. He had big plans, and what he was doing now was just the beginning!

Things were getting a little wild, though. He couldn't really stay on the down-low with Summer. He had to communicate with her more effectively. Waiting to have a five-minute conversation with her at the money machine while she was going to pill line, limited his communication with her.

It was time for him to splurge a bit, and he called his wife Shonda.

"Hey, baby. You are truly too much!" She sounded excited, and he knew why.

"Tyler must have gotten those things to you guys?"

"I'm wearing the diamond necklace and the bracelet right now. Mason and Macy didn't wait five minutes to leave after the BMWs you bought them showed up. This scares me."

He should have known. "Shonda, chill out and enjoy what I got for you. I promise it's all good."

"I hope it doesn't have anything to do with Tyler because I'll give it back!"

Atwater laughed. "Alright, I'll call him right now and tell him to come back and get everything."

"Well, just let me keep the bracelet." They laughed. "Just tell me that when you come home, you're never ever going to go back to jail?"

"I promise, baby. I'm going to tuck you in every single night. Damn, what's that I hear in the background? Sounds like water."

Shonda smiled. "I'm taking a hot bubble bath, and I'm drinking champagne."

"Ooo-weeee! I have three weeks and I can't wait."

"Just remember you promised to tuck me in at night," Shonda said seductively.

"I want to tuck you in right now. Slide your hand between your thighs and tell me how hot and wet the tub is."

"I'll tell you how hot and wet it is if you tell me what you're going to do to me when you get out."

"After or before the candlelit dinner?"

"After, baby," Shonda moaned as she massaged her pussy and imagined it was Atwater sucking on it. The phone call ended with the sound of her climaxing and Atwater's simmering plans once he was released in three weeks.

CHAPTER 36
OUT OF THE CLOSET AND ON TO THE FLOOR...

"ATWATER IS a good man and a hustler, let me tell you," Buffy said as she took another gulp of the strong and savory jailhouse hooch that had him feeling good.

Britney, Buffy, and Summer were in their cell, eating a lavish nacho bowl with refried beans, melted cheese, chopped vegetables, diced beef, and turkey log over nacho chips. Summer had paid somebody to make her a sweet potato pie, and they sat around drinking hooch, feeling good.

"Ain't that the truth. Summer has been able to put money on my account, and I've spent my commissary limit three times in a row. If I keep this up, I'm going to tell Mrs. Bowers to go to hell with that Unicor job. I'll just sit here all day and eat, drink, and get fucked," Britney said as all three of them laughed.

"Yes, Atwater is my hero," Summer added.

"He must be," she smacked. "Because he has you geeking on his dick. Bitch, you act like you too good to get high with us now."

"He don't want me to! He doesn't like when I do that stuff, but he don't mind if I drink a little."

Britney mimicked her. "He don't like when I do that stuff."

"Maybe he needs an X-pill and to fuck you with a choo-choo

train of other niggas to relax his ass, let me tell you!"

"Fuck you, freak bitch. All this is enough for him." Summer smacked her ass. "And he's enough for me. He don't need X."

"Oh, he likes deep pussy, huh?" They all laughed, and Summer flipped Britney the finger. "I'm just playing, girl. He's really good for you. Since you've been with him, you've been taking care of yourself and looking superb, and your confidence has gone through the roof."

Buffy smacked her lips. "I wish I had a dick that could transport me," Buffy said.

"You got Ray Ray's stank ass," Britney said, trying to sound encouraging.

"Please!" Buffy said.

"He ain't no Atwater," Summer added, smiling because of her luck.

"But Summer, you have to worry about that pretty bitch he's going home to."

"Why you bringing that up, stank 'ho?" Britney asked the obvious.

"It's the truth, let me tell you. He's been with her a long time."

"And I hate it! But he's with me now, and he loves fucking me. That bitch will never be able to replicate what I do." Summer had a real attitude and a jealous streak.

"I know what you mean, gurgle-throat," Buffy said.

"Who told you that?" Summer was surprised.

"Love told me while I was sucking his dick. He told me that I don't gurgle in the back of my throat while he's busting a nut. I ain't never heard no shit like that, bitch. But I'll be sure to learn it, let me tell you."

"Gurgling in the back of your throat!" Britney said, as if hurt that Summer could hold such a technique to herself.

"Trade secrets, bitch. Gurgle in your ass," Buffy said, and they all laughed.

CHAPTER 37
DOWN-LOW SUSPECT

IN PRISON, whispers create rumors and rumors create what prisoners take as hard-core facts. When the whispers started about Atwater and Summer meeting every night at the automatic money machine, accompanying her to pill line at times, and being locked up with Summer in the chapel's library during the morning hours, Atwater was under suspicion.

The suspicion first came from the Moors, which was the organization he was not only a member of, but a leading official. Then Craze-zo started to get a whiff of it.

Atwater knew he was weeks away from going home, and he didn't like the fact that his reputation was getting tarnished. But it was something that came with the territory.

He knew that if he just put money into a number of individuals' accounts, it would all be hush-hush. But even when he tried to put money on Craze-zo's account, Craze-zo had become even more suspicious. When the rumors had finally surfaced, that's when Craze-zo brought the issue to him.

They were about to lift weights, and Craze-zo couldn't put the thought behind him.

"Moor, cuz, I've been hearing some strange shit, and I don't know if to believe them, or just take it as some hating ass niggas that we need to holler at with some straps. But niggas is saying that you fucking with that punk, Summer." Craze-zo kept his eyes on Atwater because he wanted to see his reaction. He had to read his partner, no matter what his partner said.

"Fucking with the punk . . ." Atwater looked his younger partner straight in the face. "Like what?"

"Atwater, what you mean like what?" The shit was too much to grasp for Craze-zo, and his nigga, whom he would have ridden to the depths of hell with, didn't give him an outright answer. He couldn't believe that he could have fallen victim to some fag shit!

"Craze-zo, the shit is bigger than what you think. But trust me when I tell you that I ain't gonna ever do something that'd be on some punk shit."

"Come on, Atwater. Give me more than that. We're like fam'."

"Sit down." They were standing by the squat rack, and there was a bench at the side of it.

Atwater sat down and Craze-zo sat next to him. "I'm pimping the punk."

It took Craze-zo a minute to digest what he had just heard, and it was worse than what he'd thought. "Cuz, you're getting money to let fools run trains on him like what happened to him in 4B?"

"No, I ain't no sucker like that. I'm gonna let you in on what's going on, so you'll be on point. I got a list of millionaire punks that I got from the white boy who works in education. I put a couple of Summer's flicks on a social media app and gave him the game. You know I work in the chapel with him, so I've been giving him the game. I've made $80k off him already." Atwater underestimated the money. If he had said the real amount, he knew Craze-zo wouldn't have believed his story.

It was a relief for Craze-zo. He didn't believe for one second that his partner had fallen victim, and now it was all confirmed.

"I'm glad to hear that. They was saying it like you was fucking the punk or something."

"Never that. I can't take nothing home to wifey. That's my word!"

"I don't know why I ever doubted you in the first place. You my nigga."

And that was how he had kept Craze-zo's respect and friendship with a lie. He knew that Craze-zo wouldn't be ready for the truth, and he knew the best thing would be to lie.

"And I'll show you how a real nigga do it. I'm going to have my partner send you a gee to show you how I'm living."

"A gee, my nigga!"

"Yeah, get some new shoes and send your son something."

They worked out, and after they had finished, they were about to leave when Old School called Atwater.

"Got a sec, Atwater?"

"Yeah. Craze, I'll be right back. Hold up a minute." Atwater ran into the gym where Old School was sitting in the bleachers and a couple of guys were playing one-on-one.

When Atwater sat at his side, Old School said, "You know everybody's talking about you and that boy?"

"I ain't trippin', Old Timer. I'm getting money though. She's an investment to me, and I want these fools to know not to mess around with mine."

"I know you're sharp, Atwater, and I thank you for the eight grand you put on my books."

"It's nothing, Old Timer."

"No, listen. I really appreciate that shit. And you're going to have to start feeding your wolves around here just in case some drama pops off."

"I already know, and I'm already over it. It feels good to be able to look out and have something put away for when I get out. And when I hit the streets, I'm gonna show you innovation. I'm taking my pimping to the next level. And I ain't like the fools that say they're gonna do something for you and never give back. Trust me. When I get out, I got you, Old School."

"You make me proud." They embraced.

"I'm about to continue on my journey," Atwater said.

Old School laughed because he knew the obstacles that lay ahead of Atwater. And he knew it was going to be very difficult.

CHAPTER 38
THE DAY WAS NAUGHTY

ATWATER WAS TOO close to going home. He only had two more days, and the thought was killing him.

Summer, on the other hand, was getting her head together for being in jail alone. She knew it would be a challenge in itself, but one that she was willing to take. She had gone to work, and she and Kathy were rearranging the chapel's library. They were trying to make room for more religious apparatus that had come in.

Kathy wore tight slacks, doorknocker earrings, and a smart blouse. She looked like the kind of middle-aged white girl who'd be married to an NBA star. She had scaled a small ladder to put some books on the top shelf.

"Put this in the Catholic section. Can you reach it?" Summer asked.

"Yes, I got it. I'm not that short." Kathy's blouse loosened from her slacks and Summer could see the skin on her butt.

"Damn, girl, you got an ass of steel."

Kathy laughed. "Almost as big as yours." She got down from the ladder.

"No, you got me," Summer joked. "Everybody on the compound says you got the phattest ass."

"I don't believe you. My hips are only thirty-six! Here, let me feel yours. Umph, it feels good." Kathy grabbed Summer's ass and held onto it.

"Okay, girl, let my ass go," Summer joked, looking at her strangely.

"I don't really want to," Kathy said, giving Summer a weird look.

Summer had to be blunt with her. "Are you coming on to me?"

"You've never ever thought about being with a woman?"

This was the worst thing that Summer could have imagined possible. "Have a seat." After they sat, Summer broke it down to her. "You have to understand that I'm a woman that's trapped inside a man's body. If I were to even think about being with a woman, it would seem completely weird to me. I love men and men only."

"Plus, you're my girl, and without you, I wouldn't have ever known this love that I have for Atwater. And it goes beyond words my appreciation for you."

"I don't know what I was thinking," Kathy said. "It's just that you have this strong sexual aura. And I want to tell you the honest truth. Lately, when I make love to my husband, all I can see is your face. I'm always turned on when I'm around you. You just seem so exotic and erotic. It's just a spell."

Kathy couldn't tell her the rest. She hadn't yet felt embarrassed to tell her what she already had, but if she had continued, she would have said how she thought Summer was so beautiful and how she wanted to see Summer get ravished by Atwater in front of her while she watched and played with a dildo at the same time. The thought was unnerving, and she felt the moisture between her thighs fall. She had to cross her legs. Kathy followed every word that came off Summer's lips, and she wanted to feel those fluffy, velvet lips kiss all over her body, starting from her perky tits to her full mound between her legs! It was all stimulating and mesmerizing at the same time, but it was just shadows overcast over her sex life. She didn't know what she'd do, but the thought lingered, and it was one that had to be fulfilled.

She wished Lazy Eyes was still there so that she could tell him what she always wanted to tell him; she wanted him to fuck her with raucous abandon while Summer fucked her in the ass. And it would amount to double penetration and double the orgasmic relief!

Summer smiled, full of herself. "Really?" Summer asked, thinking it was funny that even women were attracted to her.

Kathy shook her head, looking intoxicating, and sultry, and her eyes were like a romantic evening sky. It was just that she was extremely horny, and hell had raised her temperature to the level of fever.

"Lock that door. I want to show you something."

Summer studied her for a minute. Seeing mischief behind Kathy's eyes, which she didn't trust, she hesitated to comply. She got up and put the 'Do Not Disturb' sign on the door and locked it.

"What you want to show me?" Summer asked suspiciously.

"Look how wet I am around you." Kathy unfastened her slacks, pulled them down, and stepped out of them. Her body was perfect.

She looked like a model from *Curve* Magazine. Summer couldn't help but be slightly turned on, and the thought was weird to her.

"You have a great body."

"Come here, Summer. I won't bite you. I want to show you something."

It took Summer a moment to start moving her legs, but she moved closer to Kathy, who took her hand and placed it between her thighs. Her pussy was soaking wet, and the moisture had seeped through her hot pink G-string.

"Girl, a woman's pussy gets wet like that?" It was Summer's first time touching a woman's pussy. She had never seen one except on TV.

"You've never touched a pussy?" Kathy was shocked.

"Why would I?"

"Here, I'll show you more." Kathy pulled down her G-string. She took off her blouse and then her bra. There was no fat on her tanned body, and her pussy was plump and shaved.

"Kathy, girl, this shit is turning me on. Put your clothes back on." Summer, who always thought women made her feel nauseated, was feeling an urge she had never felt before, and she didn't like it at all!

"Kiss me."

"I ain't kissing a woman!" Summer protested, but it was too late. Kathy had already kissed her.

At first, Kathy's kiss felt weird, but Kathy tasted good. The kiss turned passionate, and Kathy grabbed Summer's breasts and soft ass. The gesture relaxed Summer and she . . . she . . . she . . . didn't know exactly what gave her the urge to do something that had crossed her mind a number of times. But she went along with the urge, and she touched Kathy's pussy. It was clammy, and soft, but it was wonderful to touch, and she got an immediate reaction from Kathy, who moaned softly grinded into her fingers. Summer slid one of her fingers into Kathy's pussy, and it felt slick and tender, and she couldn't imagine how an ass could feel as good as a pussy for a man.

It awakened a new curiosity inside Summer to want to understand women better because her body limited her in so many ways.

She pulled Kathy to the ground and kissed all over her body until she made her way down to her pussy. She stuck her tongue into the pussy. It was slimy and gooey, but the reaction she got from Kathy made her want to continue. Kathy put her face against her pussy and fucked Summer's lips. Summer thought she would suffocate from how hard Kathy had grinded into her face, and then she felt Kathy's body shiver uncontrollably. Her pussy squirted forth and a stream of pussy juice shot on Summer's face. It was wet, murky, and powerful, and it took all that Kathy had not to scream out loudly.

"Girl, what was that?"

"That's a woman's orgasm," Kathy responded as she panted for air.

"I'm talking about this stuff on my face."

Kathy laughed. "You hit my g-spot."

Kathy leaned up and licked her juices from Summer's lips, still turned on. Summer thought she was a nympho, how horny she seemed. Kathy turned the lights off and then started to undress Summer, who laughed because she was still embarrassed and thought this was all crazy.

"What are you doing, Kathy?"

"Just hush up," Kathy said playfully.

Summer laid on her back after she was completely naked. Kathy gently trailed her fingers over Summer's skin, and her goosebumps loosened. She kissed all over Summer's nipples and kissed her lips. Kathy made her way down to Summer's small penis and rested it in her mouth. She ran her tongue under the head. It felt incredibly good!

"Girl . . ." Summer wasn't too sure of the feeling and the feeling heightened when Kathy stuck three of her fingers in her ass and started to fuck her with them while she fondled one of Summer's breasts with her free hand.

Summer felt her whole body throbbing uncontrollably, and she beat her thighs into the whirling of Kathy's tongue while her fingers slammed into her ass. Summer couldn't contain it anymore. She shot a wad down Kathy's throat, and she bit down on her own clothes so that she wouldn't cry out! As Kathy's tongue lingered and whirled, she had Summer in the grips of a screeching orgasm three minutes later.

"Kathy, that was wonderful!" Summer said. Kathy spit her cum out in the trashcan, and lay at Summer's side, trying to catch her breath.

"I thought it would be. You know there's more," she said.

Summer thought there was no way in hell that she was going to fuck a girl. It was unlikely to happen anyway because her dick was so small.

"I'm fine with what we've just done."

"Damn, I needed that!" Kathy exclaimed. She couldn't help but think how tired she was fucking her husband. She had been taken with having an excellent body, and she worked out and took supplements to achieve those results. Her husband, on the other hand, could care less. Kathy had other needs; she had a hunger that was exciting, adventurous, and wild. She just couldn't tell him that she thought about Summer, Lazy Eyes, and now Atwater, when they had sex.

"You have a freak inside you, Kathy." Summer laughed so hard that it was impossible for her to stop.

"You laugh like that's bad or something."

"It's not that at all. But I should've known something was up with you. You have that perfect body, and you can't keep it preserved like that for nothing."

"It is for nothing. I've tried to be honest with my husband one time, and I told him that maybe we should consider becoming swingers. And he went berserk."

Summer laughed. "What did you think he'd say?"

"I don't know. I didn't even think about it."

"I can't believe we just did that. But I can't lie; it was different."

"Different? Is that all?" Kathy was shocked and pleased as well.

"I don't think women are for me. I'm strictly-dickly." They laughed, and Kathy sat up.

"How is it being with black guys?"

Summer couldn't believe the question. "You've never slept with a black man?"

"You had never slept with a woman, so don't act surprised."

"That's fair. But it's different."

"Here we go with it's *different* again."

"Not like that, girl. I mean, my first love, Clayton was white. I've had sex with him a thousand times before. It's different with him and Black men because Black dick feels like fire is inside you."

"How was Lonny?" Kathy's eyes said it all.

"Girl, don't tell me you were barking up that tree?"

"I can't lie, Summer. I wanted him so bad! He had the sexiest eyes and smoothest voice. My God, I wanted him."

"He was . . . I think he was the best ever." Summer wasn't lying. She could remember how he would slam his dick into her without end. Damn, she still missed him!

"Was he big?"

Summer shook her head wanly and smiled.

"My I'm missing out on life!"

Kathy was a true friend. She had shared such a wonderful and vivid experience with Summer that would never be forgotten, and she wanted to share something very special with Kathy in return.

"I have something for you . . ."

Chapter Forty-Eight Naughty . . . Again And Again . . .

The day was still young, and Atwater had to go on what the prison called a Merry-go-Round, which was when an inmate who was about to get released, he had to go to each department and have them sign him out. He also had to pack out all of his belongings and get everything ready so that he could leave.

He didn't have to go to work anymore, and he knew that even on the streets he'd miss Summer's sweet ass for however long they'd be apart, which wasn't that long, considering she was about to get released in one month.

So, he headed over to their honeycomb hideout. When he went to the door of the chapel's library, the 'Do Not Disturb' sign was on the door, and for a minute it threw him for a loop. Atwater placed his ear to the door, but he couldn't hear anything. So, he lightly tapped on the door, and seconds later, he heard Summer whisper, "Atwater, is that you?"

"Yeah."

Summer unlocked the door and pulled him in.

Once he was in, candles lit up the room, and Summer and Kathy were butt naked on the floor! His jaw dropped in sheer disbelief.

Kathy had always been somebody who had a perfect body, and he had caught himself on many occasions imagining sex with her. Her body looked ten times better naked. She didn't have an ounce of body fat, and her body had curves in all the right places.

"What are you all doing?"

Summer laughed and laid back down with Kathy. They kissed. Kathy pushed Summer onto her back and climbed on top of her while she grinded her hips against Summer. The scene made Atwater's penis stiffen in his pants. He wanted in.

"Atwater, aren't you going to join us?" Kathy asked, wagging her ass as if it were a tail.

Summer laughed because she knew this would be the perfect present she could give both of them.

"What?" he asked, still in disbelief.

Kathy got up and grabbed him. She didn't kiss him or anything, but she went straight for his pants and snatched his dick out before he could even protest.

"Your dick is gigantic!" she said and slammed it into her mouth.

Summer went around to indulge in tasting Kathy's sapping pussy, and the shit was so raw and savage to Atwater!

Kathy placed a condom on him and pushed him down into a chair and turned around to ride him reverse cowgirl. She guided his dick inside of her and rode him while she kissed Summer.

"Your dick is like fire!" She slammed her hips down faster into the pending tide. Her body lurched and twisted, and she wrung herself of a blinding orgasm as she squeezed Summer.

Kathy was so tired that she collapsed on the ground.

"You can't hang," Summer said. Atwater laughed.

Summer got on all fours, and after Atwater changed his condom, he kneeled behind her and slammed his dick in her. He fucked her fast and hard, and the erotic grunts brought Kathy out of her fatigue. She was revived by the moans between the two.

Summer looked back at Atwater and gave it back to him as much as he had given to her. She was feral and savage.

Kathy played with her soaking wet pussy, and she wanted to feel Atwater's ramrod again, or feel Summer's lips! She laid down in front of Summer, and Summer feasted on her buffet.

Atwater felt the condom burst, and he stopped to put on another one. But while he was putting it on, Summer and Kathy lathered his dick with kisses between the two of them . . . dick worship. He could have split both of their heads if he nutted in their faces, but Summer kept coaching Kathy to let Atwater fuck her in the ass. It was too much to think about getting his massive member inside her little asshole. Summer wouldn't accept no, and after Atwater sat back down, Summer greased Kathy up and guided Atwater's dick into her ass.

Kathy had to sit up while holding the arm of the chair and resting her feet on Atwater's knees. At first, she rode him slow. But once Summer administered her tongue while Kathy was riding him, Kathy loosened up more and bounced up and down on his dick as fast as she could while Summer sucked on her clit. When the contractions of a swift orgasm hit her this time, she gushed all over the place. While she came, Summer and Atwater hugged her between the two of them as they kissed. Kathy joined in their kiss, and all three of them were kissing and fucking. The day was naughty!

Chapter Forty-Nine Don't Leave Him with Nothing...

Atwater told Summer to come back to the chapel after lunch. They had a lot to talk about. He went back to the unit and thought about what had just happened, and it was an occasion to celebrate. He had to keep something for Shonda when he went home. He couldn't go home after Summer had sexed him out.

After lunch, he went back to the chapel, and it was just as he thought. Summer was naked on the floor. He didn't have anything left after the escapade earlier that day, and he had a lot to talk to her about. But Summer wouldn't relent. She wanted to suck his dick for what seemed like hours, and he nutted two more times.

"Suck that big dick!" he coached her and nutted again. "Damn, you got my shit tender as fuck!"

He had to pull her up because there was no end to her industry. He needed to be focused on getting released.

"Damn, you ain't trying to leave nothing for Shonda?"

"Now why would I do that?" Summer didn't even look convincing.

"How did you get Mrs. Hoover in here?"

"She came on to me! You know I'm strictly-dickly."

"But did you like it with her?"

"Fuck yeah! She had some wet ass pussy, but her ass ain't like yours." They laughed.

"We have to concentrate. I go home tomorrow. And you'll go home on the 16th of August. I got some plans for you." Atwater snatched his dick out of Summer's hands. "Stop fucking with my dick! Stay focused for a minute."

"What!" Summer was mad because she wanted to get fucked again. She didn't want to hear about his endless plotting and planning. He was always scamming on something.

"Have you ever thought about being a pimp?" Summer thought the question wasn't only crazy funny, but she thought it was completely ridiculous!

"Are you out of your mind?" she asked as she laughed.

"Do I look like I'm laughing?" Atwater was dead fucking serious.

"Hell no, I haven't thought about being a pimp!"

"That's right, because I'm the mutha fuckin' pimp, and you're going to be my bottom hoe," Atwater was convinced. He wouldn't let his bitches plot or rebel or even think about bucking.

"Atwater, I ain't 'hoeing for you or nobody!" It was too much to think about Atwater wanting their relationship to end on such a horrid note.

"You still don't trust me? Understand greatness when it's right in your face. Know when you're amongst the stars? Understand when the sun is shining on your pretty face? I'll never put us in harm's way. I'm going to be here for you. I'm not going to hurt or run out on you. Every move I'm going to make in the future is to give us power and prestige. I haven't done this bid to return to the streets and be a gnat on the wall. You're in all my future plans. So, I can't believe you're still questioning me." Atwater was livid. He always showed people genuine love, so her suspicion of him being a fake was uncalled for.

"I'm sorry. I didn't mean it like that."

"You meant it like that!" He got up and dressed as if he was going to leave.

"I'm sorry. Don't leave me! I'm sorry. I'll do it, Atwater. I'll do anything you want. Anything!"

Atwater turned his back to Summer because it was exactly what he wanted to hear. It's exactly what he had plotted to hear, and it fell right into his lap.

He turned around. "What did you say?"

"I said I'll do anything you want. I'm sorry, baby." Summer hugged him and held him close.

"You'll fuck a hundred men and will do it happily if I tell you?"

"I'll fuck a thousand men if you want me to."

Atwater studied her to see if there was any sincerity in what she said. The truth couldn't have been gleaned any easier. Summer was his bottom hoe.

"You won't ever question me again? You'd walk naked in the bitter cold until your toes blistered and bloodied, and you would know that I have the map to the treasure. You'd follow that map until we got that treasure?"

"I'd do it, Atwater." Summer kissed him on his neck. "I swear to God, I'd do it!"

"Good, because I have a plan."

An hour later, Atwater said goodbye to his friends on the compound. He had hit a couple of laps with Craze-zo and told him that when he got out in one year, he could come and live with him and get money. Atwater then went to his brothers in faith and gave them things and said his goodbyes. He was just anxious, weary, and sleepless. He couldn't wait to get out and prove his merit.

He only had one person who was above all others on the compound he wanted to see and nobody else mattered. It was Old School. At 7:00 p.m. he had snuck up on Old School, who was reading the Wall Street Journal, in the law library.

"I don't pray, I prey," Atwater said behind Old School's back, and Old School laughed.

"Prey on the weak, not the strong and the wise, because who else is going to rule the world."

Atwater hugged him and sat at his side. "I'm out tomorrow, Old School."

"Seems like you're going to be leaving me, little brother."

"But not for long. I have something for you. And I ain't like all these pussy ass, weak mutha fuckas who say one thing, but when they get out, they do something else. Old School, with my hand over my heart and my hand to Allah, I'm going to get you out of here."

"Sounds like you're saluting an American flag."

"I'm saluting an American hero. I owe you everything. You developed me from nothing."

"The talent has always been there, Atwater. It's in all the brothers, the Hispanics, and all the other underprivileged, but there are those who'd want to keep them in place. Riddle me that."

Atwater smiled cleverly. "I'm going to get you out."

"The powers-that-be…"

Atwater interrupted him. "I'm gone, Old School, and I don't want to hear any defeatist bullshit shit. I got you, and you should know that's coming from a man's mouth. You taught me that a real man's words have magical properties to them that could make the impossible possible. Just know that I'm a real man, and it was you who birthed me. You gave me the real resurrection."

Old School had tears in his eyes, and he knew that Atwater was the son he'd never had.

Atwater got up to leave. "I'll see you on the streets."

And that was all that needed to be said. The rest was understood.

CHAPTER 39
AND IT WAS AS IF - AS IF, HE HAD NEVER LEFT

ATWATER COULDN'T SLEEP the whole night. He had been so anxious that he tossed and turned in his bed. To kill some of the tension he was feeling, he had gotten out of the bed around dawn and did push-ups.

Morning had come, and he was out of the cell as soon as the doors popped open. He made his rounds around the prison and said goodbye to everybody except Summer and Old School.

At 9:00 a.m. he dressed out in Ferragamo threads that Shonda had sent him. Atwater had been processed out of prison, and he stepped out into freedom!

Shonda had pulled up in a crispy white 2014 Mercedes Benz S550. She jumped out of the car and ran into his arms. She didn't even have time to remove her Prada Aviator sunglasses as she held onto him as if life had stopped moving for her.

"You're finally home!" She couldn't believe it.

"And they'll never take me again. Damn, you look good!"

He did a once-over, and she was fine to death. Her hair was pinned down to one side and cascaded over her shoulder in long, soft waves. She wore a black lace blouse that displayed her breasts with taste and a knee-length dress with black platform sandals, earrings, a heart pendant attached to a thin gold chain that hung to her belly, and an edgy and elegant perfume.

"You're going to get in trouble looking that good." Atwater spun her in a circle, but he was ready to get away from the prison to make it all official. "Let's get out of here."

Once they got inside the car, he didn't know whose car it was because she drove an Escalade.

"Whose car is this?"

"Yours." She kissed him and they drove off, heading for D.C., where they went to a restaurant and ate soul food. From there, they went stepping at a small club in Adams Morgan. The DJ played old school Maxwell and Sade.

"This reminds me of when we were young," Shonda said as Atwater spun her.

"We still are young." They laughed.

"I'm going to show you in a minute. You just wait." He winked his eye, and he was ready to go to their Marriott Suite and get it on.

They were all over one another once they were in the elevator, heading to the suite. They couldn't even walk because they were kissing and fondling each other. Atwater took off his clothes until he was clad in only boxers. By the time they made it to their suite, a trail of their discarded clothes led to their room. Shonda laughed because it was indecent that they were damn near naked, but after eighteen years, she could care less! Once he opened the door, he carried her across the threshold and took her straight to the king-sized bed and flung her down.

"Hold up, baby, just give me five minutes to look at you," Atwater said, trying to stop his heart from pounding so hard with lust pumping adrenaline.

Shonda looked beautiful under the dimly lit room that made her skin look golden. Her body was better than how he had remembered because now she had the right thickness in all the right places. When they were younger, she was thinner, but now she was well-roportioned in all the right places. Atwater cherished the moment, thinking that. But because of Shonda, he never had unprotected sex with Summer. Shonda wasn't only his children's mother; she was his best friend. The memory he cherished most about her shot him in the chest with instant guilt. Damn, he had been fucking a boy and loving it!

At that moment, he wanted to curl up with Shonda and feel the heat from her body, hear her heartbeat against his ears, and cherish the softness of a woman that nobody would ever be able to replace. His thoughts were instantly gone as Shonda crawled on him and took his dick into her hands. He felt her small and soft hands running over the shaft of his penis. He smiled for having been so hard on himself.

Shit, his time away left a lot of room for trial and error, growth, and development. As Shonda kissed the tip of his erect dick, he made peace with himself that he'd accept the past for the past and the future for the future. In that moment, there was only one person aching in his heart, body, and soul. Shonda.

Atwater went straight to tasting her wet pussy, and he dragged his tongue from her toes to her thighs. She tried to get away from the impending stimulation, but he had a vice-grip on her. He feasted until she gushed out rivulets of an explosive orgasm.

He climbed on top of her and slammed his dick into her; she was as tight as a virgin.

"My God, Atwater!" she cried out as he went deep inside.

He kissed her passionately, and they made love until the moon withered in the midnight sky beyond. His incessant days with Summer would have to be revisited—he knew. But tonight, was all about his lovely Shonda.

Chapter Fifty-One Back To Business...

When Monday had come, they headed to St. Louis. The city

was nothing like how he remembered, and he knew it would take him some time to get used to it. But he had bigger things to focus on. Atwater had plans, and he was focused. He couldn't let anything keep him from accomplishing them.

He went to his house in Baden where his whole family was. They threw him a welcome home party, and he caught up on old times with everybody.

After the party had ended, he had taken Mason and Tyler for a spin in his new car.

"Thank you all for everything. This was good to come home to family and friends."

"Good to have you back, my nigga," Tyler said, who sat in the front seat. "I know you're about to do something big."

"That's right, and I'm going to need y'alls help. I got some big plans, and I'm trying to hit these streets running, if you understand what I mean."

"Dad, you're not going to sell drugs again, are you?"

Atwater had to look at his son in the rearview mirror.

"No, fool. I have bigger plans, and I'm going to need you especially. You remember telling me about your friend, Liam Val, who you said has an inside scoop on different people in politics and the gossip about them."

"Yes, I remember telling you. But why?"

"Wait till we get to a bar and all sit down and talk."

They went to a sports bar, and Atwater checked out the scene. Everybody was chatting and telling jokes. It was peaceful. He remembered all the days that he wished he was out and about, chilling with his family, and now he had that. He didn't have to worry about the jail stuff anymore, and it made him feel good.

"What were you talking about, Dad?" Mason brought him out of his reverie.

Atwater studied his son and Tyler. Tyler looked like the average dope dealer, and his son looked like he was being groomed to be a politician or something. But Atwater knew he had to take the reins on everyone in his inner-circle, and he would have to let them in on his plans.

"I got something big I'm putting together, and your friend is going to be critical for me putting it together. Tell me more about him?"

"What do you want to know?"

Atwater had to take it slow with his son. His son was conscious of the game, but at the same time, going to all those private schools made him naïve, or at least that's what he led one to believe.

"Is he for game?" Atwater asked.

Mason couldn't believe that after his father had done all that time, he would come back to the streets and want to sell drugs. It was contrary to all the stuff he spoke about strategizing success. Although Mason loved Tyler, he always thought people could make money in all types of ways that didn't include selling drugs.

"Pops, you're talking about selling that stuff again?" Even Tyler was shocked by Mason's insistence that Atwater wanted to sell drugs, but it was as if Atwater expected it.

"I'm not going to even entertain that question again. But I'm about to break it all down to y'all. We're going to use your friend to gather information on politicians, entertainers, law enforcement officials, you name it. We're going to use this information to barter power."

Tyler laughed. "Fool, you done lost your mind in there. You're trying to get a nigga killed!"

Atwater smirked, and his son saw that it was dangerous. "Pops, you tripping."

"Mason and Tyler, you mutha fuckas betta not ever doubt me! I work off of trust and loyalty, and I don't need nobody under me who's scared or fearful. I'm about to get super rich and powerful, and if you two are shortsighted and fearful, you can get up from this table right now."

"In this age of information, I want to be the one who not only barters and sells it. I want to be the one who's manufacturing the shit."

Neither of them had left the table, and they sat feeling chastised. Tyler saw it then. Atwater was still the leader he had remembered, and he knew it wouldn't be long before he would gather a mob together that was stronger than the first one they had.

Plus, Atwater didn't want anybody to question his judgment. He wasn't a weak ass follower, a flunky, or a yes-man.

"How can you manufacture information?" Tyler asked.

"Now you're ready . . ." Atwater looked at Tyler. "What did you do with the letter I sent you?"

Tyler took the letter out of his front pocket. "It's right here."

"Did you get me a crew that ain't tied into no drug shit because that's the worst thing that can happen is for me to get on some ongoing investigation."

Tyler chuckled. "No, these fools ain't no hustlers like that. They street niggas, though, that need plenty direction. They good niggas though."

Atwater looked over at his son. Fuck the food and the drinks. It was time to go. "Let's wrap this up. I want to meet them right now, and I want you to call Liam Val and tell him I want to meet him asap."

"Dad, we haven't eaten yet." Mason and Tyler looked at one another with confusion.

"Come on. Fuck that shit. I have catching up to do."

As soon as they got in the car, both Mason and Tyler were making calls as Atwater had ordered them to do. They went to a nearby park where Atwater was supposed to meet his new crew. By now, the sun was setting, and it set a tangerine-colored glow that enveloped the city. It was the first time since Atwater left that he finally felt at home.

He still felt messed up, realizing that so much had changed. He just wanted to keep himself busy with building his empire, so he wouldn't have to cry over all the years he had lost for a mistake Tyler had made.

When they drove up to the park, Atwater noticed about eight cars in the parking area. When Atwater, Tyler, and Mason got out of the car, all the other guys exited their cars. There were twelve people, but Atwater only needed four or five.

Tyler greeted them with a pound and dap as Atwater studied them calmly. Tyler came back, and he began to introduce them. "That's Lil Rogg, Big Rogg's middle son—"

Atwater held up his hand because he didn't need to know them all. He looked for something else that an introduction couldn't fully determine. He studied their eyes. When he looked into eyes that were too ambitious, he looked them over. If he saw envy or conceit, he looked them over. When he saw admiration, with a hint of camaraderie, he knew he had his men.

"Let's go," Atwater said as everybody looked puzzled.

Tyler was tripping by now. He thought jail had messed up Atwater's head. He looked over at the crew he had assembled and told them he'd holler at them later. When Tyler got back into the car, Atwater pulled off.

"You alright, Atwater?" Tyler asked, knowing Mason was thinking the same thing.

"I only saw three I could use. I need the cat with the Saint Louis baseball cap, the cat with the Jesus cross chain, and the biggest one that was there."

"That's Biggie, Q, and Tre," Tyler said as he laughed. Atwater was still sharp.

"What's up with Liam?" Atwater asked.

"We can go over to his apartment right now," Mason said as he guided Atwater to the apartment complex.

Liam was Hawaiian, with the red complexion of a Native American. His long hair was matted with dreadlocks. His body, although short, was chiseled with rock-hard muscles that needed to be on display. Liam had on a wife beater, cargo pants, and sandals. He looked like he was dressed for far warmer climates than the muggy spring day that was approaching summer.

"Y'all smoke weed?" Liam asked after they greeted each other.

"What you got?" Atwater asked

"I got some granddaddy-purp."

"Blaze it up," Atwater said.

It was just what was needed to let the tension out of every-body. After being gone so long, people become a bit estranged, and it's only so much a visit and phone calls can do to compensate for being in person. Liam was playing Bob Marley over the sound system. He had Popular Mechanics, Hacking, Scientific American, and Popular Science magazines scattered on the coffee table in a stack in front of body building books.

"Mason tells me you have something I can make some money from," Liam said. He needed to pay his college tuition, and if he had anything left over, he wanted to buy a motorcycle.

Atwater felt so relaxed after the weed hit his system that he almost forgot the pending business at hand.

"I need to find out certain information about people in high places," Atwater said.

Liam looked at Mason, and they both laughed.

"What kind of information?" Liam asked as Tyler studied Atwater cautiously.

"I need any information on anybody who's a sexual deviant."

"Dad, that's impossible to find out," Mason said, who was on the edge of having a bout of giggles. But the more he looked at Liam, he wasn't so sure about that.

"I don't know. There may be a way." When Liam said that everybody scooted to the edge of their seats as Liam went over to turn the sound system down. "Look, all the major companies in the world gather tons of information on people based on their buying habits, the things they read, and the websites they visit on the computer. Basically, it has a lot to do—"

"Edward Snowden, the WikiLeaks guy. All the stuff with the NSA," Mason interrupted.

"That's my boy," Liam added. "Basically, what I'm saying is that I could tap into certain porn industry databases and get a profile on anybody they have a file on." Atwater and Tyler were tripping about what they were hearing.

If what Liam was saying was right, and he could do what he was proposing, Atwater could make a fortune far beyond anything he had ever expected. With a little ingenuity, he could lock himself in a monarch of not only wealth but power and influence. And power and influence were prized far more than wealth.

"So, all I'd have to do is give you a list of the people in high places, and you could give me any info as to if they are sexual deviants?" Atwater asked, amazed at the power this kid, who was not even twenty-one years old, was about to give him.

"Pops," Liam said, "I'm not only going to be able to give you a yes or no answer as to if they are sexual deevs, but I'm also going to be able to tell you exactly what gets them off as if you were in their heads."

"That's bullshit!" Tyler said. Of course, he couldn't understand why Atwater wanted to know that type of information, but he didn't believe it was held on people.

Atwater was already writing down names on a sheet of paper that was on the coffee table. He already knew the names by memory from what he had planned from day one. He handed the paper to Liam, and Liam laughed at the twenty-six names he saw. "Fuck!"

"Watch your mouth," Atwater said to Liam. "We're going to make each other filthy rich."

"Yeah, and very dead in the process." Contrary to Liam's statement, he had sparkles of excitement in his eyes. This cloak and dagger shit was right up his alley— living on the edge with no brakes.

After they left, Atwater went home. Shonda and Macy had cleaned everything up, and they were awaiting Atwater's arrival. Regardless of his excitement, he made it a point to spend time with his daughter. Around 8:30 p.m., he and Shonda got dressed and went to an elegant restaurant. When they returned home, they had passionate sex.

Not too long after, he was glad to find out that Shonda was pregnant. It was the best news yet because he would get a chance to take part in raising his seed. But he had a more pressing matter, which was building an empire, and the drama that lay ahead in doing it.

CHAPTER 40
TOGETHER AGAIN

AFTER ATWATER LEFT THE JAIL, Summer had gone through a deep depression. She knew she would be with him in under a month, but the thought of him being away was killing her.

On more than one occasion, Kathy had tried to rekindle their lustful fun, but it could never be rekindled. Summer was just strictly-dickly, and the thought that she had been with Kathy disgusted her. However, she kept it as friendly as possible.

Atwater had her head fucked up. He had all these dreams and goals of being wealthy and powerful, and she just didn't believe that she fit into any of them. She didn't believe she had what it took. As she told Britney and Buffy the details, they laughed like crazy although it did make sense.

Her release date came in a blink of an eye. She had an emotional farewell hug with Britney and Buffy, and she knew she would miss her support team. She was then processed through the slow and agitating release procedures, and she dressed out in her clothes.

Atwater had sent her a banging Akris gown that had a split on the side and Manolo Blahnik shoes that she thought were too fucking elegant to drive home in. After she dressed, though, she felt a hundred times better.

When the COs saw her, they laughed. "Where the fuck you think you're going? To the Grammy's?"

"To none of your fucking business!" Summer was like that! She had a little attitude, and she wasn't the scary cat she had come to jail as. Buffy and Britney had rubbed off on her. She didn't care what people thought of her, and she didn't fear getting her ass kicked anymore.

Summer was no longer the girl that Peyton had set up, or the detectives had frightened to snitch on Glen, or the girl that needed protection from Sosa, Black, or otherwise. She remembered how frightened she felt when Black had shoved her face into the wall and snatched down her pants. She believed that after being with Britney, who knew how to fight, and Buffy, who knew how to talk shit, she was a mixture of the two.

Her confidence told her she could stand up to her father and tell his hateful ass to go fuck himself and take her brother with him. She would be woman enough to take the ass whipping that would probably come with it. She felt the strongest confidence knowing that she had made her peace with her mother, had a man that truly loved her for her, and told her Uncle Kevin she never wanted to see him again.

Above all that, she was free!

When she saw Atwater, who pulled up in a rented drop-top red Ferrari, she dived into his arms. He was dressed like a Miami playboy, and he looked finer than ever.

"Damn, I missed you!" she said. She couldn't wait to get fucked tonight.

"Come on, we have a plane to catch."

"We're not going to drive?" Summer looked disappointed. She was going to give him head to the earth's end. "You know I don't have to report to my probation officer till Monday."

"Just get your fine ass in the car." Atwater's dick was already hard. He'd been wanting to fuck Summer the whole time he'd been out.

Summer sauntered her buttery hips over to the passenger seat. When she got in, Atwater had real make-up for her to use in a toiletry bag. She made her face up, and she looked good. All she needed now was to whip her hair up, and she would have been the baddest bitch on the eastern seaboard.

"Where we going?" she asked as they sped down the highway. She had just finished putting her finishing touches on her make-up, and she leaned over to rub his cock that stiffened to the touch.

"Just shut up and enjoy the ride."

"You want me to shut up?" She had a mischievous smile on her face as she massaged his dick. He smiled unevenly. "I'll keep quiet." Summer unzipped his pants and gave him the mega head he loved.

They drove to Philadelphia, where they caught a first-class flight to Florida, where he had reservations for a two-night cruise.

Carnival Cruise line had boarded, but before they embarked, Atwater took her to a beauty salon that whipped Summer's hair up with an expensive weave that they styled in big bows cascading down her back. She felt fresh, relieved, and free! Atwater was amazed at what a good weave could do, and he took her to the mall to get some clothes for the trip. While she was there, she got a pedicure and manicure.

They then headed on the high seas for the Bahamas: Nassau and Freeport.

After dinner, they went to the dance floor. "Tender Love" by Force MDs was playing, and after the song, they went back to their small cabin. They had wild and savage sex until they couldn't move anymore. Afterward, Atwater had to prepare her mind for what he needed next.

"I got everything lined up, and now I need you to get me some bitches that look like you."

"Not right now, Atwater. Damn, come back and get in the bed."

Atwater made himself a drink. Sleep was the last thing he needed. "I need you to focus. We'll relax soon enough, but right now I want you to get your ass up and grab a paper and pencil."

Summer fumed but did as she was asked. She wrapped herself up in the bedsheets and came to Atwater's side as he sat on the edge of the bed with a laptop. He went to a website that had ads for transvestites, and he and Summer poured over different people until they had the names of who they wanted to interview.

"You have qualities that I know I'm right about why I chose you to do this job. You're going to be able to relate to these girls, and they're going to look up to you for a lot of reasons."

After the two-day cruise, they went their separate ways. But Summer knew what she had to do.

CHAPTER 41
RECRUITMENT...

A MONTH LATER, it had been exactly as Atwater had said it would be. She didn't even know that she could have that much influence on other people. But she carried out his instructions to the tee, and she only recruited people who were classy and loyal to them.

She just didn't know he was going to be so persistent, and anal retentive, pressuring her about everything. She thought that their weekend on the cruise ship would be spent full of wild sex, but all he wanted to do was tell her what she had to do! The simple fact was she loved him harder than ever, more than ever, and it paled the love she felt for him when they were in jail together. Now she'd ache if she wasn't with him, and she hated it. She hated that he was so different now.

Damn, he had turned into a drill sergeant overnight, and she felt like she was losing her identity in his. He told her how she would have to use pleasure to attain information, how they were going to use cameras and spyware to catch politicians, entertainers, and law enforcement officials in embarrassing and compromising positions. He went as far as to actually want to use truth serum drugs. She thought it wasn't only funny but crazy!

Maybe she didn't see his ideas at all as being practical, and that's why he had been on her so hard. But she did do her part, and she recruited her fair share. Atwater's project was in its beginning stages, and he was edgy. He'd fly back and forth from St. Louis to D.C., or he'd do visual conference calls over Zoom from his home office. But he took the shit as seriously as a heart attack.

Summer had recruited ten people; one was a white girl who was no older than seventeen, but she looked the part, and she was sharp for a kid. Her name was Faith, and she was best friends with a transvestite who was nineteen, whose name was Lacy.

Lacy was most definitely the greatest asset to Atwater's project. She was a slender Dominican girl without a blemish on her creamy and milky white skin. She had dashing features and pink succulent lips. She was by far a clever talker, and her wit was beyond her years. And she was as sassy.

And that's when the big opportunity came. Lacy had gotten a video of her fucking a mayor of a city in Maryland, and his name was protected for obvious reasons. Although Lacy was a transvestite who loved to dip, she air dropped the file to Summer, and Atwater did what he was best at.

He sent pictures of the video to the mayor's office with a contact number. Within minutes, Atwater was on the phone with him. He was able to negotiate one million dollars to an offshore account to keep quiet, but it was a source of income that Atwater could always use.

The next big item scheme came from Faith, who had slept with a married pastor of a mega-church. To keep the statutory rape issue hush hush, he had paid Atwater two million dollars, and the two schemes had been finalized within a week of each other.

Summer was busy doing the boring part of instructing everybody she recruited where to stash the equipment, how to attract the men, and how to conceal their identity, which included how they were supposed to wipe the place down of their fingerprints.

Their real identity would never be revealed, and whenever Atwater presented anything to the tricks he was scheming on, he would use the real identity of somebody else who fits the bill.

But nothing could compare to when Lacy had set up a federal judge. She had made a tape of her fucking him in the ass! It was their greatest achievement, and when Summer had called Atwater with the news, he had chartered a leer jet to fly him there immediately. He didn't want anybody to get a copy of the video.

Summer had flown out of town for two nights with a senator she was baiting. Lacy and Faith were at the airport terminal, awaiting Atwater's arrival.

When the private jet landed, he walked out into the glistening sky, looking like a million bucks. With this video of the sex scandal, the sky was the limit. He was about to put his phone with a copy of the video up somewhere safe in St. Louis.

It was the third time he had seen Lacy, and while he thought Summer was gorgeous, Lacy was fine to death! She wore a pink DKNY miniskirt, and her tits were a bit smaller than Summer's. She didn't have nearly as much ass. Faith trailed her. And they both were five-star ladies; their hair had been whipped by hell!

He hugged them, and as he hugged Lacy, she slipped him the video. It wasn't long before they were above the clouds, headed toward St. Louis.

Atwater put the video on. It was the best! The video had clarity and the judge's voice could be heard all too well. It was all he could hope for, and much more. He couldn't help but reach over and kiss Lacy on the cheek.

"Ain't no looking back!" he said repeatedly. And the expression foretold their future blow.

Faith was at a table in a corner, making lines of cocaine. Atwater didn't know that Lacy or Faith were heavy users. He didn't realize it until he got up to get a glass of champagne and saw her making perfect white lines.

"What the fuck is this!" He was livid. He didn't want the pretty little bitch in the back of his privately chartered jet getting high off that shit.

Faith didn't know what to say, and Lacy came to her rescue. "Papi, it's just for celebration. Don't have a heart attack. We've worked our vaginas off, and we're going to celebrate. All of us!"

Atwater eyed her for a second. That sassy ass Latina shit was mesmerizing.

"Go ahead then. I need to take a piss." Atwater had popped the video out and placed it in his front pocket. He wasn't going to let it out of his sight for one second. When he came out of the bathroom, Lacy and Faith were snorting the long lines off the table. Their noses were white, and they laughed like little girls. "This some good stuff. It has my pussy tingling," Faith said, leaning back in her chair. She was just too advanced to be so damn young and fine.

Her little body looked like sex on the beach and fuck on the ocean. "Shut up, mami. Watch your tongue. Our boss is here."

Atwater laughed. "Quit with that boss shit, you pretty mutha fucka."

"Papi, you're the one acting like you got something stuck up your ass." They all laughed.

"Come over here and do a line and chill your uptight ass un poquito."

"I ain't doing that shit." Atwater sat at Faith's side. She was one of the finest white girls he'd ever seen, even though she was a bit on the slim side.

"Fine, papi. More for us."

"Summer told us about when you all were in jail," Faith said.

"She runs her mouth too much."

"She said you had a big dick," Lacy said, snorting another line of cocaine.

Atwater laughed. He knew what they were trying to do, and he wasn't having it. He thought it was just a senseless game, but Faith reached over and caressed his dick.

"What the fuck are you doing?" But she stroked his dick, and the little bitch looked like she wanted to be stuffed. The energy was so fucking erotic that he had to stand up for a second. His dick was hard as hell, and they both saw it.

"You never tried this shit before, Boss?" Another stupid ass pestering question, but this time it didn't sound so dumb, and the shit didn't look so bad.

"Move the fuck out of the way. Let me see what this shit is working with." Atwater threw caution to the wind because he was so happy with the shit that was in his front pocket that he knew he was going to celebrate tonight anyway. He took a deep whiff of the white powder, and it seemed like fire was being rammed in his head. But his head instantly felt numb, and then a feeling of extreme euphoria followed.

The girls didn't pay him any attention. Faith went over to Lacy, and they kissed passionately and groped one another's breasts. The shit was so stimulating to watch that Atwater's dick was throbbing.

Lacy grabbed his dick, and he was fucked up because if Summer found out, she would go berserk. He was too far gone to say no, and his altered state had no resistance. Lacy sucked his dick, and the shit was the bomb. He fell back into a seat behind him as she slurped his dick.

Lacy had heard so much about Atwater that from the first time she saw him, she was in love with him. He was more than Summer had described, and she and Faith would always talk about him behind Summer's back. They would say that they each would have his love, no matter what Summer thought. They worshipped him as much as Summer did, and when they started seeing the money come in that he had promised them, he was all that and then some.

Faith played with her pussy and Atwater watched her. Her pussy looked pristine, and he knew he was going to fuck her young ass. His dick felt like it would explode, and Lacy grabbed KY jelly from her Louis Vuitton purse and greased her ass. She wanted the shit so much that she turned and slammed his dick in her ass as she rode him reverse cowgirl.

She fucked better than Summer, but her head could never compare. Atwater fucked her good, and she brought her head back to him and stuck her tongue into his mouth.

Faith's pussy was tingling, and she wanted to get fucked too. She went over and kissed Lacy after she had yanked her face from Atwater. Faith straddled Lacy, who was getting fucked from the back by Atwater, and Faith put Lacy's six-inch dick inside her.

The shit was wild! When Atwater thought the shit with Kathy and Summer was crazy—this shit was bananas! Faith leaned over and kissed Atwater as he slammed his dick into Lacy's ass and all three of them fucked one another.

Lacy sucked on Faith's perky tits and slid inside of her pussy as she felt Atwater ram his dick inside her.

She grinded down into his dick as Faith bounced up and down on top of her and they were all so coked up that they could fuck for hours.

Atwater motioned Faith to get up, and she got on all fours. Lacy got behind her and fucked her. Atwater climbed on Lacy and fucked her from the back, and Lacy and Faith were screaming with bliss!

Atwater couldn't nut for nothing because he was so high. But Lacy's ass was so good that he put in work on her.

Faith had seen Atwater's fat ten-inch dick, and she had never been with a guy that big. She was scared, but she wanted him so badly that she begged him to fuck her.

Atwater laid on the ground and the young bitch slid down on his dick. It was some of the best pussy he'd ever had. The shit was tight and wet and she grinded back into his dick and screamed like he was killing her. Lacy didn't just stand and watch. She slid her dick into Faith's ass, and they double penetrated her until she was biting and scratching from heart shattering orgasms. She had three orgasms before Lacy and Atwater had one.

Atwater wanted some more of Lacy's ass, and Faith sat on his face while Lacy smothered his dick with her ass. His dick slid in and he almost fainted. The ass was better than any pussy he'd ever had, and she slammed back into his dick as Faith moaned and groaned and grinded her young pussy against his face. His dick flared, and he exploded inside Lacy's ass, and it was the hardest he had ever nutted before!

Chapter Fifty-Four Fed Up

What seemed to Summer like the other side of the world, was actually Seattle, and she was whisked off to a banquet by a senator who patronized the escort service that Atwater had set up. It was clear now that Atwater had somehow converted her into a high-class call girl because she was encouraged to sleep with the past five clients, they had gathered intel on. These clients would be extorted by the week's end.

The banquet was immaculate, but the ceremonies were boring, with a lot of brown-nosing and ass-kissing.

But the threads Summer wore made her look the nicest she thought she'd ever looked. She wanted to fall asleep in the soft material and dream about the love of her life. Atwater.

Everything up until now was hard work, and she had to stay positive to keep up with this facade. She wanted him to herself, and she was tired of sharing him with Shonda. She had to go weeks without seeing him, and it made her crazy! It was always the same excuse that Atwater had: "Shonda's pregnant, emotional, and she needs me right now."

She downed her glass of sparkling champagne, and it took everything in her power not to blow off the whole night and fly back to D.C. on a redeye flight. How much of this would she have to take!

Summer longed to feel Atwater inside her. She loved the sex they had.

She had to re-cross her silky, shaven legs because she felt her insides quiver at the thought of it all.

Foolishly, she was in love, and nothing could change that. She only wanted all the money that was pouring in to help him manifest the dreams he held so dear to his heart.

Summer was twenty-one at that moment, and her life up until that point had been something she hated. Everybody had judged her, and the more she thought about it, it was just because she had a dick! The hate she had for her dick made her certain that her past thoughts about getting a sex change were etched in stone. It was something she was going to do as early as next month.

Chapter Fifty-Five There Was Nothing Atwater Couldn't Do...

Two days after Atwater had gotten his hands on the tape of the federal judge, he had set up an appointment with one of the most powerful mob bosses out of Chicago.

Atwater, Tyler, and their crew had rented a private jet and flown to Chicago where they were chauffeured to a mansion in the suburbs.

Atwater's party of ten was escorted to a conference room in the mansion where an Italian boss, Joey Bispucci, sat behind a desk. He was strikingly handsome, but he had the eyes of a killer, which Atwater noticed immediately. He was surrounded by security guards, an attorney, and other wise guys who were all dressed in expensive suits.

Once Atwater was seated, Joey asked, "So you're saying you can help my Uncle Pauli?" Joey's question was filled with sarcasm, and if Atwater was bullshitting, none of his crew would leave alive. His Uncle Pauli was serving a double life sentence at ADX, and if the highest paid attorneys in the nation couldn't get his uncle out, how could this fucking hooligan get him out?

Biggie, Atwater's bodyguard, tossed a manilla envelope on the desk.

"What's this?" Joey opened the envelope to see a picture of the scandal.

"One of those faces should look familiar to you." "What kind of friggin' homo shit is this?" was

Joey's first reaction. But as he looked closer and closer, he noticed who Atwater was talking about. "Get the fuck out of here! That's Judge Snider! These are fucking impressive."

Atwater smirked because he knew he had him. "To say the least. Which one of these gentlemen is your uncle's attorney?"

"You asked for the attorney to be here; he's here," Joey said, with his uncle's attorney standing at his side.

"I wanted to ask what stage Mr. Bispucci's

Subsection 2255 was at?" Atwater knew all the answers he asked because he did his homework before he made the appointment. He knew everything about the Bispucci family. He had found out all the in-and-outs, and he knew he had them by the balls.

The attorney was just as lavish and as snobbish as the bosses around him. "He's on his subsection 2255."

Atwater knew exactly what a U.S.C. Subsection 2255 was. It was a procedure that allowed somebody to appeal their conviction in front of the judge who originally sentenced them, and it all made more sense because this was the same judge that they now had by the balls.

"Who has the final say-so in a subsection 2255?" Atwater enjoyed himself.

"Judge Snider." The attorney looked over at Joey with eyes that told him they had to pay whatever Atwater was asking. However, the attorney had yet to see the photos that Joey then handed to him.

"Oh my God!"

That was music to Atwater's ears. "You think you could score a favorable decision with those?"

"Without a doubt," the attorney said.

"What do you want?" Joey was tired of the beating around the bush.

"Considering that Bispucci Inc. has an estimated wealth of a quarter of a billion, and when he was arrested, the feds seized a little over $20 million in cash and assets, which they'll have to cough over once his case is overturned, I'm thinking $30 million."

Joey was livid, and it took his bodyguards to calm him down. "Are you outta your fucking mind! What do you think? We have $30 million just laying around in the house?" He'd have Atwater's head on a platter before he'd let this smart nigga with photos get that kind of money from his family.

Atwater had remained an esteemed gentleman. "I understand your frustration, and I truly sympathize with the whole shock of it all. But if you don't put this judge in your front pocket now, he's going to let the feds take all of this." Atwater looked around the luxurious mansion.

"Frankly, my friend, you don't have a choice."

That's when it dawned on Joey that Atwater had done his homework. He looked over at his attorney, who read his mind.

"Joey, I'll have to agree with him. The feds are already closing in on the gambling operations, the overseas investments, the butcher shops, the restaurants—hell, everything. I advise you to take this as a major breakthrough and a major turning point. You can keep the feds at bay now by simply controlling the judge."

"Get him the friggin' money," Joey spat.

"All of it?" his banker, who was a part of the Bispucci family, asked.

"Get him the friggin' money already!"

Chapter Fifty-Six The Boss Is In The Building...

The breaking news aired on every station:

"Shocking news just in. The Bispucci crime family's head, Pauliano Bispucci, has been immediately released from ADX maximum security. His conviction was overturned when District Judge Snider declared that his conviction was based on an illegal search and seizure, and his twenty-four-count indictment for the following crimes, money laundering, tax evasion, drug trafficking, murder for hire, and a continuing criminal enterprise, was unconstitutionally attained."

The news showed Bispucci leaving the federal courthouse a free man. There was a crowd to welcome him, and journalists were asking him questions and snapping pictures.

"How do you feel about the judge's decision?" a journalist asked Bispucci.

"Let our forefathers who drafted the US Constitution praise the judge's decision."

Atwater laughed. He was a different person now. He was in a huge Jacuzzi that was built into the ground at the decked-out penthouse flat in D.C. that he shared with Summer. He was smoking a cigar and wore a gold necklace, a bracelet that shimmered with diamonds, and a Rolex, which was just as dazzling.

"You like that, don't you?" Summer asked, who looked like a million bucks in her swanky pale silk robe and her expensive weave that fell to the small fall of her back. Her diamond stud earrings and the perfect make-up on her face made her look more like a movie star than a model.

"Fuck yeah. Justice served. Fuck that judge. I did eighteen

years because I didn't have nobody who was laced with game like me. We ain't even been out a year yet and we're multi-millionaires, and I have that sweet ass of yours to thank. I got a springboard on power."

It was now or never for Summer to speak her mind as she slipped into the hot water with him once she disrobed.

"That's what I wanted to talk to you about. I'm tired of this. This was your idea, and I only did it because I promised you I would. I'm not complaining like I promised I wouldn't, but now that I got everything in line, I want to quit. I've been thinking about doing the surgery."

"Where the fuck is all this coming from?"

"I just want to be with you, Atwater! I've stopped doing drugs because of you. I'm not even bipolar anymore. You always make me feel complete. I just want to be with you." Summer looked coy and sexy. Atwater truly loved her. It was sheer ambition, hunger, and drive that made him desperate enough to turn her into a high-class call girl.

He could afford for her to quit. The decision he was making was only because he did love her and wanted her to himself. He coveted her to such a degree that he made her and the rest of his workers take HIV tests monthly as an added incentive to his clients that the product was healthy and clean. But on Summer's account, he wanted it so he could have unprotected sex without having to worry about bringing anything home to Shonda.

"That's all I'm saying." She kissed his lips. She didn't know that he had been doing lines of coke ever since he started fucking Lacy and Faith. His attitude had changed, but she attributed it to the money and power.

"If that's what you really want to do, we can make it happen. But you got to find somebody you trust to hand over your responsibility to."

Summer smacked her lips. That would be the easiest thing to do in the world. "Lacy can do it much better than me. It's like she's made for this stuff, and what's more important, she's loyal to you."

By now, Summer's hand was under the water, caressing Atwater's dick. She straddled him and slid his dick inside her ass as she stuck her tongue down his throat and let him bust a mega nut inside her. Yes, he most definitely loved Summer! The love he had for her was some shit he didn't think possible. It made the years he had spent with Shonda seem like nothing, and it made Lacy's fire ass and Faith's pussy, pale in comparison. It was her heart he loved most and the chemistry that made everything else seem like nothing.

But Atwater could hardly think about his flailing love with her. He had the most exciting news of all. Tomorrow was a really big day for him, and Summer would be at his side when he received it.

CHAPTER 42
AIN'T NOTHIN' LIKE THE OLD SCHOOL

THE NEXT DAY WAS A BREEZE. Atwater and Summer had traveled to a place that they thought they'd never see again. But when they arrived, the place seemed foreign to them, as if they had never been there before.

They were chauffeured in a limo from D.C. to Schuylkill, Pennsylvania, and they traveled the whole way with a fine girl who looked no older than twenty-one years old.

They were going there to pick up Old School!

Old School looked completely debonair in his Italian cut suit and his slicked-back salt and pepper ponytail and Aviator sunglasses once he left out of the jail. He was being escorted by the DEA agent who had cracked him many years ago. Atwater had dug up so much shit on the DEA agent until he knew all the agent's fetishes and quirks. He had found out that the agent was not only a married man who was a homosexual on the down-low, but he also liked to smoke meth. Summer had matched a guy up with the agent who worked for their service. After the episode went according to plan, the agent was more than happy to lie to Old School's prosecutor and say that Old School had given critical assistance that resulted in the arrest of a big-time ecstasy ring out of Buffalo, New York. The prosecutor filed a motion to

Old School's judge, asking for an immediate release for Old School's substantial assistance, as they styled it. It was too funny to believe that it was all a lie in the first place, and Old School would get out of jail because Atwater had set the DEA agent up! Imagine that.

Old School broke down when he walked into freedom. He had never thought he'd ever see the outside of the prison's gates, and now it had truly happened. He hugged Atwater, knowing this was the son he'd never had, and they were family for life.

When Old School got into the limo, he saw the young girl who Atwater had brought for him. She was a young tender, and Old School had to get used to affection because she was all over him.

"What Craze-zo doing in there?" Atwater asked. He had spoken to him frequently and sent him money.

"He's still a fool." They laughed.

"And Buffy and Britney say you should write them, Summer."

Summer smiled. She'd get around to it, but it wasn't like she didn't send them any money. It wasn't that she didn't want to write them. Atwater had her doing so much stuff, and she couldn't think about anyone or anything else other than being with him.

They flew back to D.C. and Atwater showed Old School the sky-blue Bentley Brooklyn he had bought for him and the penthouse suite that was across from the building where his penthouse suite was that he shared with Summer.

It was funny, but after Old School made love to the young girl, he felt like one of the tricks he had condemned all those years. The young girl's name was Michaela, and her skin was golden, her hair blonde and wavy, and she had green eyes. Damn, was she fine!

Old School expired within minutes after he had given her mind-boggling orgasms and showed her tricks she never knew existed. He laid there and tickled her brain with his strongest asset, his mind.

"Oh God," he exclaimed pleasurably. "I see a lot has changed since I've been gone."

"What's changed?" she said. Her voice sounded sweet to his ears.

"When I was young, these kittens here walked on all four legs." He caressed her pussy gently. "Now they have wings that can fly."

"No, they don't!" she laughed.

"Yes, they do; I swear to God they do!"

"How does it feel when you're inside me?"

"Like I'm king in heaven." She laughed at Old School. She thought he was the smartest man in the world and the best lover she'd ever met. "Riddle me this: a man's mind or a woman's pussy? Where does the power lie?"

It didn't take much to think about how men ruled the world. "A man's mind?"

"You're very wrong, sweet thighs. A woman's pussy has the power of life, death, and influence.

On the right bed, the whisper in the right ear can change the world. This is magic if you learn to use it. As long as you don't ever allow yourself to become like one of those women who forgets that their power over men lies in their beauty and femininity. I can show you how to get the world at your doorsteps. Baby, you have all it takes and much more.

If you can say what I'm about to say next, you can have it all."

"What? What is it? Tell me, I'll say it?"

Old School was going to have to spend the rest of his day catching up on endless fantasies.

"Say this: I don't pray, I prey."

"I don't pray, I prey." She laughed; he lusted for her for it. She was the first girl he had sex with since the female CO he had a sexual affair with five years ago. Old School, unlike Atwater, had compromised over ten female COs, and he had never once been tempted to have sex with a boy.

"That's it. Now give me some more of that power of yours." He made love to her for hours until she fell asleep in his arms, dreaming of one day owning the world.

Old School called Atwater on his iPhone that took him hours to figure out how it worked.

"Come and get me out of here before this girl has me addled-brained."

Atwater laughed. "I'm on my way."

Atwater walked over to Old School's building, and they went back to Atwater's flat. All the opulence, including the flat Atwater had gotten for him, was too much to be thrown back into.

It looked so clean, spotless, plush, and luxurious and that it would take some getting used to.

They went into Atwater's lounge. Atwater poured them some Remy Martin, and they sat down on the leather couches. Atwater drank two glasses of the Remy Martin, and Old School knew Atwater had something to say.

"What's going on, young blood?"

"Old School, I started using that stuff." When Atwater said "that stuff", he implied cocaine.

"So what? Don't get hung up over it. Look how you're living? You're driving fast cars; you have your boy, millions, living in plush lofts. It's a rush, but you're going to get back into the groove." Old School already knew what "'that stuff'" meant. The signs were there, and Atwater couldn't hide them, even if he wanted to.

"Damn, I love you, Old School. That's exactly what it is! I feel like I'm out of control. Shit is just coming at me in high speeds. And it ain't only that, I've been fucking Lacy, who's a boy. The shit is getting bad to where I like fucking transvestites now. Old School, I'm losing my soul."

Old School laughed. "Young blood, if you had a soul, I wouldn't have dealt with you a long time ago. A man doesn't need a soul; he needs a brain and a high-IQ. When was the last time a person made millions or changed the world and he attributed it to his soul? You wanna know why nobody can ever judge you? There is no right or wrong. There ain't no good or evil. It's just how your computer's programmed, and that's why I always tell you to think outside the box. All you have to do is get control of yourself again with these circumstances of having freedom. Just get control."

Atwater knew he could do it. He thought about what it would take, and it wasn't anything other than coming to grips with his new situation of having everything he wanted when he wanted. Cocaine, he could stop or manage, along with his family life and his love affair with Summer. Everything was manageable, and he could hold it all in the palm of his hand. One thing was for certain, Old School gave him back his poise.

He ran everything down to Old School about how he had schemed, set people up, used cutting edge technology and spyware to get the evidence to ransom millions from politicians, entertainers, and law enforcement officers, and how he had nego-tiated over thirty million dollars in proceeds. They sat up and talked all night, and now Atwater had his foundation and mental support back.

Fifty-Eight Done By Design…

Months later, Lacy wore a pink Hugo Boss long sleeve lounge robe, which was actually a minidress that exposed her flawless, long legs. It was tied loosely in the front and showed that she didn't have on a bra and her flat, sexy stomach.

She and Faith were inseparable sex demons. Faith wore an Emilio Pucci Greek bleached printed scarf with tassel details over a fluid red dress and her perky breasts dangled erotically in the thin material. The both of them had just the right amount of wrong. They were in a fashion contest and both of their coifs were whipped by hell. They could only be topped by Summer, whose pinch of peach Gucci bodysuit and flowery vest and stilettos, would only be considered the height of fashion. Her hair was pulled into a tight ponytail that hung to the bottom of her back. She had on doorknocker earrings, gold bangles that covered her forearms, and a gold chain that hung past her belly button. Her vest was open to show her tasty collarbone and supple neck that Atwater had sucked on as he fucked her from dusk until the twilight of the next day.

They headed for Vegas, and Atwater knew he was pressing his luck because he had been gone all week. Shonda was due any day now, and she wanted him home at her side.

They spent the weekend in Las Vegas partying and gambling. Atwater had finally decided to hand the reins over to Lacy, who had recruited many of her friends and was running most of the operation. Through Atwater's connect, Liam Val, whom she would never meet, arranged for more than one hundred million dollars in set-ups. They were bathing in cash!

Everything was good until they were on the way back to D.C. Lacy rubbed Atwater's dick and Summer had seen it. They were about to fight on the plane, and Atwater had to break it up by slapping Lacy for the disrespect to his girl, but it wasn't enough for Summer. By now, she had the idea that he had been fucking Lacy.

Atwater couldn't believe the clumsy move played on Lacy's part, and now he wasn't so sure the move was clumsy. When they touched down, Summer stormed off the plane, still in tears. Atwater didn't have time for this shit! He headed back to St. Louis to chill with his wife.

CHAPTER 43
IT'S A GIRL

THE FOLLOWING DAY, Summer was scheduled to fly to Miami to have her operation. She had been doing the psychological evaluation for five months to make sure it was what she wanted to do. She could live without a penis. It wasn't like she ever used it anyway, other than to piss. It was disgusting for her that it was attached to her body, no matter how small and ridiculous it was.

When she arrived at the airport, she was whisked off to the doctor's office. Once there, she was placed in a small room where she was given anesthesia. Two cosmetic surgeons went to work as the anesthesia worked on Summer.

She was at the hospital and Atwater was standing there at her bedside. He was yelling for her to push, and the more she pushed, the more pain Summer felt. It was almost as if her body was being ripped in two. She felt sharp knives cutting on her, and she felt the blood pour from between her legs, and she pushed harder and harder.

Atwater grabbed her hand and sweat poured from her head as she pushed harder and harder.

The doctor was screaming for her to run and never turn back! But Atwater was there, and she'd never run from him.

The more she pushed, the harder he held her hand. And at that instant, the doctors cried out victoriously and celebrated as Atwater looked on in amusement and smoked a cigar.

"It's a girl!" they screamed

When the anesthesia had worn off, Summer came to. She was now a full-fledged woman, but what was more apparent from her dream was Shonda had had a baby girl.

Summer flew back to D.C. three days later. It was the most amazing feeling that she was now complete. She had to heal fast so she could lose her virginity to Atwater. She was still in pain, which made her temper quick and edgy.

She had called Atwater, and he didn't answer his phone. She didn't know somebody had stolen his phone, and he'd have to get a new one. When he didn't answer his phone, Summer freaked out and called his house.

Shonda picked up the phone on the first ring. "Is Atwater in?"

"No. May I ask who's calling?"

What Summer said next was done on purpose. "Can you tell him Summer called?"

It took a minute for it to register in Shonda's ear, but then it dawned on her instantly. "This wouldn't be the Summer he was in jail with?"

Summer knew she had taken it too far, and she hung up.

Chapter Sixty Jail Talk Versus Street Talk...

That night, when Atwater came home, Shonda had leaned into him. She couldn't even finish making dinner, and the baby kept crying as if she knew what her mother was going through. Shonda was livid!

"Why the hell is that boy calling here? I heard you talking

about him to Tyler, and I distinctly remember the way he looked at me during a visit when you were in jail."

Atwater had to play it cool because this was not ok at all. "You're overreacting. I had her…"

"Her? What the hell do you mean her?" Shonda had heard it all! This was ridiculous!

"I put *him* on the internet, and we used him to get some tricks to get some money. That's the honest to God truth."

Atwater had thought about those tricks, many of whom were heartbroken when Summer had gotten released from jail, and they'd never heard from her again. They tried to find her, but Summer had changed her name, and it was as if she were a ghost. The tricks felt scandalized. But what could they do now?

"You're lying, Atwater!"

"What the hell you saying then? You saying I'm fucking a punk?" This was the hour of truth, and when Atwater leveled the question at her like that, it sounded impossible.

"I didn't say that, but why would he hang up when I asked him a simple question?"

"I don't know?"

"You think I'm stupid, don't you?" she asked. She knew because she'd never believe that Atwater would be one of those creeps who were on the down-low and leading a double life, fucking a punk! The thought was unnerving, impossible even! But she just couldn't let the idea go that easily, because it all made her feel ambivalent. "I remember how he looked at me during the visit, Atwater!" she screamed.

"I don't know. Maybe he thought you were cute."

"Damn it, Atwater!" Shonda could have laughed or cried because Atwater was making light of it.

"That wasn't the look he gave me. It was a look like you all had something going on."

"You know what? You need to stop watching those talk shows. That shit is messing with your head."

"I'm going to get to the bottom of this!"

"Just keep your snooping ass out of my office."

"This is my house too!" Shonda retorted, mad with grief. Her hands were shaking. Atwater had only been home ten months, and he had already begun to run the streets all in the name of "I got to catch up!" She could almost spit the words back in his face because now they had three beautiful kids together, and for at least one of them, he could be there.

She never expected to get pregnant so soon, but his dick felt so good after all those unrighteous years of her forced celibacy that she made sure she sexed him nightly. That only lasted a month, until he started flying all over the country and chasing a dream that consisted of power, influence, mansions, exotic cars, and money in the bank that would ensure their children's future.

But what was it with this Summer thing coming back into the picture? She remembered seeing that "thing" and thinking that their lives were somehow tied in - something she still could not understand. The thought of it was enough to get a gun and kill Atwater! Yet she could never believe that her Atwater, the father of their three beautiful children, could ever lay up with a thing like Summer.

She was brought out of her grief when she heard their three-week-old daughter, Nyla, crying. As she gave her daughter a warm bottle of formula, she could see how she could forgive Atwater for even the gravest unpardonable sin if she had to.

CHAPTER 44
CHAPTER FORTY-FOUR ~ IT WAS THE GIRLIE THING TO DO...

ATWATER COULD KILL SUMMER! He couldn't believe this imbecile-shit. It was the least he'd ever expect coming from her. She was trying to tear at the seams of his life after all the shit he had explained to her while they were locked down.

He hopped on his chartered private jet and flew to D.C. immediately. He walked into the penthouse suite and slammed the door.

"Summer, what kind of idiot shit caused you to call my wife!"

Summer was in pain, and she could barely move her legs as she lay on the couch, looking at the HD TV big screen. She was agitated, in love, lonely, and she just exploded, "I don't care! Fuck that bitch! Just leave her so it can be me and you."

"Was that your plan all along?"

"What the hell do you think? I've given the better part of myself to you! That bitch just rode the wave, and she's reaping the reward of my hard work."

Atwater couldn't believe what he just heard. He loved Summer more than life, but his life had order, and he wasn't willing to throw it all to the wind.

"You know this means I have to chill on you until things calm down?"

"What do you mean? You said you'd never leave me!" Summer couldn't even stand. Atwater was about to walk to the door, and she couldn't stop him because she wanted to run into his arms and tell him that she was sorry and everything was all right and would be all right; they would be together forever, and she would always have his love.

"That was before you tried to destroy my family! Yo, you're on your own!" Atwater started for the door, but Summer's piercing cries shredded his heart in two. She had to learn a lesson. There was no way she would be allowed to ruin his life. He turned around. "I did nothing but love you, and this is how you repay me?"

"Don't leave!" Summer cried as she tried to crawl toward him. "Don't leave! You said you'd never leave. You're my life!"

Atwater hesitated. He didn't feel so bad now that he saw her like that on the ground, and it was easier to forgive and forget. He wanted to pick her up and hold her in his arms. But she had to learn!

"I'm out." Atwater stormed out of the door and went to see Old School across the way.

Summer panicked. She went berserk and grabbed her phone and called Atwater over and over again, but he didn't answer! She went crazy.

She thought she had arrived at the end of her life and all her beauty and youth could be summed up in two words. Those two words had haunted her forever, and she saw it every time her father and brother looked at her. It was so disturbing and confusing that she went to great lengths to cure how people viewed her.

It was two words that described why she had to find pleasure in a man slamming his dick up her ass when it was on rare occasions that she could get her own pleasure. She hated to face the truth of it, but the same words came hurling back into her face, and it felt like a sharp slap.

Summer wouldn't accept it, but somehow, she already had. She had carved her body out and divested it of its wholeness because of the words that so neatly described her. She had to say it to herself! She had to confess it, and she hollered out the words that were once leveled at her: "TWISTED FREAK!"

It was those words that caused her great grief. She crawled to her wet bar and guzzled down liquor that spilled down her silk robe. She just had to make it to her bathroom. She knew she'd never feel pain ever again.

Her stitches had torn, and she was bleeding profusely. She hobbled to the bathroom, rummaged through her medicine cabinet, and took as many pills as she could. Summer took all of them, and miraculously enough, the pain was deadened.

She floated and felt much like a butterfly in this bogged mental state. Her head felt numb, and her heart slowed. Her mind played tricks on her, and the floor under her moved. She tripped and fell to the ground.

Her father was on top of her pummeling her with his fists, and when she thought it to be her father, it was then Clayton. Her father had Clayton's face and Clayton had her father's face.

Her heart sped up, and it was beating too fast. She cried out for help. But when the help didn't come, she cried out, "Stop, Daddy! I love you. I swear I do!

Please, just stop beating me! I'm going to die, Daddy, and I love you. I love you! Please stop, Daddy. Please save me, Daddy! Please don't kill me!"

But it was Clayton who pounded away and threatened her. "I wish I never met you, faggot! You killed my mother, you faggot bitch! Die, sissy!"

"No, I didn't! Please don't kill me, Clayton! I deserve to live!"

But then kids appeared, and they danced in a circle around

Summer and teased her. "You're a sissy, you're a fag, you're a girl, and you're on your rag." And they repeated the song infinitely.

"I'm not-I'm not! Stop it! Shut up! Shut up! I'm not a fag or a sissy! I'm a human being! Why won't y'all just let me live!" Her cries went unheard as she imagined Peyton smacking her again and hearing Peyton's hateful words. "I hope you kill yourself, you TWISTED FREAK!"

Summer found the strength to make it to her feet, and the ground rocked under her. She hobbled to her penthouse balcony, looked over the lights of the city, and they were moving. Her mind was foggy. She saw tall blades of grass and her arms brushed the grass as she ran into her favorite orchard that was filled with butterflies. She ran to catch one, but the butterfly floated beyond her reach. Summer tried to catch it because she was blinded by the butterfly's beauty. It flew so softly in the sun-drenched wind that Summer longed to have wings to fly. She stood on the banister of the balcony and when she felt the warm current of the wind, she thought she could fly. Before she could leap, she slipped off the ledge and fell back into her penthouse suite.

Atwater had been across the street at Old School's penthouse suite. Old School had the young girl eating out of the palm of his hand. Atwater spoke to Old School for about an hour, and Old School explained to him that you never ever leave emotionally unstable people alone with the threat of you leaving their life forever -- especially after being the force that had enabled them to change. Old School's experience revealed to him that was how you turn a good girl bad.

Atwater, as always, agreed with Old School. They walked

across the street to the penthouse suite that Atwater shared with Summer.

"Summer, where the hell are you?" It was the third time Atwater had yelled her name, and now he had grown worried after Old School gave him an "I told you so" look.

Atwater went to his bedroom and saw the doors to his balcony wide open. When he walked over to shut them, he found Summer lying in a pool of blood.

"Old School, call 911! Hurry up and call 911!" Atwater's cries pierced through the silence of the night as he heard Old School dialing the number.

"Wake up, Summer!" Atwater screamed as he held her in his arms and checked her pulse. It was beating slow enough for her to be as good as dead! "Call 911, Old School!"

"They're on their way," Old School said as he returned to Atwater's side.

Moments later, the ambulance arrived, and they did CPR as they rushed Summer to Howard University Hospital.

The doctors had pumped her stomach and had lost her twice. She struggled for her life as Atwater sat with Old School in the waiting area.

Atwater's mind flashed on all the good times they had up until that point. For all it was worth, the love he had for her helped him to see past everything. He had taken her out of the context of being a social evil and realized she was a human being with fears, love, and aspirations, like everybody else. But nothing was evil about Summer, and she was the best, prettiest person he had ever met. It made him think about when Old School told him there wasn't anything evil—it was the programming. People always programmed themselves to hate anything that was different. But his mind couldn't grasp why she would want to kill herself. Between tearful eyes, he asked Old School, "Why would she try and kill herself?"

Old School looked at him with knowing eyes as he said, "It was the girlie thing to do."

The cruelty of realizing and understanding what Old School had said summed up Summer's whole existence—what she had always tried to make Atwater understand. She was a black woman one hundred percent.

As those thoughts sunk in, the sun was rising in the distance as Summer continued to fight for her life.

CHAPTER 45
THE END

OR IS IT?

READING GROUP QUESTIONS

1. How do you think readers who have been molested by close family members and those who were no relation to them could learn something from Summer's story?
2. Is there anything Summer's family could have done to keep her from using drugs or becoming a homosexual?
3. Do you think Summer should forgive her mother, possibly her father and brother, or her uncle for what they had done to her?
4. What do you believe the reader could take from the double life Summer's uncle led? Does it send the wrong message regarding prosperous pastors of mega- churches?
5. Do you think there are transgenders who can lead a successful modeling career and model in some of our most widely viewed magazines, movies, and clothing lines as the opposite sex without anybody knowing?
6. Why do Old School and Atwater have so much ambition for being powerful? Do you believe their experiences with the judicial system, being

incarcerated, and their harsh sentences have anything to do with it?

7. Do you think that Atwater is gay? And if so, do you believe he should tell his wife Shonda and his children?

8. Do you think it's right for Atwater to set up politicians and judges to acquire wealth and power?

9. Do you think the politicians and judges will try and take revenge on Atwater because of the dirt he holds over them?

10. If there was one message in the book that Summer wanted to convey the most to the readers, what do you believe it would be?

ABOUT THE AUTHOR

Rodney Roussell, known as M.C. Shakie, is the author of several books. He is from New Orleans, Louisiana where he works as a celebrity vlogger, New Orleans Bounce Music Emcee, and businessman. He is the former victim of prison rape and advocates for its end.

He is hard at work on his next release from Wahida Clark Presents …

CLASSIC
STREET LIT
—S–E–R–I–E–S—

FROM WAHIDA CLARK PRESENTS
INNOVATIVE PUBLISHING

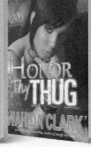

NEW RELEASE

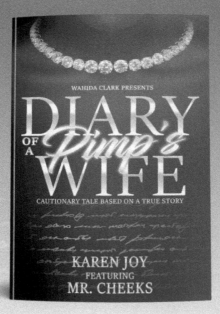

WAHIDA CLARK PRESENTS

DIARY
OF A Pimp's
WIFE

CAUTIONARY TALE BASED ON A TRUE STORY

KAREN JOY
FEATURING
MR. CHEEKS

WAHIDA CLARK

WAHIDA CLARK PRESENTS

ANNA GRISTINA

SECRET
DESIRES

OF THE
ONE PERCENT:

A SHORT STORY COLLECTION FROM THE WORLD'S
MOST NOTORIOUS MADAM

WAHIDA CLARK PRESENTS

A HOOD TALE:
Beyond
B.E.T. WITH

Big Fifty

IN-DEPTH WITH DELRHONDA HOOD

AVAILABLE NOW

WCLARKPUBLISHING.COM

Lightning Source UK Ltd.
Milton Keynes UK
UKHW010632120922
408721UK00001B/183